I0687538

# The Heart Gem

## by

## Isabella Macotte

**The Heart Gem**

Cover Art by *Angela Anderson*

The Wild Rose Press
PO Box 708
Adams Basin, NY 14410-0708
Visit us at www.thewildrosepress.com

Publishing History
First English Tea Rose Edition, 2012
Digital ISBN 978-1-61217-111-1
Print ISBN 978-1-61217-048-0

Published in the United States of America

## Dedication

To Frank, my Heart Match.
And to my daughter, Rachel—
may you find your Heart Match too.

To my friends and colleagues at the Mount Prospect
Public Library and Chicago-North RWA.
I wouldn't be here without you, and am grateful for
treasured friendships and advice.

To my editor, Cindy Davis, thank you
for your support and guidance.

Chapter One

*West Coast of England, Merseyside County, 1885*

Damn! She'd lost her chaperone again. The fates were merciless today, just as they had been over the past month.

This one last act of responsibility, Hallie Pinefoy promised, and she was done with correctness. Of all the places the irritating Mrs. Black could have gone, the note left in their room at the Wrightsville Inn announced a jaunt to Webber's Tavern for a dose of daily "tonic." Once again, that woman had to be retrieved before venturing into another difficult situation.

The chambermaid, Carol, whined while struggling to keep up the pace, "But Miss Pinefoy, perhaps Mrs. Black will return on her own. Must we fetch her?"

This "escort" provided by the inn was already proving to be as much trouble as the other. "As I said to the innkeeper, Mrs. Black has a propensity for wandering off and not returning until late the next day. Our train leaves in the early morning. Besides, Webber's is just six short blocks away: a right at the next corner then down a straight path. Not far at this hour."

Hallie drew the grey silk cape about her slim frame and made the first turn north. A full moon lit the sky, and gas lamps illuminated the shadowed path as their booted feet tapped sharply on the ground. The number of walkers dwindled with each block until the street was quiet, an unsettling sensation of emptiness permeating the air.

They came to the end of the block and she relaxed a little, straightening away the shakiness in her knees. A cold wind blew along her skin and made her long for the comfort of the warm, plain room at the inn. Only three more blocks.

As they crossed the street an unfamiliar tightness clenched in her stomach and nervous acid rose, but pushing reluctant feet forward, she pointedly ignored the growing fear welling up and flooding through every inch of her body.

Something was wrong.

Then Hallie heard it. Men. At least three or four, loud and crude, speaking in a manner she'd only heard on a few occasions. The revelers were proceeding in their direction.

"Carol," she whispered in a calm voice, "we must turn back."

Too late. The men had spotted them. The group laughed, pointed, and then moved forward with an alarming pace. Her eyes scanned the block, searching for some escape, but the buildings and shops lining the road all appeared closed and sinister.

"This way." She led the maid across the street, sprinting now, calculating if the two of them could outrun the band. She cringed as her toe hit a loose stone. Hallie stumbled, her arms flailing before catching herself from falling. The raucous laughter of the men jeered at the clumsiness.

"I'll take the tall one! Looks like she needs a little fun," an inebriated voice roared.

"Wait your turn. Oldest goes first, I say," responded a more sober, rough voice.

"Take the chits off into that alley. Just make sure you put something in their mouths to keep them quiet. But leave some for me," a third ordered.

Her heart pounded. "Help us!" she shouted as

they ran.

Then to Hallie's horror, Carol began sobbing hysterically and threw herself to the ground. Hallie yanked on the maid's arm. "Please compose yourself. We must remain moving." She grasped the girl's hand and tugged to no avail.

Hallie thought about the items in her purse: a couple of coins, a comb and a small metal nail file. Taking a ragged breath, she removed the file and placed it in gloved hand, ready to use. The press of the sharp object was comforting. She waited.

She opened her mouth to scream, but a deep male voice came from behind the carousers, "Stop! Step away from them!"

She and the pursuers turned. Just a few yards distance, a gentleman aimed a small pistol at the group of aggressors. His shadowy outline almost melted against the dark building, the light from the lamps casting an eerie glow. Tall and strong jawed, ebony-black hair waved over the side of his forehead. He presented a fearsome sight while eyes blazed as the wind swirled his black overcoat around.

"I said..." he repeated, the words resonating in the air that now seemed ten degrees colder. "Leave. Them. Alone."

"Yes, leave us alone!" Hallie clutched the metal nail file. She pushed out her right hand from underneath the cape and slashed the night air. The illumination from the street light caught the smooth object, making it appear as though she held a small stiletto.

The pack looked at each other, their bravery dissipating at the loss of their defenseless prey. Eyes flitted back and forth between both gun and dagger, weighing each risk. "Just wishing to give the ladies a little fun," said the shortest of the men in a jovial voice. "Why not join us? You can even go first. Take your pick."

The sound of the gun cocking reverberated through the quiet night. With a dangerous gritted expression, one that made *her* step away, the stranger pointed the pistol at the man's head. "Walk away right now, or I'll shoot." The look on his face attested to the fact he had no qualms about resorting to violence.

One of the gang went forward with arms up halfway. "Come now, the women were in no danger." The man took another step closer. The stranger's leg swept out, hooked the man's ankle, and thudded him to the ground. Hallie jumped at the slam as skull hit stone. He rolled over with a painful groan, a dark smear of blood spread across the back of the man's head.

Hallie ordered her feet to run but instead took a couple of steps toward the group, raising the makeshift dagger while approaching, not quite sure what to do, but ready to fight for the three of them.

The stranger fired a warning shot into the air before his eyes met hers. "Hold this," he ordered and tossed the pistol to her, but missing the catch, the gun slid across the ground. Carol lunged for the gun.

The maid picked it up and stared, horrified.

"Carol, hand me the pistol."

Instead, the girl shrieked and scurried back in the direction of the inn carrying the firearm. Hallie and the stranger exchanged glances.

While unsure if her expression demonstrated the dismay and embarrassment she felt, his expression certainly could have stricken down the assailants better than a bullet. Except the look was directed at her.

The three men moved in unison to ambush the stranger.

"Watch out!" she yelled.

Suddenly eight fists flew, some connecting, some punching the air, until the shortest assailant fell to the ground holding his midsection in pain. The stoutest held the stranger's right arm in place, but the powerful left fist of the stranger connected with a hook to his jaw sending the man down hard on his backside with a loud cry.

Before her eyes could focus, the stranger broke the hold of the last man and sent him to the ground.

The stranger addressed the group sprawled across the cobblestones. "You are fortunate I didn't consider any of you a fair fight. But this *is* your last chance to leave alive."

Faces grimaced in pain, the men scrambled up to slink down the nearest alley.

The tension eased from her face. Hallie proffered a hand in thanks.

"What in hell do you think you two women were doing?"

"What?" She straightened the smile away and re-clenched both lips.

"Are you completely mad to go wandering around at night?"

She stiffened her back. "We were looking for someone."

"Apparently you found *four* someones."

"I beg your pardon! There is no need to speak to me as if I were a child."

"Do you realize how dangerous it is to wander about the street? In the dark? Do you realize you could have got us all killed?"

"I don't remember asking for your assistance."

"You needed assistance."

"I was told the area was safe at this hour. Particularly with a companion."

"A useless companion? You need more than that."

"I'll have you know we were searching for my chaperone."

"Next time, think before escaping a chaperone.

5

It is evident you are sorely in need of a protector."

Hallie marched past the onerous man. "Excuse me, but I'm continuing toward Webber's to find my companion."

"At the tavern?" His mouth curled and strong eyebrows rose. "Surely you can come up with a better explanation."

Tight muscles bristling, she propelled her stature to a full five and a half feet. Hand poised just inches away, the inclination to take the handy nail file and finally put it to good use was fought down.

The exotic-looking man loomed tall, a sweeping gaze revealing quiet amusement at the choice of weapon.

"I don't care what you think, sir. Please step away."

The stranger straightened the black overcoat collar. "I'll offer accompaniment in light of your maid having fled."

"There is no need. I see Webber's in the distance. I bid you goodnight."

"A gentleman wouldn't allow a woman to wander about alone. Notably one who seems inept in taking sensible precautions."

"A gentleman?" With a doubtful expression, Hallie scrutinized the stranger from head to toe to make clear the insinuation the man was not considered in such high esteem. "I don't need assistance."

An entertained expression danced in his eyes, the muscular frame patiently enduring the arrogant appraisal. "Are you sure you don't require assistance?"

"I am. In fact, I order you to stay out of my way."

He shrugged broad shoulders. "As you wish. Nonetheless, I'll accompany you." He stretched out a wool-clad arm toward the cobblestone street.

She frowned. There was no way possible to stop

the stranger's unwanted attendance; however, she wouldn't wait or even walk next to the insolent man. Turning on a suede heel, Hallie whirled, quickening the pace until approaching the front doors of Webber's Tavern. The stranger's strong footfalls drummed behind, but she fought the urge to glance back. Traversing the town was safer with an escort, any sensible lady would admit with a measure of resentment. Therefore in the current situation, Hallie would accept assistance, as it might be impossible to accomplish the task alone. She allowed a smug smile. How supremely satisfying to think she was using the oaf.

She thrust the door ajar and ventured into the small building. Her vision didn't need adjustment from the evening light to the dark room. A dozen round pub tables circled the bar, and the smell of stale beer and dirty smoke permeated the rank air. She examined the faces of each patron about the room.

Mrs. Black was not there. Hallie's shoulders sagged and a slight ache began across her brow.

The hoary barkeep set down two glasses and drew out a wine bottle.

"Excuse me, sir. I'm looking for an older lady. White hair, brown dress. Wire-rimmed spectacles. Do you recall if she visited this establishment tonight?"

"No one like that today. What is it you and your husband will have?"

"Nothing. And he isn't my husband. You're sure the lady I described wasn't served this evening?"

"I can remember every customer ever stepped foot in here. Not her."

Was this awful evening experienced for nothing? "Is there another establishment, within walking distance to the Wrightsville Inn?"

"There's one other place in town right by the

docks. But that's no place for a lady. Maybe your man should go alone? You can wait for him here," the barkeep offered.

That awful old woman should have been allowed to fend for herself. "I appreciate your counsel, but please guide me in the right direction."

With a jerk of his bald head, the man pointed a crooked digit south. "Go half mile or so that way. It's called the Dockhouse. Follow the smell of fish and you can't miss."

She refused to meet the stranger's questioning eyes, and even for a moment debated returning to the inn to procure another escort, but the outrage flowing through her blood urged the continuation of the quest. In fact, she almost dared anyone to disturb her on the way.

The odor of brackish sea air became stronger with each passing block. Still holding the nail file, her fists were clenched at the sides and ready to snap. Behind, the hard steps of the stranger followed. She would give anything to know what was going through that head. No doubt laughter at a powerless woman's plight.

A grimy, toothless vagrant heaved from a stoop ready to engage in conversation. She heard the growl of a whisper from the stranger. "If you know what's good for you, man, step back."

The unkempt beggar did.

The wooden sign of the Dockhouse hung at a crooked angle. She forged through the creaky swinging doors, and there was Mrs. Black, perched in one of the corners, an empty bottle of cheap Madeira wine set on the plank. The woman's iron-colored hair was pulled tight into a dowager bun, and the high-necked mousey dress exuded an air of prim decorum. Except for when a loud hiccup escaped the chaperone's throat.

"Mrs. Black! I have been searching the past

hour. Why did you leave the inn?" To think father was paying *this* woman good money to take care of *her* was insufferable.

With a sheepish expression, the woman admired the wine glass, and slurred, "Well, Miss, I needed my evening constitution. The liquor keeps the blood clean, you should know. The inn was rude and would not provide service."

Hallie counted out three deep breaths. "It appears you've finished your evening constitution, ma'am. We'll adjourn now to the inn. If you recall, we have tickets for an early morning train." She slid over to the woman to grasp a thin arm in assistance from the stool.

"Wait," warned the burly barkeep. "That'll be one shilling."

Wringing skinny veined hands, Mrs. Black paled. "Oh dear. I'm afraid I may be lacking." After making a great show of searching through the small reticule, the lady finally fished out a penny piece.

Ready to scream in frustration, Hallie reached into her cape pocket also finding a penny piece. "I'm afraid I'm short, but promise to return first thing tomorrow morning with the balance."

The barman's face reddened, "Not tomorrow. Payment is due now." The patrons lolling in the tavern paused in their card playing and drinking, and silence filled the damp room. All eyes followed the tense interaction.

The dark stranger stood at the door, but Hallie bit her lip to keep from speaking. She refused to ask for help, when she'd made it clear she did not need assistance. She met the bartender's eye. "Unfortunately it *will* have to be tomorrow."

"I say today. Someone will have to pay."

"And I say payment will be made promptly in the morning. Mrs. Black, shall we leave?" An expectant silence filled the room, and Hallie dragged on the chaperone's arm again.

The barman waved to the opposite wall. A well-dressed portly gentleman lounging in a dark corner ambled toward the group. "I know how you can earn that money, lady. One shilling it is."

Gasping at the insinuation, heart hammering as the patrons' excited murmurs filled the small space, Hallie took a protective stride backward, only to step squarely into a broad, hard chest.

The stranger slammed a few coins on the counter. "The lady is with me. Payment is made." His ominous voice brooked no further discussion.

She turned in grateful relief but was alarmed at the wrath across his face. The stranger's expansive frame filled the room. His enraged eyes made contact with the men looking for trouble, holding each gaze until the patrons backed down one by one, shifting trouble-seeking gazes away.

Satisfied by the money, the barkeep resumed working behind the counter.

She reached for Mrs. Black's arm in an effort to help the woman stand. The lady wobbled a bit, then straightened her spindly legs. While guiding the old woman to the door Hallie glanced at the stranger, embarrassed at having to rely on his help.

He gave a questioning look, took Mrs. Black's arm and led her to the door. "Where are you staying?"

"At the Wrightsville Inn." Hallie refrained from offering thanks. The man really did make it difficult to be grateful, and implied her efforts were ineffectual. "If you can lead us to the entrance, the staff will help us to the room."

"I'll make sure you are safely situated."

"I assure you we'll be all right." The sooner rid of him the better.

"Nonetheless, I'll confirm Mrs. Black is safely ensconced."

At mention of her name, the woman rolled both shoulders in a coquettish curl, "What a wonderful gentleman. So helpful and charming. You must learn to show your gratitude better, miss." The old woman stuck out a flat chest and fluttered sparse eyelashes at the stranger. "Such a handsome man, if I can say so. Don't you think so, my dear? Isn't he one of the handsomest men you've ever seen?"

Hallie felt a blush rising over her face and neck. In such close proximity, the man was indeed quite good looking, in a dangerous, out-of-the-ordinary way. But certainly quite boorish and haughty in disposition, and she couldn't wait to depart from his offensive company.

Keeping her eyes to the ground for the remaining journey, barely listening as Mrs. Black prattled on about the limitations of the town, relief swept through Hallie as the frame of the Wrightsville Inn came into view. "We'll be fine now." She tugged on Mrs. Black's arm trying to move ahead of the stranger.

Mrs. Black bent double and groaned. "Oh my, I believe I may be ill."

Hallie felt the blood drain from her face. Would she ever think of this evening under a different name than, "the nightmare that was Wrightsville"?

The stranger swept Mrs. Black off the lawn, bounded up the stone steps and through the entry doors. "Direct me to your room."

With the elderly chaperone draped in his muscled arms, the man stood in the lobby as Hallie retrieved the room key from the desk. Hallie led the way down the long hallway and up the oak staircase to the door. "Well, I thank you for your assistance, but I'm quite capable of handling things now."

He shot her a scowl before entering the small room to lay the drowsy Mrs. Black upon one of the beds. Within seconds the woman was snoring.

Hallie stepped over to the small desk. "Please wait. I'll get the monies owed from the payment made at the Dockhouse."

"No."

"No?"

"Partake of a glass of wine with me instead."

Surprised, she looked to the man's face and paused. Those dark eyes seemed almost hypnotic, and a sudden vision came to mind of looking into those eyes right before his lips moved in closer and closer, toward her mouth. She forced herself to look away.

He held out a hand. "Just a glass of wine? Perhaps we can pretend to have just been introduced under less dramatic circumstances?"

"I think not. However I'm grateful for your assistance." She held out the coin.

"I never accept money from a lady."

"Do you make a lady feel obligated then? That's your preference?"

"I'd hope the lady would forgive me for my churlish behavior by allowing a contrite man to make amends."

Was he mocking her?

"One glass of wine. Please." He seemed to notice the hesitation. "On the Wrightsville Inn's front porch in full view of all." His face softened. "With a repentant gentleman." He held out a hand. "I'm Bremen Tyler. The apologetic Bremen Tyler who wishes to make restitution to a lady offended with loutish behavior."

"Again, I must decline the offer."

He paused for a moment. "Are you afraid?"

"Afraid? Of you? I most certainly am not."

"Sit with me then. You can berate me for my temper, comment on my lack of good manners, and insult me for my lack of wholesome attributes. I put myself in your hands for as long as you wish to

12

partake of my poor company."

Being the one in control was intriguing. After having spent the past hour feeling foolish and taking directions, she found these pleas for forgiveness and companionship quite appealing.

She bit the inside of her lower lip. Her aunt had modeled excellent behavior whenever confronted by rudeness in the doll shop, and the lady had dealt with boorish gentlemen on a regular basis. Perhaps this would be good practice now, as, if she could manage Mr. Bremen Tyler, there was no limit to who she could manage. Extending a hand, she assumed a gracious manner, "Hallie Pinefoy."

When their palms met, she received a shock, almost the same as when crossing over the carpets in the cold winter months. But this current was quite pleasant, and it must have been for him too for a pleased smile crossed the man's lips.

Leaving the bed chamber, an intense awareness of his close proximity filtered through her. Even the simple act of taking the strong arm was thrilling, and the vibrant warmth of his body seared through the cloth of his coat.

"It's my pleasure to make your acquaintance, Miss Hallie Pinefoy." The word *pleasure* seemed to roll off his tongue in a tantalizing way, bringing shivers up her spine.

"Thank you again for your aid." It was important to prove she was no helpless country bumpkin, but a grown woman who had acquired the traits of sophistication during her time with Aunt Agnes.

Bremen smiled, face transformed by the tiny crinkles around his eyes and curve of manly lips. "I'm happy to be of use. I've recently traveled from Wales to Wrightsville and haven't seen calamities as those encountered tonight. Hopefully the disturbing events will not leave an enduring impression."

"No, of course not." She waved away as trivial the past hour's adventure.

On the porch Bremen guided her to a seat at one of the round lantern-lit tables. She sat and took a few deep breaths, and composure recovered, studied him through lowered lashes. He was a tall man, dressed in good-quality, although not fancy attire. He had a wonderful deep voice with a slight indefinable accent, and hair and eyes glowed dark in the night, so dusky the features blended into the shadows.

A waiter clad in a short black jacket sauntered over to take their order.

"Is white wine acceptable, Miss Pinefoy?"

"In truth, I prefer red."

Bremen nodded and ordered an excellent-quality red wine. "It is my wish to make the rest of your evening more enjoyable than the beginning." With a charming smile he drew his chair in closer.

He was so near she could smell the clean scent of the man and see the straight whiteness of perfect teeth. There was something about Mr. Tyler which awoke a feminine awareness, and for some inexplicable reason Hallie found his closeness tantalizing. Had the temperature outside risen to tropical? "After what has transpired, the evening shouldn't be difficult to improve."

His eyes smoldered with a sensuous gleam as an eyebrow rose. "I'll do my best to make our time together as memorable as possible."

Suddenly feeling out of her element Hallie looked at her folded hands. "Your timing earlier was opportune. I must confess I've never had such a dangerous episode and my helplessness was somewhat embarrassing."

"On the contrary, you'd prepared a weapon and kept your sorely-tested composure commendably. You also held your emotions well in the tavern.

14

Many ladies would have fainted or been in hysterics."

She laughed, "Yes, I suppose so. Hopefully there won't be a repeat of tonight during the rest of the voyage."

"To where you are traveling?" Bremen inquired, nodding his thanks to the waiter bringing two glasses and a wine bottle to the table.

"Back home after a few years training with my aunt; I wish to start working again soon."

"Shall we toast, my dear Miss Pinefoy?" He raised the glass. "To new beginnings."

"Yes. New beginnings." She gulped a restorative sip of the drink. Something was certainly beginning here that could lead to tantalizing circumstances.

"You were speaking of home. Where is that?"

"Cheshire County."

"A lovely place it's been said." He watched with such a measure of intentness she was sure Bremen could see the booming of her heart in her chest.

"Yes, it is. You're not from the area, Mr. Tyler?"

"No, but it's unlikely you've heard of the place. Few have. However, at this time I'm traveling to investigate a new business venture."

Hallie was fascinated by the man. His conversation was intelligent and charming, and his mannerisms both flirtatious and mysterious. Bremen knew just what questions to ask to draw her out, but after some time she realized she didn't learn much about him.

"Have you traveled much, Mr. Tyler?"

"Yes, particularly during my childhood. How exciting to make a fresh start, Miss Pinefoy. Do you find your venture exhilarating or frightening?"

"A little of both, I must say," she admitted without hesitation.

Bremen smiled in sympathy across the table. "I would enjoy hearing about which of those two you find it more so. May I call upon you once you're settled in?"

Flattered, she looked over the edge of the wineglass to meet his eyes.

The moment thudded to a sudden stop.

Fascinated, she saw the silver flecks in those dark orbs catch the light from the full moon. It was frightening how attractive Bremen was, and the mystery exuded was of a delicious sort. Her glance swept from eyes to perfectly proportioned lips. Unwittingly Hallie parted her mouth and wondered how it would feel to place it on Bremen's. Of its own volition, body tilting toward his as though two magnets inching to join together, she shifted forward.

He must have been thinking similar thoughts as a strong hand lifted, but then paused. "Hallie, I must see you again."

Surely a few sips of wine could not be so strong as to induce a total disregard for restraint?

He must have comprehended the hesitation. "I understand you may be reluctant to leave your address with a stranger, but as I've no permanent residence at the moment and am staying at the Wrightsville Lodge for only one more day, I am not able to reciprocate by leaving mine. Must I plead? Just say the word."

Hallie was surprised by the uncertainty in the man's voice, and in fact, had a strong feeling uncertainty did not come naturally to Bremen. However, that didn't mean she was obligated to offer reassurance. "Unfortunately we are not well acquainted, and it would be preferable to go our separate ways after this evening."

He reached across the table and placed his hand on hers. There was nothing on this earth which could induce Hallie to move that hand away. How could that be?

"You feel it, don't you? The connection?"

She did but wouldn't allow her head to bob in agreement.

"Are you so ready to never meet again? Will you take that chance? I'm asking again, are you afraid?"

"No."

"Then...just tell me where you live, a town is sufficient. Would you rather I follow you there? I would follow you anywhere, Hallie."

While a mere half hour ago she'd wished to have the man removed from her sight forever, the situation had reversed. Could any harm come of a future meeting? Especially returning to the respectable home shared with her father. "It would be pleasant to continue our conversation." She spoke the words with care not wanting to admit how interesting the possibility was.

Bremen patted jacket pockets, searching for something. "I must have lost my pen in the scuffle. Meet me in the lobby tomorrow morning? We can speak together before the train."

"I will."

"I'll hold you to your promise then. Are you departing early?"

"Yes, the first passage." With some satisfaction she saw disappointment settle in his eyes.

"That's regrettable; however, I look forward to tomorrow and sharing a few hours."

"Perhaps I should return to my chamber. My chaperone may be worrying."

He lifted the skeptical eyebrow. "I'll walk back with you."

Once more, they advanced through the inn, down the long hallway, and up the stairs to the room she shared with Mrs. Black. Fumbling a bit, Hallie took the key out and turned, standing closer to him than anticipated. "Thank you again, Mr. Tyler, for your heroic rescue."

He closed the gap even more. "It was my honor to act as your hero."

His warm, strong hand took hers and holding the gaze, lifted it to place a kiss. She shivered as his lips touched her skin. He turned her hand over and pressed a kiss upon the palm.

Bremen looked into her eyes. She saw mystery and heat and recognition there in the gaze.

"Although I would not wish such a harrowing experience on a lady, it was fortuitous in that I was able to make your acquaintance."

"Would you then say fate had a hand in this evening's events?"

"I believe in fate. Do you?"

She couldn't breathe, or think of a proper response.

"Goodnight, Hallie, until we meet again." Transfixed, she watched as Bremen leaned, pressing his mouth to hers.

A warm melting went through her limbs, and if Bremen didn't hold her she would swoon. Swoon! Wasn't that something silly girls did?

Now those wonderful lips were moving, warming, exploring, blocking out any further thoughts while hands were touching and caressing, making each pause on her skin feel like a heated claim through the thin fabric. Bremen encircled her waist. She knew they should stop. Instead her mind stopped thinking, breasts almost aching for the man's touch as strong fingers brushed her ribcage.

His mouth moved with sensual slowness down her neck and lower to the upper curve of her breast just below the collarbone. Excitement coursed through her body as her breaths came faster, eliciting sweet groans of pleasure. Her knees swayed and Bremen moved closer against the wall, holding her. He kissed with more force now, and her traitorous hands swept to his back, pressing harder, and pulling in, her body acting without any regard for commonsense.

He moved her hips against his, and Hallie could feel his excitement. Not shocked at the motion, her body craved the pressure. Finally it was Bremen who pushed away. "Hallie." His voice was rough as he leaned his forehead against the top of her head.

Embarrassed, she couldn't believe the wanton behavior exhibited by kissing a man she'd just met. "I need to go."

Bremen held her body pressed while smoothing her hair gently into place. "I must see you again. Meet me in the lobby in the morning as early as possible."

"I must think."

"Just a meeting, as soon as you awaken," Bremen said. "Will you? Tell me the truth."

"I promise."

"I'll be waiting for you at first light."

She gave a quick smile and rushed into the room, closing the door. After shutting her eyes for a few moments to slow the deep breaths, she glanced over at the still-snoring Mrs. Black. Perhaps the woman had some redeeming qualities. Fate worked in inexplicable ways.

Hallie undressed for bed and washed in the basin provided in the room before slipping into the narrow bed. There was something magical about the man, making her whole being feel alive and in tune. Tired, she closed her eyes and fell asleep thinking of Bremen Tyler with those tantalizing kisses.

Sometime in deepest sleep, pleasant dreams took a turn toward something more primitive and lustful. She was with Bremen in the dark night, his warm, hard body next to hers filling and touching her naked and heated skin in the most intimate places. He held Hallie in a feverish embrace, kissing and whispering wicked suggestions, caressing, giving intense pleasure. She cried out his name and he rolled her under him, moving with exquisite, powerful slowness until both were spent.

He gave a satisfied groan before taking her face in both large hands and kissing her once again. "I'll be waiting for you at first light."

Chapter Two

Bremen stared at the ceiling of the hushed Wrightsville Lodge bedchamber. His instincts had almost done him in. Urges held in check for a prolonged time had inevitably threatened to take over. While he prided himself on remaining controlled and keeping emotions reined, there was something about Hallie. Some deep connection had been made from the moment he first saw the lady.

He emitted a frustrated growl and rolled over, hoping to find some comfortable spot to rest upon while waiting out the long interim until dawn. Bremen reached to the nightstand table to take yet another look at the gold pocket watch, the piece indicating the time was well past midnight. Hours since the intriguing Miss Hallie Pinefoy was escorted to her room at the Wrightsville Inn a few buildings away from his lodging.

Unbeknownst to her, he'd seen the lady earlier that evening in the main dining area of the inn while partaking of a solitary supper. He had been alone in the elegant room where heavy red velvet drapes outlined the windows and dark oak paneling surrounded the large central fireplace. The flames' amber glow brushed the chandeliers hanging from the ceiling, brightening the noisy room filled with smoke from pipes and cigars. A typical British dining hall.

Hallie had been escorted to a side table in an alcove near the patio. Bremen hadn't been able to place where he had seen her before and although he could swear they had never met, that lovely face seemed so familiar. It was rude to stare, the elders had taught, but there was something about the lady that made him want to break a few other more serious rules.

A vibrant radiance emanated while the woman sat poised at the small table watching the patrons and surroundings with curious, beautiful green eyes. Hair a glorious color, shiny toffee-brown, was pinned up at the base of her long creamy neck. The white blouse was cut at just the right depth, barely skimming the top of her high breasts.

While waiting for an opportunity to follow and be introduced, she'd risen in a hurry before he could leave the table. His senses had prompted a search outside, and a few blocks from the inn he spotted the woman and a young maid unaware of the hooligans' approach. The vision of Hallie standing small and defenseless, except for a little metal nail file ready to take on the attackers, was a moment never to be forgotten. And she was even ready to protect him and the maid. He'd wanted her at that instant and knew she was for him.

The unexplainable fear for her safety had made him angry enough to lose control. He knew his behavior was uncouth, but she was so independent, he'd been determined to put the woman in her place with harsh words. And her place was next to him.

Soon, he would go to the Wrightsville Inn lobby to be able to be with Hallie again. The link between them was forged now, and she needed to realize the connection. If only he could get a few hours of sleep before dawn. Bremen stretched out and rolled to the other side of the bed.

Then there were the sounds outside the room: careful steps and an urgent light tap pulsed on the door.

"Tyler," a man's familiar voice hissed.

Bremen rose to open the door, irritated by the

interruption. Malone stood in the hall, his tall frame filling the doorway and elegant Tilda standing at his side.

"Malone. Cousin Tilda. What's happened now?" Nothing good could come from a late-night visit.

"Tilda and I regret to inform you Uncle Roman has passed away."

"Come in, We don't want to draw any attention in the hallway. Roman will be missed by many. Have you come to inform me of the final services?"

Tilda shook her head. "The Ancestrals have requested your presence at the Stronghold."

"Requested?" he countered. "Ordered is a more accurate word." Although an outright refusal was impossible, the meeting with Hallie in the morning was uppermost in importance. "I'll be there later tomorrow. There is a matter to be attended to in a few hours."

"Tilda and I are just the messengers, but the Ancestrals were adamant about your leaving right now, at this moment."

"If I delay?"

"They said to tell you any postponement would shift your responsibility to Bremma."

Bremen paused, thinking of his younger sister and the vow made to their parents to protect and care for his sibling after their passing. His teeth clenched and body tensed at the added complication. "I need to leave a message first. But wait while I get ready."

"Hurry, my friend. You know their impatience at any hindrance."

He bristled. Bremen longed for the simple life of his early youth. He tossed articles of clothing and toiletries into a black leather traveling bag, and was ready to leave the room within a few minutes.

"Malone, go find a discreet place outside to use the Veil. I must leave a message at the Wrightsville

Inn."

"I'll go with you," Tilda offered to Bremen with a sad smile.

He squeezed her hand before starting down the staircase. "I'm sorry to hear Uncle Roman has departed. He was a good man."

"Yes, we'll miss him. He did live a long full life, though, and in the manner he wished."

"Bremma is all right? She's still in Scotland with our relatives?"

"Yes. Malone and I keep a watchful eye on her, but I know she misses you. As do we. You are well?"

"Yes." He paused, needing to say the words out loud. "I think I've found my Heart Match." He stopped speaking at the lobby desk.

The clerk looked up alertly, attention fixed on Tilda. "May I help you both?" he extended obsequiously.

"Mr. Bremen Tyler wishing to return the room key and end my stay."

"Of course, sir and madam. I hope your visit was pleasant?"

Bremen signed the register and guided his cousin outside toward the Wrightsville Inn where Hallie was staying.

Near the top of the stone steps, the doorman allowed entry, and at the desk, Bremen took up a pen and paper. After writing in bold strokes, he folded the note and sealed it in an envelope. "There will be a Miss Hallie Pinefoy waiting for me this morning. Please give this message to her."

The clerk stared at Tilda as if dumbstruck by her beauty, his mouth gaping open.

"The note, man. I need you to give Miss Pinefoy the note. It's very important."

Tilda smiled, used to the attention. "Sir, if you would be so kind as to pass this to Miss Pinefoy?"

"Y-yes, of course, my Lady."

Bremen gave a gentle roll of his eyes. Why Malone and most of the male population fawned over the girl was beyond him. Until a couple of years ago, his cousin was a gangly, awkward brat putting mud in his shoes and labeling him a mixed blood. "You will give Miss Pinefoy the note? I can be assured of that?"

The clerk nodded, his eyes unblinking while he stared at Tilda.

Bremen stifled a frustrated glance, then directed them out of the Wrightsville Inn.

Malone stood waiting at the bottom of the steps. "Follow me." The man led them into an alley out of view. Bremen waited while he unfolded a tiny gossamer cloth over and over until the inch-square fabric became an opaque film about four feet wide and long.

The group stepped through the shimmering fabric and transported.

****

Bremen grounded his feet until the spinning stopped. The swirling colors were the first indication of a very different place, shades so unique they were nameless in the outside world. His nostrils filled with the smells of flowers and herbs unlike scents found elsewhere—sweet and bitter, sharp and smooth; even the air had a different, electric quality. This was where his family originated, but it wasn't home. Nor would this place ever be.

As a slight twinge of pain rolled through Bremen's body, all five senses heightened back to the point they were before leaving the Ancestral world. The many senses were not missed as those extra attributes came with many restrictions and conditions.

Malone folded the veil into a minute package and placed the item in his pocket. Bremen gave a short nod to his companions to move, and started walking on the smooth path leading to the Ancestral Stronghold in the distance. Of inestimable age, it was a fortress built of dark grey stones of immense size which fit perfectly against each other; the lines almost imperceptible even when viewed up close. Against the blue-green sky the small Keepers fluttered around, their reddish gold leathery wings whipping against the brisk wind.

The red sun was setting over the Stronghold and the hot light filtered through his eyes. "Have you any idea what they want?" he asked Malone as the trio continued the walk toward the fortress.

"No. Although you can be sure they are self-serving, as usual."

"Let's hope it is just a ceremonial gesture toward Uncle Roman," Tilda added.

Malone took her hand. "I hope you are right, my love."

The double-width metal doors inlaid with cryptic rectangular symbols automatically opened inward at their entry. Gold brightly-lit sconces lined the walls, illuminating into all but the deepest recesses of the Stronghold. It was preferable not to venture into some places; some of the Ancestrals who'd wandered into the forbidden places never returned.

A grey hush settled in the rectangular entry room when a stout man approached, face grimly set with a deep frown slashed across the short forehead. Scarpello greeted Bremen without acknowledgment. "The council awaits."

"Scribe."

Flanked by Scarpello, with Malone and Tilda in his wake, Bremen went into a round large black chamber with an enormous open skylight in the center. The open area in the middle was circled by seats in rowed levels; each place was filled by a shrouded council member. Climbing the stairs to the central platform, all eyes fixed at his entry.

The Head Council in the front row stood and spoke without preamble, "Bremen Tyler, you have heard the news of Roman Tyler's passing. He was given the choice to live outside of the Ancestral world in deference to esteemed service to the Ancestrals. Now, all possessions and responsibilities pass to you."

Bremen bowed his head to cover a grimace. He had no wish to live among the politics and rules of the Stronghold, and these short years had enjoyed life on the outside. He would remain there.

"To better serve your people and responsibilities, the council has decided it is time for you to wed."

Bremen took a sharp look at the Head Council. "It has decided?" he asked with sarcasm.

"Yes. The council has allowed a number of years of freedom. Now a man of your age and stature must take a wife."

Bremen's jaw softened as an image of Hallie Pinefoy entered his thoughts; the council's edict might not be so bad after all. He had realized during this long night his intention was to wed the woman.

"The council has determined to keep the Tyler bloodline strong. Your cousin Tilda has been selected as your bride."

A feeling of heaviness dropped across both shoulders as Bremen attempted to control the anger and frustration starting to rage. Looking into the figures of the members, he tried in vain to find a pair of sympathetic eyes. "You are directing me to marry my cousin?"

"As is customary, you and Tilda will partake in a viewing ceremony using the Heart Gem. If no disastrous marriage is foretold by the Artifact, you will wed."

Bremen sensed Malone's body tightening just a few yards away, as though a jaguar ready to fly. With an almost imperceptible movement, he raised a

27

hand at his side to stay the other man.

"Tilda and I are promised," Malone stated in a terse voice as he took her hand.

"It is not a promise recognized by the council," the Head dismissed.

"Nonetheless, it is our promise," Tilda added with conviction.

Bremen took control, wanting to make sure nothing was spoken which could make the already impossible situation into an untenable nightmare. "We are not medieval here. No one is forced, correct?"

Light, whispered words speaking of impertinence and irresponsibility could be felt throughout the chamber. The Head Council continued, "Prepare for the ceremony, Bremen Tyler and Tilda Tyler. It will be held in one cycle."

Chapter Three

Hallie glanced at the new wristwatch once again. Could it be wrong? Bremen Tyler had promised to be waiting at first light, but that time had passed almost two hours ago and the lobby had turned from a quiet room which would have been appropriate for an intimate conversation to a place bustling with the activity of a busy staff and patrons.

She leaned on the wing-tip chair and crossed both slim ankles in a ladylike way. However the thoughts flowing through her mind were far removed from any noble contemplations. The time spent sitting in the lobby of the Wrightsville Inn listening to her stomach growl had swelled the growing irritation with each tummy rumble. In retrospect, she reflected on the now-foolish decision to miss breakfast in an effort to be able to spend every extra moment with the man.

With care, she turned her gaze around again, trying not to appear too eager. A gentleman with black hair stepped into the stairway, his back toward her. Ready, she stood and smoothed the navy linen skirt. At last. With a smile on her lips, Hallie took a few steps as the gentleman turned around. The welcoming expression fell off her face as the mustached big-bellied guest moved away from the lobby desk.

She was foolish and rejected. Had she misunderstood Bremen's intentions? Her head was still a little fuzzy from the passionate dreams she'd had the night before, and even this morning it was almost possible to smell him on her skin and feel the thick silky hair on her fingertips. The attraction last night was palpable and flowed like a rush through her body, every inch of skin aching to be held even closer than outside the room. She took a deep breath, trying to expel some of the alarming feelings he'd incited.

What was needed was to relieve some of the tension winding her up like a top. Instead, the last person she wanted to see right now was coming down the steps. It was unbelievable. To see Mrs. Black's sweet face, one would think the woman was beyond reproach, and it was amazing this person never appeared to suffer any ill effects from such inebriations.

"Good morning, Mrs. Black."

"How quickly morning has come. I feel as though I was just rescued by our handsome helper. What a gentleman."

Hallie felt a blush rise over both cheeks. "And fortunate we were, ma'am, to have the help. I'm not sure what would have resulted at the tavern, and must say your care during our voyage back to England has not been such as my father would have expected."

Having the grace to show some shame, Mrs. Black responded, "Fortunate we were indeed, miss. Have you eaten already?"

"I will forgo breakfast this morning. Shall we meet here in the lobby in half an hour? We will have ample time to procure a porter and arrive at the train station."

The chaperone gave a sharp upturn of a bony chin and moved toward the dining hall.

Alone again, Hallie tapped a toe on the rose fleur-de-lis carpet. Perhaps there was confusion in the meeting place, and instead of the Wrightsville Inn, they were to meet at the Wrightsville Lodge where Bremen was staying? That must be the misunderstanding as this reason would provide the only possible explanation for the tardiness.

In a hurry now, she bustled out of the building and over to the lodge. It was a smaller establishment with a modest lobby but also empty. She approached the desk. "Good morning. I am Hallie Pinefoy. Have you a message waiting by any chance?"

The clerk shook a sleepy head and mumbled, "No, I don't believe so."

"May I have a pen and paper then?" She took both and jotted a short note. "There'll be a Mr. Bremen Tyler down some time today. I'm sure the gentleman will ask if there's a message waiting at the desk. Could you please forward this?"

"Yes, ma'am, of course." He placed the missive into an envelope.

Should she wait any longer? The statement informing of an early morning train had been clear last night. "Excuse me again, sir. Can you tell me if Mr. Tyler has come down to the lobby yet? Perhaps very early and I missed him?"

The clerk fumbled through the ledger and desk, and then the distracted look suddenly cleared. "Mr. Bremen Tyler checked out in the middle of the night accompanied by a lovely lady. In quite a hurry to leave too. Lovely lady, I must say." The words seemed to drift off as memories appeared to fix on an image of this "lovely lady."

He was gone? With another woman? Was this the reason Bremen left so suddenly in the middle of the night—the wife had come to fetch an errant husband home to the children?

"You're saying Mr. Tyler left with a woman?" She needed to clarify. "Was she his wife?"

"Oh, not sure about that, miss. But her I couldn't forget. Almost put me in a trance. Unforgettable, really. They made quite an attractive couple. Such a beautiful woman."

"Well. Your assistance is appreciated."

Hallie stomped back to the Wrightsville Inn. There was of course no assurance the other woman was a spouse, and if Bremen was an honorable man a message may well be waiting at the Wrightsville Inn begging forgiveness and offering explanation for not being present this morning.

Adding to the frustration of the morning, Mrs. Black was already seated on one of the velvet couches waiting for transport to the train station. Hallie decided to make one more attempt and approached the clerk. "Could you tell me please, have you a message for a Miss Hallie Pinefoy?"

Surrounded by numerous patrons, the distracted clerk tried to brush away the interruption. "Please wait your turn, miss, there are others before you."

"Miss Pinefoy, the porter has arrived and is ready to provide transport to the train," Mrs. Black piped up from the lounge.

Hallie's empty stomach churned even more, "Just one moment, please."

A few interminable minutes ticked by until the clerk finally gave his attention. "What was it you wanted again?"

"A message for me, sir. Is there a message for a Miss Hallie Pinefoy?"

He gave a cursory glance across the desk. "No. Don't see one."

"You are certain?"

"Yes, miss. No time to dawdle now, the porter is here."

It became quite obvious at that moment her first impression of the cad, Mr. Tyler, had been correct.

****

After an unbearably long and dull ride home in the stuffy ladies' car, Hallie and Mrs. Black's train pulled into the town of Mooreland. The mid-day sun heated the humid air and contributed to her sour temper of the past few hours. It would be uplifting to return home and forget the unpleasant incidents of the prior two days.

She scooped the smaller articles and made sure Mrs. Black had the ever-empty purse and old carpet bag.

"This is a filthy way to travel! The noise, the soot, the press of people!" Mrs. Black complained.

She preferred Mrs. Black inebriated and silent, but nodded in appeasement while guiding the woman to an open area. Hallie was determined not to converse at length with the troublemaking chaperone who had triggered the unfortunate incident in Wrightsville. The less said to the woman the better.

A plainly dressed family standing near a worn-out wagon waved. "Good luck then, Miss Pinefoy. Do you want me to wait with you until your father comes?" Mrs. Black offered without enthusiasm.

"No, please go ahead. I see your family is waiting." Alone, she gathered the remaining bags and trunks to wait for her ever-late father. The noise of the train engines was deafening and a layer of haze hung over the crowd. She peered through the air at the hurrying people to catch a glimpse of him. The train pulled away as a bead of sweat rolled down her neck.

At long last, Edgar Pinefoy came into sight, waving a well-tanned hand. Short and thin, the man had a sharp brain and persuasive manner beneficial in many diversified business dealings. It was obvious the trip to the Islands these past years had been successful.

"Father."

"Hallie, dear. You're well?"

With satisfaction, she noted the voice tinged in guilt. He'd abruptly dispatched his daughter to

Boston, and ordered a return back home to Mooreland as hastily. "I am happy to be home in England."

"High time for you to return." He motioned for the footman to load the trunks. "The city has grown a great deal. Not as big as Boston, of course, but the place is a bustling metropolis with many new shops and restaurants." Edward Pinefoy assisted her into the buggy. "Your trip home was uneventful?"

The man couldn't imagine how eventful the voyage was in truth. "I do believe I'm now capable of traveling alone."

They settled into the vehicle and the driver started to navigate the noisy paved streets.

"Agnes wrote of your immense help in the toy shop."

"I wasn't a burden, and now hope to follow in my aunt's footsteps. My own business plans will be successful, as there is an associate here in Mooreland already arranged and eager for a partnership in my new enterprise."

"That's interesting, dear, but quite unnecessary. Instead now would be a time to think on a spouse. In fact, Clay Nash is still available. I've taken the liberty of speaking with the gentleman and the elder Mr. Nash." A frown crossed a brown wide brow. "Most women your age are wed. Or at least betrothed."

His questioning inspection attempted to determine which faults had brought about her impending spinsterhood.

"Dear father, I'm quite content to be unattached and am looking forward to my immediate future without a husband."

"Hmmm. But at your age, my dear…"

She cringed. Already upon the shelf in her twenties? The machinations working in the man's brain were alarming, and her sire didn't comprehend the extent of the independent life she'd led for the past few years. "Aunt Agnes has been encouraging during your absence, Father. I'm looking forward to implementing successful plans in Mooreland."

Edgar swiped a disdainful hand. "Perhaps we can talk about this whim once you settle in."

She turned toward the window. Instead of arguing the first day back, she would show by example that she was not the malleable child who'd left home. A great deal of preparation would ensure success, and in addition to the shop owner in town she'd corresponded with, there was a toy store in Mooreland which might want to form a consignment agreement. Interesting possibilities were inspired in just a few moments. New markets and shops were waiting to be visited, and this endeavor could be quite fruitful with hard work and some luck.

More residents, more patrons for her dolls. "So unlike the quiet town of a few years ago."

Edgar Pinefoy nodded, already preoccupied with plans of his own.

The buggy sped out of town onto a dirt road, and her mind returned to the mystery of Bremen Tyler. The man had been so believable in his request to meet in the morning. Had he found her wanton behavior shocking, or was his conduct appalling? Either one or both might be correct, but she'd be glad to never meet again.

The horse halted on the curving drive in front of home: a low, brick building in the wooded area not far from the center of town. Energized now, Hallie alighted. She greeted the staff warmly and proceeded to her bedroom to unpack a few things and wait for the trunks to be brought in.

Hallie removed the latest creation from the blue carpetbag, and with care, pulled on the elaborate garment sewn the day before yesterday. First, the new doll was fitted with a set of silk petticoats, the type any fine lady would be thrilled to wear. Layered on next, a rose satin dress in the latest style, with tight sleeves expanding at the top of the shoulder and tapered down the arm. Hallie fluffed the small bustle before fastening tiny matching gloves onto the hands and securing the elaborate plumed hat on the doll's head with a final touch.

Aunt Agnes' store, Pinefoy's Playthings, specialized in unique and unusual toy and collector items for both children and adults. The shop carried checker and chess sets of fine ivory and unusual stones. Also offered were master-crafted miniature castles and mansions accompanied with delicate doll furniture and accessories for display. Rare marble sets and detailed marionettes were available for the discerning buyer. The shelves filled with a wide selection of antique first edition and new children's books. Some were printed on heavy stock paper, others hand lettered and bound in carved leather.

The handmade doll in her hand was the same as the specialty of Pinefoy's Playthings. Exquisite custom-made wax-over-composition dolls were crafted for the wealthier families of Boston. First Agnes sketched the faces of the well-heeled children with great care and a true artist's touch. Then, the wax doll faces were shaped over papier-mâché before painting to resemble the children they represented. Finally the dolls' dresses and suits were sewn using fabric provided by the clients who insisted the figure's clothing matched their child's attire.

The outrageous cost of these handmade dolls could only be affordable for the most prosperous of society. The price, however, did not deter the exclusive clientele, and the objects had become a status symbol for those affluent enough to afford the items.

As these dolls were unlike anything offered in Mooreland, or even Cheshire County, Hallie determined to learn the intricate craft of creating them.

Correspondence with Mr. Roman during her stay in Boston was fruitful, and the venerable gentleman who owned the curiosity shop in Mooreland had indicated his great pleasure in taking her on as a partner in a new joint venture.

Finished with the prepping of the doll, Hallie packed up two of the less expensive baby dolls and three custom dolls into a large wicker basket.

After washing and changing, she checked the mirror, pleased at the very professional appearance projected on the glass. Attired in a serge-grey dress and a neat hat perched at just the correct angle, she smoothed the sides of thick brown hair styled into a coiled braid at the nape of the neck.

****

The horse's hooves clicked on the cobblestones of the road, and the rhythm of the noise started to swing around the vehicle for the short trip.

Roman's Curiosity Shop held many happy memories within its walls. With childhood friends Viola and Clay, the three children would watch Mr. Roman open new packages filled with goods shipped from all over the world. Sometimes, it seemed he put the wrapped boxes aside, as though waiting for Hallie to come to the shop and see the objects first-hand with him.

After tying the horse, she lifted the basket from the back of the buggy and climbed down from the seat.

She rapped on the locked front door of Roman's. "Hello?" Unusual. Mr. Roman was always in the shop. There had not been a time the sign showed Closed as today. She walked back toward the living apartment, and peered through the window. Everything inside looked untouched.

"May I help you, miss?" A washerwoman stood

in the courtyard next to the neighbor's door.

"Yes, I'm looking for Mr. Roman. It appears he is out."

"He is permanently out, I'm afraid. The dear old man passed away just a few days ago."

Hallie's head swam. She bent to place the basket on the ground. "How unfortunate. Was he ill?"

"Not ill, I believe. Had always been the picture of health, in spite of his advanced age. Always a head for business, the man had. When last we spoke, he even told me he'd put plans in place for a new venture. Then, he was found passed away in his sleep. Always a pleasant gentleman to talk with, I must say."

"What's to become of the curiosity shop?"

"Heard his nephew inherited everything. Haven't seen him come to settle matters yet."

"Do you know when his nephew is to arrive?"

"I'd thought this week, but no one's been here."

She offered thanks to the woman and stepped away. The wonderful old man. He came to town over fifteen years ago, from where, no one knew. Hair white as bleached cotton and alert grey eyes that sparkled when he spoke, Mr. Roman had the most interesting merchandise from all over the world.

When she'd written of her business plans, Mr. Roman had promised to devote part of the curiosity shop to the dolls, offering encouragement, in fact, to continue the tutelage under Aunt Agnes. He'd even predicted these plans would bring Hallie much happiness in life.

But now, her perfectly laid arrangement had met its first impediment.

Chapter Four

Bremen paced the room, wincing when a tap sounded on the chamber door. "Enter."

Most men considered Tilda a stunning woman. Blessed with jet black hair, the lightest blue eyes and a figure molded into a cast of feminine perfection, the whole package exuded a dangerous sensuality. But she was as close to him as his sister, Bremma. "What do you and Malone think of the upcoming ceremony?"

Pausing, the woman took a deep breath. "You know how we feel. We've been waiting for the right moment to push our case before the council again, and desire to be wed as soon as possible. The difficulty rests with Malone not being one of the Ancestrals, so our marriage is outlawed."

He'd have to give some thought to helping the couple, *after* this situation was resolved. "It is forbidden to refuse participation in the Heart Gem ceremony, and the directive can't be ignored. Reluctant candidates have endured severe punishments, even death. Let's hope a horrible marriage between us is foretold, shall we? That would solve our dilemma quite neatly."

Tilda didn't smile at the weak attempt at humor. "We understand, however Malone has a plan. Will you be prepared to assist?"

"Of course, but this timing couldn't be less opportune. I've met her, cousin."

"Your Heart Match?"

"Yes. I must tell you of the lovely Miss Hallie Pinefoy later, but for now, follow me to the Assembly

39

Chamber. The drumming of the next cycle started."

Bremen would never agree to a forced marriage. His parents had broken tradition by not marrying within the same circle of the Ancestrals; however, the couple had been unequivocally in love. True love had been the only acceptable possibility for them, and nothing less would suffice for him either.

Waiting outside the assembly room, he glanced into the ornate platinum mirror at the door and observed his angry, glittering eyes. Those dark eyes with flashing flecks of silver were the only sign his patience was stretched thin, but anger would not serve well now. It would have to be reserved for later if needed.

Scarpello opened the door and swept a mocking gaze. "They're ready."

Bremen caught the hungry glance the scribe gave Tilda when she turned and walked from the room.

His sharp mind continued to work at a way out of the situation, but one by one, each solution to the predicament was rejected. He climbed the circled granite steps to the platform and took a place next to Tilda. His vision skimmed the seated observers surrounding the stage: the council members who might attempt to decide his fate.

Smells of musky jasmine and frangipani wafted through the air and thin grey-blue mists swirled along the floor. Drums beat a harsh rhythm. Aware of the observant eyes of the crowd, he bowed to Tilda with reluctance. She looked over at Malone standing to the side, arms crossed over chest, watching with an intense gaze. A worried frown crossed her face, and he knew she was afraid the man would interrupt the ceremony.

Bremen held her cold hand in his right as the Heart Gem was placed on his open left palm. The Artifact was a clear crystal disk, about three inches wide. After a few moments, the Heart Gem glowed brown around the edges. An image formed in the center. In spite of wanting to wrench away, he held onto Tilda as the object performed a forecast.

The picture reflected on the surface of the Gem flickered before showing a future-view portraying an image of him much older, with Tilda. In the view, the grey-haired couple was seated at the long dining table in the Great Hall, each deep in separate thoughts. In the moving picture shown on the flat top of the Heart Gem, he and Tilda looked listlessly across the table, sad faces showing no joy in being together. They returned their attention to the golden dinner plates and stared with resignation.

The Heart Gem image shimmered before disappearing, leaving the smooth surface transparent once again.

With dread, he heard the excited murmurs flowing through the council, a consensus reached. The Head spoke, "As no ruinous marriage has been foretold, the council has decreed Bremen and Tilda must wed and thus the Tyler family will continue strong and true." With an air of finality, the council members filed out of the chamber satisfied with their decision.

He was just able to catch Tilda before she fell to the ground in a faint.

Malone rushed over. "I'll bring her to our residence."

"We'll meet later to discuss the plan you have?"

"Yes, we'll come to your room to speak in private." Malone carried Tilda from the chamber.

Bremen's obligation to partake in the ceremony was met now. Nothing else could be forced, could it? He'd been able to direct his life these past years except for the token acknowledgments to the Ancestrals' link, and wouldn't allow the group to dictate his existence.

He rubbed his chin, feeling the lower jaw clench tight. What he needed was advice from someone clear headed and without any underlying motive but revealing the truth. For the first time, he followed the sconces down the long hall of the entry-room chamber. The lights flickered and darkened further into the recesses of the Stronghold, the grey walls changing from light to dark as the hall went deeper. At the end of the passage, an abrupt stop led to a curling staircase, and with a resolute stride, he climbed the narrow winding steps.

At the highest recesses of the Stronghold was a vast round room, the highest residence of the Stronghold. He entered and bowed to a petite woman with a young unlined face topped by thick white-silver hair. The Seer was seated on a large cushion embroidered in gold symbols, the small table near her feet set with various stones and cards. Forehead knotted above large grey iridescent eyes, the woman greeted, "I was expecting you, Bremen Tyler."

"I was sure you were, Seer," he countered with a tight smile.

"I want to hear from your own lips what you want to know."

"I've participated in the ceremony, but won't wed Tilda. In spite of breaking many rules, my parents lived in great happiness. I will too, whatever the consequences will be."

The Seer paused for a moment then ventured inside his mind, reading the most secret thoughts there. "I won't advise to go against the council's choice, as made through the Heart Gem, but you'll find your one true Heart Match out in the world, that is already known. If you choose this path together, there will be many difficulties, and danger will mark the course with numerous obstacles. But in the end, if you are both Matched to each other, your love will bring everlasting happiness." Waiting, the Seer inclined her head.

"Tell me more. Tell me what to do," he persuaded.

"I'll say no more, as much is obscured, but from the moment your Heart Match comes across your life's path, all changes and there will be no one else. Go now, Bremen Tyler."

He knelt and kissed a tiny hand and turned to the long staircase. There must be an alternative. If there was the possibility to escape now, could he persuade Hallie to marry immediately? For once married, the Ancestrals would not separate them, would they?

He opened the door to the bedchamber. Malone and Tilda were already waiting on the massive couch. "We must devise a plan to benefit all, without any possibility of further harm. You both agree?"

"No. Destroy the Heart Gem and the other Artifacts of Love so the objects may never again be used to force a marriage." Malone pounded a fist on the table.

Bremen exchanged a glance with Tilda. "It's not that easy," he reasoned.

"It is that easy. None of the Artifacts, including the accursed Heart Gem, are protected in the fortress."

"I'm just as adverse to this situation, but there must be a coherent plan."

"Bremen, I've powerful friends who will help to hide the Artifacts. In secret places, locations which will remain unknown to the Ancestrals."

His mind sifted over the proposal. "You can trust these friends?"

"Yes, yes."

"No, Malone. Too many things may go wrong if others are involved. Let's wait a day or two."

"I can't live the next few days knowing Tilda is

promised to you."

"Only in word. That means nothing to either of us."

"I won't accept the council believing it," Malone countered.

Tilda took his hand. "I won't wait for our fate to be decided either."

Bremen eyed Malone carefully, concerned about allowing the man's impulsiveness to make matters more difficult. "Then we must go separate ways. Malone, you and Tilda leave tonight. I'll devise other plans."

Tilda held out her arms. "I wish you the best, dear cousin. I pray to see each other again one day."

He reached across to Malone, shaking the man's hand. "I'd tell you to take good care of her, but know you will."

****

It was the sweetest dream Bremen had ever experienced. Charming Hallie, with caramel-colored silky soft hair and mesmerizing green eyes unfastened the top button of a fitted low-cut dress until the summits of both tempting breasts were exposed. They were stunning from this angle. With a teasing wink, she paused, and opened one more button displaying more tempting flesh. He waited for that last button, and there, it was almost out of the eyelet. Now she was pulling the fabric apart…

His bedroom door burst open. He bolted from the cot. "Who is there?" Privacy was strictly observed in the Stronghold, in spite of doors never being locked. Who dared come into the bedchamber without permission?

Scarpello, surrounded by a legion of half a dozen soldiers hefting glowing night torches, stood in the doorway. "You stole them! Where are they?"

"Where is what? Are you mad?"

"The Artifacts of Love. They're missing. Search

the room now." Scarpello barked out orders sending the men scattering in all directions of the chamber.

"The Artifacts are not here." In the recesses of Bremen's mind a terrible thought arose. Surely Malone would not be so foolish? He and Tilda were only to escape into the night.

He leaped out of bed and pulled on black trousers. The beautiful dream had shifted into this real-life nightmare. Knowing it was fruitless to stop the attendants, Bremen waited while they tore through his few personal effects searching for the Artifacts.

A messenger burst into the room and addressed the group. "Tilda has requested to speak with the council and is waiting for the assembly."

Bremen jogged ahead of the party to the chamber and witnessed a sobbing Tilda hunched over a beaten and bruised Malone. The man had a swelling black eye and bloodstained clothes and lay moaning in a semi-unconscious state. Tilda ran soft fingers over Malone's face; the woman's streaming tears mixing with the blood drying on his skin.

Bremen rushed to her side, fearing the worst of the night was yet to be. "What happened?"

"Malone's injured," she murmured. "H-he took the Artifacts. Not for personal gain, but to ensure the council would not use one of the Artifacts of Love to separate us. Or to separate any other couple. He was furious to learn the council wouldn't allow us to view the image of the Heart Gem together."

An atmosphere of rage filled the chamber, and whispered dark curses grew louder. Bremen took a step closer to Tilda, ready to protect the three of them if necessary.

She addressed the seething crowd, "Malone's intention was to hide the items so no one could be forced to wed against their will. He must have revealed information to associates who robbed the

Artifacts."

"Where are the thieves now?" Scarpello demanded.

"I don't know. Malone tried to stop them, but the men attacked and left him for dead. I found him this way. He was able to tell me part of the story, but then became unconscious and wouldn't wake."

Inciting words of "death" and "punishment" swam in the electric atmosphere. A coldness seeped into the room that went beyond the most frigid winter night.

"Wake him," the Head Council directed. A tiny man stepped forward to place a hand against Malone's forehead. The injured man fought the healer's effects but after a few moments opened pained glazed eyes.

The imposing figure of the Head Council moved closer. "What happened to the Artifacts? Where are they?"

Malone's eyes tried to focus on Tilda. "I believed they could be trusted. The men were frequent visitors at the estate, both Jacques L'Ormond and Franc D'Arget. I..." His words became incomprehensible, and he drifted back into unresponsiveness.

Bremen knew not speaking immediately would be fatal. "The Artifacts will be located, I promise. These objects cannot remain hidden for long. I vow to find the Heart Gem."

A grateful expression filled Tilda's face. "I'll find the Heart Compass."

Fury filled the room, the crescendo of noise threatening to snuff the accused.

Bremen extended both arms to the assembly. "The Artifacts will be found."

The Head Council was still for a few moments. "First, we must make an example of Malone." He paused to consider the man's fate. "We won't kill him—such an action is against our ways. But he'll be banished and forget all seen and known in this place. Oblivion will be the curse."

Tilda began sobbing and screaming, and Bremen stepped forward to comfort the distraught woman.

The now-silent chamber listened in attention to the Head Council. "The Artifacts have been given to the Ancestrals to protect, and each object has special powers and abilities. The best of our group will be selected to retrieve the four Artifacts. But I instruct the seekers to remember these words. You are forbidden from killing to retrieve an object. The punishment for disregarding this directive will be death for the seeker. Take heed also of this most important caution: the objects are spelled with a deadly curse. Those not of the Ancestral people who possess any of the Artifacts of Love go mad."

Bremen felt the impenetrable eyes of the Head Council rest upon his head. "We are expecting you to hold to this promise. You will return the Heart Gem quickly, Bremen Tyler."

"I have a request of the council." Bremen forced a gaze toward the disapproving eyes of the council members circled around the center of the platform. Finally his eyes rested on the Seer's gentle gaze.

"My request of the Ancestrals is this. If I find and marry my true Heart Match, I may remain in the outside world. Never to return to the Stronghold unless I wish to do so. I ask to be granted this favor."

He controlled ragged breathing while the Head Council reflected. "Enough damage has already been done, but power must be exerted and the wishes of the Ancestrals may not be flouted." He paused, "We agree. However, the woman must wed willingly with no undue coercion, and with no proof you are each other's Heart Match. Any deviations from these two instructions will result in this council deciding your fate."

Bremen bowed his head, thankful at least for this.

****

As the train sped through the English countryside, Bremen considered the false evidence he'd just hunted. The informant had provided clues asserting the thief and the Heart Gem had been seen in London, but the contact had been wrong. The chase cost Bremen a wasted week. Nonetheless, his life would not consist of a constant search for the Gem.

Hours later, the train pulled into the Wrightsville station, and he rushed off the platform and to the inn. A message from the lovely Miss Hallie Pinefoy would at last be retrieved. Moving into the lobby, he glanced around for his Heart Match in spite of the impossibility. He uttered a frustrated curse at the knowledge of having to make due with the information Hallie left at the lobby desk. An in-person meeting could not happen soon enough.

The bored clerk came to nervous attention as he towered the counter, "My name is Bremen Tyler. I have a letter waiting here."

The man searched the reception counter, "No sir, nothing here."

The air rushed from his lungs. "What do you mean there is no message? You must be wrong. A communication must be here."

Flustered, the clerk flipped through numerous jumbled envelopes and papers set to the side. "I'm sorry, Mr. Tyler, but there doesn't appear to be a note."

"There must be a letter from Miss Hallie Pinefoy. It's of utmost importance."

"Oh, here. I see there is a note *for* Miss Pinefoy, but not a note for *you.*"

Bremen's stomach knotted. "Let me see that."

He took the envelope and pulled it open. It was the missive he'd written last week to Hallie explaining being called away on an urgent family matter. "How could this not have been given to her?"

The clerk jerked and a fearful expression filled his face. "I-I don't know. Someone must have missed giving the paper to the lady. If you have an address we can mail it," he offered.

He cursed the Ancestrals' call that fateful night. "If I had an address I would have given it to the lady myself. Do you know where she lives?"

"No, sir. Those records are not retained."

*Dammit!* Had Hallie decided against leaving an address? She'd awoken a sensual hunger never felt before, but he needed to reassure the woman his intensions were honorable. Was she frightened by those passionate kisses? Or had she played with his affections?

Bremen sprinted from the lobby and toward the train station, covering the ground in a few minutes. Which way could Hallie have gone?

Around the platform various people milled about, both waiting for the next train and arriving for a stay in town. The smoky air hung around the station rooftop and the noise was rough as a slight drizzle started to spit out from the murky sky. The chatter of excited voices swirled about, but his mind blocked the noise.

Hallie was gone. He stared down the many rows of railroad track seeing pinpoints of movement going north, south, west and east, fading in all directions. She had gone. Away from him.

His plan had just encountered an enormous obstacle.

Chapter Five

He was right behind! Hallie ran through the fields, the white ruffles at the hem of the blue dress fluttering, and the tall stalks of grass slapping pink marks on her arms.

The ground pounded as the man ran closer and closer, the harsh breath more labored with each step but each step as strong as the last. She pushed with a powerful burst of speed and shot further ahead. Once more he pressed and gained distance. The new black velvet short boots were hurting and the laces were undone, but all she could focus on was to get to the trees first.

Ducking and darting through the triangle of trees, the crunch of the branches popping, she tried to step where her feet would meet the least resistance. The mottled light gave a spotted appearance against the ground until the thinning trees opened into a clearing.

The man moved closer and she shrieked. Startled birds screamed then scattered as the meadow was disturbed by the chase. Hallie glanced to catch the blur of her dress floating behind as he closed in again. The man grabbed the back of the billowing fabric, then pulled to a stop.

Hallie fell to the ground laughing.

When she had caught a few breaths, Clay Nash was frowning. "How can a woman run so fast? It's not fair!"

She threw the wildflowers onto his heaving chest and sat up. "That is what you get for thinking you are better. *And* you were silly enough to give me a head start."

Clay grinned while picking up the flowers.

A childhood friend, he appeared very interested in spending time together since her return to England last week. In spite of having no romantic feelings for each other in the past, his feelings had taken a turn.

She pulled the loose tresses to the side and started to re-braid the strands which had fallen.

"I think you cheated!" Clay accused in a harsh voice.

She was taken aback by the vehemence. Matching the same tone, she straightened both shoulders and shot back, "Cheated? You are calling me a cheater? You, sir, are a sore loser. Cheater indeed, I should leave now and never speak with you again."

She made to rise, but Clay grabbed her arm. "Well, not a cheater then, you're just too fast for a girl. Didn't you ever hear of letting the man win? What about my feelings?"

"When I race a man," she teased with a smile, "I may consider letting him win."

He threw the flowers back and plopped down on the ground. He took her hand and moved it to lie on his chest. "Your mistake, Hallie, is you don't think of me as a man. I am one now, and older by two years."

She eased away. "You're a good friend, Clay." Then to break the seriousness added, "No matter that you run slower than a girl."

She rose and tightened the bootlaces, catching Clay's covert sideways glance at the ankle revealed. For the first time, she was uncomfortable about his gaze.

Clay took a deep breath before speaking, "I've missed you every day during your absence. Let us go and tell our families our intentions. I've taken the liberty of speaking with your father. We can be wed within a month."

"Married? But I've just returned. Besides, I have no interest in marriage."

"Why? We've known each other since childhood. This plan would suit all of us quite well."

She took a seat on the one of the old stumps in the clearing. While she had no intention of marrying Clay, it was better to ease the good friend into realizing the impossibility. "Yes, but it has been a long time...and we've changed."

"Perhaps you've changed, but I have not. Have you met someone else?" his eyes bulged and his voice became higher.

A picture of Bremen Tyler floated across her eyes. "No, but I've lived independently for a number of years, I have plans to earn a living now."

Waving away her intentions with a dubious swipe, Clay continued, "You are a grown woman now, Hallie, the time of independence is over. I'll take care of you, and you'll have no concerns or responsibilities except those of a wife and mother."

It irritated her to know the man was not listening. "Tell me what you have been doing during my absence."

He took a seat on the second of the three tree stumps. "I've been busy with various property acquisitions. They're somewhat complicated. I'll tell you this; join me tomorrow for luncheon in town. We can dine at a fashionable restaurant, and then visit some of the new businesses. I've connections with owners you may not have yet met."

"That would be pleasant; however, a lunch as old friends sharing a meal. Nothing else, agreed?"

"Of course, my dear, but I reserve the right to convince you of a deeper feeling."

She didn't smile at the attempt at wit. "I must return home now. Viola is stopping for tea. Will you join us?"

"I've a prior engagement but will walk with you to the house."

They covered the distance within a few minutes and he bowed before continuing. She was surprised Clay had declined the invitation without a second thought. Before her time in Boston, the three of them frequently enjoyed tea together.

She entered the drawing room and observed Viola sitting near the fireplace. "I apologize for my lateness. I'd intended to have a short walk with Clay but strolled a bit further than intended."

Viola glanced behind Hallie's shoulder. "Is he joining us then?"

"No, he had another engagement."

"Oh."

"Come into the kitchen and we can fix tea. I've missed my proper English tea time."

"I've heard the gentlemen of Boston are quite good looking. Did you meet anyone interesting there?" Viola inquired.

Hallie wiped both hands dry on the front of an old apron and handed over the plate of bread for slicing. "There were some handsome gentlemen in town, but I didn't have the opportunity to experience the attention of anyone in particular." She paused, wondering if she should tell Viola of the other encounter. "However, I did meet a certain man during my overnight stay in Wrightsville before taking the train home to Mooreland." She pictured Bremen and the kiss and felt her cheeks glowing.

"He sounds fascinating. Tell me more."

Hallie sliced the cucumbers paper-thin. "The man was good-looking," she admitted. "I'd gone out in the evening, and he saved me from some unscrupulous characters. While his manners were quite irritating in the beginning, our moments together after the episode were admittedly very intriguing."

Viola placed the kettle on the stove. "So, what happened then? Don't make me beg for details."

"He pleaded to meet in the morning, and was very urgent and sincere in this request. But when I went to the lobby, he was not there. I learned, in fact, that he had departed in the middle of the night. And in the company of a stunning woman."

A thoughtful expression settled on Viola's serene face. "I suppose there could have been a number of explanations. Have you no word since last week?"

"No. However I did leave a message at his lodging." Hallie moved to cutting the cheddar cheese with hard, deliberate strokes, eyes unwavering from the task.

"If you are fated to see this gentleman again, you will."

"The interest must have only been in my imagination."

"There is no such thing as 'your imagination.' Sometimes there's a strong connection between people that can't be explained by anything on this earth. They can be great distances apart but still feel each other's presence."

"However, in this case, I'll give up on the future possibility of seeing Mr. Bremen Tyler. What use is a man who is unable to keep a promise? This schoolgirl pinning must not continue."

A faraway look settled on Viola's face. "My grandmother has come to stay in Mooreland. She sees things and is skilled in giving readings and would be pleased to offer one. You will be amazed at my granny's visions but must keep an open mind and not be afraid."

A shiver ran up Hallie's spine, but she was determined not to be intimidated. "How exciting."

"Granny's reading may be painful or disquieting," Viola warned.

"Let's finish our tea first." Crossing to the

kitchen table, she poured a fresh portion into Viola's Wedgewood cup and savored the delicious aroma of the brew. "I've been gone from home so long, but to have learned a new skill was wonderful."

"What of your aunt?"

"She was most welcoming, and I was pleased to work for my keep as it would've been awkward intruding on her good intentions without offering some sort of service."

"Now you will think of marriage?"

"Have you been speaking to Father? He has tried to press upon me my responsibilities."

"And Clay?" Viola focused her gaze on the delicate teaspoon resting on the china saucer.

"We corresponded on a few occasions during my absence. Our fathers have expressed an interest in joining our families. Clay has in fact voiced an interest also," she admitted.

"What? And your answer would be? You can avoid this whole upheaval of a business, then!"

Hallie laughed. "But I want the upheaval, and wouldn't miss a chance to be independent. As a married woman I would never have such freedom, Viola. To enjoy every opportunity offered without restrictions."

"I don't believe you are making the right decision, my dear. Clay is a good man. What if you lose him?"

She shrugged. "I've never had him. This is just a plan of our fathers."

"I'm not quite so convinced."

Hallie was aware her plans were not the norm. "Perhaps we should leave to see dear Granny now?"

She gave Viola her shawl, and lightly bonneted, made the short walk to Viola's cottage.

Her trepidation rose at the house. Seated on a rocker near the fireplace was an old woman. The gentle word Granny did not seem to fit, as the person was formidable and bright with harsh lined skin and deep black eyes. Coarse hair stood out from the woman's head giving an intimidating appearance.

Hallie gazed at Viola, wondering if her friend would remain. Viola shook her head, "I'll return shortly. An errand waits."

Granny smiled, wise all-seeing eyes seeming to size her up. "So you would like a reading of the future, miss." It was a statement, not a question.

"Yes ma'am, if you would be so kind and have the time."

"I have enough time, girl." The woman heaved from the rocker and motioned Hallie to a chair at the kitchen table. Granny poured some of the brew on the stove into a mug and slid the beverage forward, "Here, take this cup and drink. The liquid is warm."

She took the cup of strong coffee and drank the whole beaker with a few sips, and when done Granny took the empty mug and placed a saucer over it, inverting the pair in one deft stroke.

The old woman examined the dregs, and the atmosphere in the room changed from benign to disturbing. Granny's face whitened a bit, and the woman's eyes searched Hallie's, as though seeing her for the first time.

The old woman spoke in a voice so quiet she needed to move forward to hear the words uttered, "Your path will be marked by much uncertainty and trouble. There will be grave danger. Your life will be in jeopardy more than once. Decisions will be difficult and even the correct choice will not make life smooth until much later. If a right choice is made, love will be true and you and your man will be joined together for all eternity."

She had expected a pretty fortune: lighthearted and amusing.

"You have strange premonitions," Granny

continued.

"This isn't something I speak about."

"Trust those feelings, girl. They'll serve you well." The old woman put down the cup and took her hands. "There are varied beliefs and ancient treasures in my culture and others in this world. And beyond. You'll see and experience some things others could not even dream about."

"I, ma'am? I'm only a humble doll-maker, back to stay at home for good now."

"This is your home, for true, but you'll still see other places," Granny predicted. "There is a veil between two places, thin enough to pass through for some special people. You'll pass through this veil one day with your true love."

"My true love? Who is he?"

"He is the one who was determined for you at the beginning. You must be open to love, girl. Not so afraid and careful."

"Do you know his name?"

"A man who already knows you as his."

Goosebumps rose on her nervous skin. "What else can you tell me?"

"Some is clouded as should be. There is more to this world than we see, girl. We go about looking, but not seeing, and miss more than could ever be imagined. Open your eyes. Remember that."

## Chapter Six

George Iberville's deft fingertips felt the almost imperceptible impressions made earlier on the corners of the face cards. "I'm sure Lady Luck will be smiling on you this hand, my friends," he soothed during the final dole.

The pupils of the three men at the club table enlarged and tightened just as expected based on the cards dealt. His hearing was tuned to their quickened and slowed breaths. *Like candy from a baby. Or rather, like money from an aristocrat.*

The three men played back and forth, imagining they had him bested, until the final hand when Iberville laid down a royal flush and moved the money on the table closer in a smooth, casual sweep.

"Again, I can't believe your good fortune. You must have been born under a lucky star." The Viscount slapped down the remaining cards.

Iberville modeled a vacant, bored look. "When you play as I have since the days of the cradle, the cards do seem to go in your favor." He had left the men with some money; taking too much would ensure the patrons would not play the following evening.

"Enough loss for one night, gentlemen." The baron gulped his brandy in one burning draught before shoving a chair away from the table. "I expect to win back my losses tomorrow."

Iberville inclined his head with grace. "I look forward to it, dear sir."

The men gathered what was left and rose from the table. They staggered, drunk from both the depletion of their pockets, and the addition of strong liquor to their bellies.

Iberville relaxed in the elegant chair and motioned the waiter to bring a glass of champagne. He felt very satisfied. This was the sort of establishment he'd wanted to belong to his whole life: discreet, cultured, and French. The francs and guineas passing across the gaming tables were staggering, even to his jaded eye.

The corners of his mouth pulled up in a smirk. If the owners knew he wasn't the cream of the aristocratic milk he purported to be, they'd have him booted out, along with the other ruffians and undesirables who dwelt outside these exclusive walls.

Giving a gracious nod when the champagne glass was presented by the waiter, Iberville took a silky sip from the flute. If he were a cat, a purr would fill the room. When mixing with the true bluebloods and using the false name of George Smith, no one could link him to any previous unsavory endeavors.

He was a very clever criminal. He even liked the word "criminal." It had a dangerous, bad feel. He'd been called other more pithy names like cheat and thief, but those descriptions didn't do true justice to his nature.

Born in a run-down London neighborhood, he'd learned to survive by quick wit and hands, never afraid to say or do anything to get what he wanted or needed. When it seemed London had tired of him and was eager for a speedy departure, he had traveled to France.

Now having made the way to the Riviera with rich people, rich property, and rich food, life was excellent. Yet true wealth was still completely out of his greedy grasp. This club was closer though, catering to the kind of people who took money for granted.

He raised a hand in a welcome wave to a new friend, Henri Reynard, when the count entered the room. Iberville observed the stagger in the aristocrat's step; the man was already deep in his cups.

"My friend, George Smith," Reynard slurred. "A brandy? You'll join me?"

"Of course." He answered with a tiny bow and sauntered across the hallway to take a seat at the count's own table. "I can't let a dear friend drink alone."

Iberville forced himself to sip the brandy, resisting the urge to down its superior vintage. "You've been busy? You've not been here for days."

A look of sadness crossed Reynard's face. "I had to settle the final details of the estate business. My late wife's." The man motioned for the bottle.

Iberville's interest piqued. Estate was such a brilliant-sounding word. "All is now complete?"

Reynard waved a sophisticated hand, the crisp white lace at the cuff fluttering. "I care not one whit for it all. The estate, the lands. And the accursed treasure. An artifact, I was told by a former friend. Damn stone."

Iberville focused on the conversation. Artifacts usually meant money; he had already helped himself to a number of "artifacts" lying about Reynard's mansion during a few visits. "An artifact? What is an artifact?"

Reynard's face hardened. "It is a curse. I had intended it as a wedding gift for my Maria, but it signaled the end of our happiness, before our joy even started."

"How tragic. My condolences again, my friend. However if this artifact brings you painful memories, I'd be pleased to take it off your hands."

Reynard was befuddled. "I'm not sure. See,

someone I knew was trying to hide it. I took it to give as a gift for my future wife thinking it would please her, but made a mistake. I must do the honorable act now and hide the thing."

"I'm a collector. For museum pieces—did you know? Surely I can see this artifact, for purely scholarly reasons, of course."

Reynard cocked his head. "Your businesses are so varied, Smith. I suppose your seeing it should be all right, but you'll promise to keep it a secret?"

"Of course, my good man. I'm a keeper of innumerable secrets."

"You're a good friend. I appreciate the help given in sorting out some of my business and charity decisions this last month."

Those contributions had gone right into his pocket. "Of course, Henri."

Reynard signaled to the valet to bring their coats, and a footman slipped the cloaks onto their shoulders and escorted them outside and into Reynard's waiting coach.

Iberville kept silent until the driver stopped in front of the chateau, and then followed Reynard across the marble foyer and up the grand staircase. He had never been in the bedroom suite before. And while the room he had stayed in here once before was richly appointed, this domain was decorated with the best furnishings and decor he had ever seen. He made a mental note to examine the "artifacts" closer next time Reynard was in a drunken mood.

Going over to a small nondescript bureau, Reynard pulled a key from a waistcoat pocket and unlocked the top drawer. With a mixture of awe and hate on his face, the man pulled out a small item from the bureau. The count unwrapped an object from a white velvet cloth, and placed it on the mahogany table nearby.

"This is the Heart Gem."

Frowning, Iberville examined the unimpressive flat stone nestled on the square cloth. About the width of his palm, it appeared to be pure white cut-glass.

"Noelle," Reynard yelled, calling over the young maid cleaning in the hallway. The count grabbed the frightened girl by the hand and with his other hand picked up the stone and waited.

The Heart Gem started to glow a deep red around the edges. Suddenly the center area of the stone showed a moving picture of Reynard and the maid together in bed. In the view shown on the surface, the girl was sobbing as the count clutched her in his bony grasp, his lank, dirty hair falling over the face of the terrified girl.

Iberville clamped down his shock. What sort of magic was this?

Reynard let go of her hand, and pushed the girl away letting her scurry into the corner. "Now look at this."

The count removed a lock of his late wife's hair from a gold case in a breast pocket. Next he held the hair and the Gem, again one in each hand.

The Gem glowed black-edged now, the surface showing Reynard at the tombstone of his wife's grave. "This is the same image shown on our wedding day."

"What is that?" This Artifact could provide immense riches and prestige. Wealthy French and British individuals would have the expensive opportunity to use a new toy.

Not breaking his gaze at the tragic image, Reynard spoke in a serious tone, "I was told the Heart Gem shows the essence of what a union will be. It can show happiness or wealth or tragedy. It will show whatever the life together will become founded on."

He would have the Gem. He could sell a view into the Gem to all the nobility and wealth of Europe and beyond. He expertly plucked the stone from Reynard's hand.

"What are you doing?"

"This brings you sadness. Give it to me and be released from your burden."

"No. It was to be hidden away before it was stolen, and now I must fulfill that intention by putting it where it can never be found."

"Of course, my friend. Let me borrow it then. For a short time only."

Reynard's eyes flitted between the Gem and Iberville's face. "No. I must keep it hidden. That is what Malone should have been allowed to do."

"Well, this Malone—whoever he is—was wrong." He slipped the Gem into his pocket. "I promise to return it very soon."

Reynard spoke with more conviction now. "No." He reached toward Iberville's jacket. "Give it back now."

Iberville hit him hard in the jaw. Reynard struggled to remain standing, but a second punch in the stomach doubled the man over. Iberville slipped the count's small pistol out from under his coat, and slammed Reynard viciously across the temple with the barrel.

The unconscious man dropped hard onto the floor.

****

He was up behind the woman, hips slapping against her derriere. She was pushing back, their rhythm perfectly tuned for rough pleasure. He moaned at the same moment as her scream pierced through the darkened room then bit down on the back of her shoulder, eased off and flopped outstretched onto the bed.

George Iberville put his arm around Louise's

shoulder and stroked the lustrous light blonde hair before lifting the locks to smell the fragrant aroma.

His other hand reached to the cloth bag on the table next to the bed. "Look what I have." He pulled out the Heart Gem.

"George, what is that?" She examined the Artifact from a distance.

"This is our escape, love; our new life of luxury awaits." He held the Gem to catch the light in its unusual prism.

"Such pretty colors shining through. Is it a diamond?"

"No, even better. Watch, I'll demonstrate what this does." He took hold of her hand.

The Heart Gem started to glow black around the edges. The image reflected a sumptuous bedroom filled with expensive possessions. The bed was enormous, spread with a gold brocade cover, large pillows placed against the ornate gold headboard, and an opulent painting of naked nymphs on the wall above.

In the image portrayed on the Heart Gem, Louise stood next to the bed, jewelry draped around her neck and diamond drops at the ears. She was dressed in a luxurious negligee of filmy white froth, pupils dilated in pleasure. The Louise pictured on the surface emitted a naughty giggle as the back of a fair-headed man entered the image. The man pressed her down on the bed, and they started a wild romp.

As they lay on the bed looking into the Heart Gem's visage, George exchanged a glance with Louise, excited by the images of play. "Look now." He returned her attention to the Gem.

In the image, a sound came from the door in the corner. Louise and the romping man looked up. She wore a look of intense fear.

The Heart Gem image revealed the man on the

bed with Louise was not Iberville but another man, of the same hair color and build. In the view, Iberville burst into the room with a pistol pointed at the couple. He aimed first to the man and shot, then pointed at Louise and shot again.

In alarm Louise pulled her hand out of his, breaking the connection with the Heart Gem. "What horror is this stone you have?"

"It tells the truth," he said, feeling the blood rush as every muscle tightened. "I'm willing to give you everything, and you betray me. Who is that man?"

"I don't know who he is, but I'll not cheat on you." She glanced to the wall, fastening an old robe.

He sat and reached over to shake her. "It shows the truth. You were not faithful to me. Did you see all the gifts I showered you with? You are a whore!"

Louise squeaked in fright. "How can you be angry with me for something that has not happened?"

The tramp would betray him. He had intended to share a treasure, but she would take a lover right under his nose. "You bastard bitch. I was willing to give you everything, and this is how you repay me?"

"I want you to leave now, George. You have hurt me."

She arose from the bed, rubbing her arms.

He jumped after her and cornered the woman against the wall. And now she dared to reject him? He clamped her in a restricting grip and asked once more, "Who is the man in the image?"

"I don't know, but you must leave."

Louise started to turn away, but he grabbed her by the arms and shook roughly. She tried to break free with a squeal, but he shoved the woman down very hard onto the stone floor. Her head made a sharp "crack" noise as the bone hit the ground. He stuck out his foot to kick but she moved no more.

Chapter Seven

Bremen slid the one-hundred pound note across the table, keeping his fingers on the edge of the paper. "You are sure Count Henri Reynard has it? You've seen the object yourself?"

The coat clerk blinked at the sum of money. "Yes, he brought it in last week, ranting about it stealing what little happiness he and the countess could have had. Something about 'better not knowing their fate.'"

"And the size. About how large was the object?"

The man gestured with thumbs and forefingers. "I asked if I could hold it, but he snatched it away. Said he should never have taken it in the first place."

He let go of the money. "Which way to Reynard's home?"

The clerk glanced around before slipping the note into a pocket. "Three miles. Follow the road to your left to the large stone fence. The manor is just beyond the gardens."

At last, a concrete lead on the Heart Gem. Bremen had searched now for weeks, garnering only elusive clues that bore no definite results. Until now. If he could conclude this business today, using whatever means necessary to obtain the Gem, the search could start in earnest for another important treasure, Miss Hallie Pinefoy.

Motioning the footman for his horse, Bremen took the reins in one hand and passed a generous franc note with the other, then eased the horse into an easy canter to the estate. The French countryside was beautiful, the spring flowers in bloom and the warm sun on his back. A place for lovers, and perhaps a future honeymoon stop for him and his Heart Match.

At the stone fence, he stopped the horse and straightened in the saddle while eyeing the estate's perimeter. An acquaintance of Malone's, Henri Reynard, purportedly had taken one of the Artifacts of Love. Some small bits of information had filtered down to Bremen through contacts, and now he was ready to follow and retrieve the object belonging to the Ancestrals.

Leaping off the horse and tying reins to a post, he was surprised no staff was in attendance. In fact the grounds looked deserted, and despite their grandeur seemed neglected of late. He reached to the knocker and let it fall with a loud clang. There were footsteps, and a young maid dressed in black answered the door.

"I am here to see Count Henri Reynard. Could you tell the gentleman Mr. Bremen Tyler is here?"

Her red-rimmed eyes moistened, and hands squeezed the full-length white apron. "I am sorry to inform you the count passed the day before yesterday."

Another serious obstacle. He glanced over at the black-ribboned windows. "My regrets. May I ask how he has passed?"

"Oh, sir took his own life. He was in the bedchamber and shot himself. He was mourning the late countess these past weeks so terribly. His friend was witness to the count's last act of grief." She dabbed weeping eyes with a handkerchief.

"May I speak to his friend?"

"George Smith said he must leave the area, the sadness was too much to bear."

"Do you know where he went?"

"I don't know. The gendarmerie wished to speak

with him again, but could not locate the man. I know he was English, so perhaps he returned home. He seemed in a great hurry to leave, the horrible circumstances were so shocking. He consoled and advised the count since the countess's passing." She paused as though noticing her loose tongue. "May I ask, sir, what is your interest?"

"I believe there was an object Count Reynard had possession of which was to be returned. Had the count made any recent acquisitions? Something memorable."

The maid's face paled, matching the white cap. "I don't know what you're talking about."

He moved in closer. "May I speak to you inside, in private?"

The girl tried to push the door closed. "No, I must get back to my work."

"Had the count acquired an unusual object? Something secret and kept in safekeeping?"

She was frightened and blinked in rapid succession. "I don't know of any objects. And it is not here anyway."

"You will not be in trouble. I just need to locate the thing Count Reynard had secured."

She was very tired, shoulders drooping about her thin neck. "There was something, but it's missing now. I know the count kept it under lock and key, but the cabinet is now empty."

"This friend of the count's, Mr. Smith. What did this man look like?"

"Fair haired, blue eyes. Quite an elegant gentleman with a stocky build. But I never did like the man."

"You said he was an Englishman. Have you heard him speak of home in England? Any particular city?"

"I believe he was from London. He appeared in town about a month or so ago and became fast friends with the count." The woman paused, her eyes a vacant stare. "I must go now. I am done with the sadness in this house. I'm moving on to a happier town."

He slipped a coin into her hand. "For you to make a fresh start."

Her eyes widened. "Thank you indeed, sir."

"Is there anything else you can tell me about Mr. Smith?"

"Only that he knew of the object you are seeking. I saw the count show it to him the day he died."

Bremen didn't move, not wanting to frighten the girl. "I would appreciate hearing a description. Do you remember what the object looked like?"

Her face was more relaxed now, and a small smile peeped out as she rubbed the gold piece. "Round, sir, fitting on the palm. I never touched the thing, wouldn't want to, but it changed color and showed a picture." The nervous frown returned to her forehead, and she crossed herself.

He expelled a deep breath as the door closed. So close—only two days off. He climbed onto the horse and surveyed the lonely vista before him. Even the sun had grown colder and the flowers lost their scent. All he could do was pass on to his contacts what had just been learned and hope the network could help tighten the net around this Mr. Smith. No doubt the man was now far away from the area.

He kicked the flanks of the horse setting a course north. He needed to go now and find Hallie, his Heart Match. The contacts had been unsuccessful in tracking her whereabouts. In spite of not having the time to properly court, he must persuade her to wed with haste, but without undue pressure, as directed. No small feat with her independent nature and his demanding personality.

He could seduce her, hoping Hallie's ladylike

sensibilities would induce her to wed without the usual engagement period. Would the means justify the end if his intentions were pure? He believed so. Especially as the Ancestrals did have a reputation for getting what they wanted.

The stallion's hoofbeats drummed against the ground, kicking up a long dark cloud of dust, the staccato lulling him into thoughts of the Ancestral people. From the earliest of memories, the group had been moving when out in the world, not staying in any place longer than necessary. Most of the local people saw them as a kind of gypsy, and the Ancestrals encouraged those beliefs. It was easier than the truth. "More mysteries on earth and above that people cannot even imagine," his mother used to say.

He rode across the countryside remembering his early years with affection. Father had specialized in the handling of unique treasures and museum pieces, and knew just where to look to find the ancient sword or the golden arm cuff. Like his father, Bremen could also spot a forgery with ease.

Interested in acquiring a great knowledge of history and archeology, Bremen had benefited from formal education in America until his teens. Some of the "history" being taught was wrong, but his family considered it best for all not to correct the instructors and thus he graduated at the top of the class.

Then things changed for him and sister, Bremma. Their parents died and both children returned to the Ancestrals who had shunned his family for many years. There were benefits in living with the Ancestrals, but it was not the life he wanted.

His Uncle Roman had chosen his own path in life many years ago, and settled to a warm community in the English city of Mooreland. His work was done through correspondence and deliveries; however, Bremen knew Roman kept the shop open and stocked with various items that would provide interest and legitimacy to the business. There were weapons and collector items, jewelry and ornaments, manuscripts and books.

While the people of the town did not purchase much, as Roman had expected, the business thrived through procurement and sale of select pieces of interest for numerous clients all over the world.

Now Roman had passed on, leaving the curiosity shop business and possessions to his nephew. To inventory the items would be of the first order, then to determine what to do with the business.

Bremen also needed to ensure there was no mention of the Ancestrals in any of Roman's papers or personal effects as nothing could be left behind to draw attention to or give clues to their existence.

It was necessary to take a few days in Mooreland before venturing out again to search for Hallie Pinefoy.

Chapter Eight

Another impediment.

Hallie left the milliner's shop rejected and regretful. The rejection had been dealt by the owner, an ignorant man who didn't understand her lifelike display models would increase his business. The regret was her fault, brought on by a few sharp words when the man agreed to only consider a business deal with her "father" or "husband."

She hadn't anticipated so much difficulty; therefore the past few weeks were not as successful as expected. Fingers wound tightly about the smooth handle of the wicker basket, she made her way back to the buggy. If dear Mr. Roman had still been alive, God rest his soul, they could have entered into a financially successful business venture. The funds her late mother had left would be applied to purchase a share in the curiosity shop. That mercantile was ideally located, on one of the busiest corners directly across from town hall.

She packed the basket of dolls under the buggy seat and pulled onto the bench, arranging the navy fitted skirt and securing an elegant feathered bonnet under her chin.

The sun was dipping in the darkening sky. Except for a few restaurant patrons, the streets were clear of shoppers and pedestrians. There would be a full moon tonight.

Before raising the riding straps, Hallie glanced toward Roman's Curiosity Shop. The lights were on. That was unusual. A tiny quiver ran up her spine as various possibilities were examined.

Of course, it could not be old Mr. Roman, raised from the dead. And if he did rise from the dead, it surely was not with the intent of returning to the dusty shop. However, if the long-lost nephew who inherited the business was there, he may be interested in resuming or divesting the business held by Mr. Roman. That prospect was promising.

She slipped from the buggy, removed the bonnet and smoothed stray hair into place in the loose chignon. After brushing out the creases from the skirt, she was prepared to present a neat and ladylike first impression when meeting the new owner.

Hallie crossed the street and stopped at the shingled, well-maintained building. Was it correct to venture uninvited? A peek through the smudged window proved there had been some activity going on as items had been removed from the shelves and placed onto the table. A large ledger was laid open on the counter, and a few empty wooden boxes were stacked along the side of the shop. Packing had begun.

The door emitted a small creak when pulled open; a protest for being unused for the past month. The tinkle of the bell announced her entrance to the empty room.

Shelves filled with goods lined the walls and at the center of the shop stood a glass counter desk that ran along the width of the store. A large worktable with a couple of chairs sat off to the side. There were books, figurines, and some ornamental objects unrecognizable, but even to an untrained eye the items locked in the glass counter case appeared to be valuable and rare.

"Hello?" The apartment in the back was also lit up, and there was some quiet movement there. A thief may have broken in, but surely that was not the case as the lights were blazing.

"Hello? Is anyone here?" Hearing no response, Hallie inched toward the back of the building with trepidation.

A tall dark-haired man stepped out from the draped area of the back. She squeaked with sudden alarm at the looming size of him, and then froze, feet locked in place.

Mr. Bremen Tyler. Her eyes fastened with his in immediate recognition as high emotions leapt from happiness to curiosity to anger. Here was the man who tried to seduce her in Wrightsville. The man who escaped in the middle of the night with a beautiful woman. The man who didn't keep a rendezvous after pleading for one. She drew in a long breath. Please don't let the questionable Bremen Tyler be Mr. Roman's nephew.

"Hallie? It's you." With a grin he reached for an embrace.

She nodded with as much cool, calm confidence it was possible to muster but took a step backward, "Hello again. Was the name, Mr. Lemon Tyler?"

"*Bremen* Tyler. I've been searching for you."

"Oh? How nice. What gave you the notion to investigate in the back room? Was I there?"

"Pardon?"

"Nothing. Anyway, you've found me in Mooreland." She was being gruff but was pleased to see a confused look cross over Bremen's face.

"I was called away during the night on an urgent matter and regret we could not have met that morning."

"How interesting."

"Just interesting? You've been in my thoughts since our evening."

"Oh, that evening. I'm sorry to have caused so much trouble and interrupted your night."

"I wouldn't call it an interruption. Rather fate, my dear."

She held herself in tight check. "Mr. Tyler, are you related to the late Mr. Roman? I heard the unfortunate news of his passing."

His eyes rested upon her, reminding one of a hungry wolf seeking a tasty meal. "I'm his nephew. When you and I first met, I had been traveling to Mooreland to visit him. Again, I ask your forgiveness for not meeting in the morning."

Was he a criminal on the run from the law? She was determined not to let the formidable Mr. Tyler rattle her again. "I'd actually forgotten about our meeting until now. In fact, I believe I even overslept that morning."

"I lay awake thinking of you."

Her body tingled at the thought of this handsome man lying in his bed thinking of her. She prodded with a question, "Until dawn?"

A slightly closed expression fell over dark eyes, "Until I was called to leave."

"Ah, yes. Family business? And that matter is now closed—you are free?"

"Not quite free. It's a rather complicated story."

"I'm sure it is." She crossed arms over chest. "My deepest condolence on your uncle's passing, but perhaps we could meet now about a business venture I'm undertaking? Mr. Roman and I had communicated in depth about the matter. Now the venture could be advantageous to both of us."

"Would you like to speak about it now?" His deep voice held those tantalizing undertones she remembered so well. "We can speak about whatever you would like for as long as you would like."

His hand went out to move a lock of errant hair behind her ear. She forced two very shaky knees to lock back into place. She needed a breath of air as cool composure was swiftly evaporating. "Unfortunately I have the buggy and must return before nightfall."

"I would be pleased to escort you back home." He took her hand.

She remembered what happened last time he acted as escort. She pushed away. "No, no. It's not convenient for me at this moment."

"Stop by at your convenience then."

Unable to control a blush, she moved toward the door. "Sometime tomorrow then?" That should give enough time to gather up the racing thoughts.

"I'll be here waiting. This time there is nothing that could keep me away."

Chapter Nine

Her eyes looked too bright and eager against feverish cheeks. Hallie stared into the mirror and tested out yet another relaxed expression. In spite of the shock at seeing Bremen again, she would control any interest or feelings for the man. While acknowledging a bit of foolish attraction, nothing could persuade her to become embroiled in any more embarrassing situations, especially if there was a beautiful woman in the cad's life.

Hallie allowed one more preen before the glass. The crisp white blouse exuded primness, the black skirt—most plain. She was ready, had in fact been ready for over an hour after waking in a rush, fretful Roman's Shop would be empty, the prior day just a dream.

The sun was rising as the horse set off; the wares having been readied the night before. She promised to endeavor to do her best to ignore any awkwardness. The unusual custom-made dolls could find a good home at the shop, and everything could still proceed as planned. In addition, buying the business from Bremen would remove him from her sight. Perfect plan.

In case the man happened to be watching, she made the exit from the buggy slow and the entry to the shop unhurried and casual. She affixed one of the practiced calm expressions before entering.

Bremen sat at the counter desk writing in a ledger, a dark swath of thick hair falling over a wide forehead. "Miss Pinefoy, I've been waiting since first light."

The greeting rendered her speechless for a moment, and a blush rose while Bremen took in every detail.

"Mr. Tyler, I pray this is a good time to speak about the business venture which was mentioned yesterday?"

"Pray go ahead, ma'am," Bremen drawled while pulling out a seat at the table.

"May I propose a partnership?" She almost bit her tongue as the words came out in an ungainly, too-direct manner. He did fluster her so.

Bremen lifted that skeptical eyebrow, the gleam in his eyes indicating extreme interest. Then, placing a hand on hers as it rested on the tabletop said, "I have an interest in a partnership, also. May I speak first?"

She swallowed hard and slid away as if the table was red hot. "You've inherited a property which you don't want to keep. Sell it to me."

The man's wide mouth curved in a smile. "What makes you think I don't want to keep the property?"

She was silent. That was something unanticipated. "It seemed during our first meeting you weren't looking to settle in one place. Yesterday it appeared you were cataloging and packing goods."

"I have a...task to complete, but nonetheless am now considering the prospect of continuing my uncle's work here in Mooreland."

"I had not thought you were interested in a small venture in a small city."

"I did not realize I'd been so clear in my aspirations. May I be clear now?"

"Would you consider, then, being an absentee partner? I could run the business, both the curiosity objects and the business trade. You could leave and do...whatever your task is and take as long as you like. Away from Mooreland. For as long as you like. Forever, in fact."

"However, I want to stay in Mooreland." He moved in closer, whispering so that she needed to shift closer. "There is much here which appeals to me."

Hallie slid back with a sharp movement. "I can't convince you?"

"Miss Pinefoy, I'm sure you could convince me of anything and everything, but the mores of society would frown upon that. However, you could try. May I persuade you?"

She was speechless for a moment but nonetheless undeterred. "Then you would consider a business partnership in my venture?"

"And that venture is?"

"I've created beautiful and unique dolls which can be placed for sale in this shop."

"Dolls? Children's dolls?" His tone reflected surprise.

"Both for children and as collector's items. There are a few in my basket. May I show you?"

"Please do."

She placed one of the baby dolls and two fancy dress dolls on the table, positioning the limbs to exhibit the best details. "These items are not for sale in the county, so I believe customers will have an interest in acquiring them. There is also the prospect of custom orders to match hair, eyes and clothing."

"This might be a unique item for the shop," Bremen responded in a business-like tone. He lifted a doll and examined the meticulous smoothness of the skin and the perfection in the placement of the hair.

She was impressed by his attention to the important components of the figure and proposed an offer, "A half and half split is recommended. I can take care of all the business details in your absence."

"My dear Hallie, I assure you I've decided to stay in town."

Her heart pounded in her chest. She prayed Bremen couldn't hear the sound. No, hoped he couldn't feel the banging as it pulsed through her body and boomed through the room reverberating off the walls. "You will stay?"

"Yes, I will stay. Do you want me to stay?"

"It matters naught."

His look was one of disbelief, as though able to see inside her head. "You are certain of that, my darling?"

"Quite so."

"You have a lovely little vein fluttering at the side of your neck. What would be the reason?"

"The dolls, Mr. Tyler? May I leave them here along with a price list?"

"By all means, Hallie."

"Could I get a receipt please?"

"A receipt? Of course."

Bremen searched through the items on the counter until finding a receipt book. He wrote up the proper documentation and held the paper out.

"Thank you, Mr. Tyler. I hope this can be the start of a lucrative business relationship together."

"My pleasure, Miss Pinefoy. I greatly look forward to a relationship. A permanent one, my love."

\*\*\*\*

Bremen eased into the nearest chair. She was even lovelier than when they'd met almost a month ago. The thick light brown hair was pulled to expose a long neck, and sparkling green eyes gazed earnestly into his. He had commented on her nerves, but his heart had been racing too.

Even the demure blouse and skirt had an effect—he'd wanted to peel off the fitted layers, sweep Hallie into his arms and spend the remainder of the week in the bedroom.

He got up and started to pace. He wouldn't ask

why the woman hadn't left information on how to be reached. What mattered now was she had walked into the shop and nothing would stand in the way of making Hallie his wife.

But always an obstacle. He loosened the white shirt collar.

The edicts set forth by the Ancestrals prohibited placing undue pressure on Hallie. Instead, she must come willingly, with a true and loving heart.

While he believed she was his own Heart Match, there was the possibility he was not her Match. His lips tightened at a circumstance too horrific to consider.

Yesterday he'd intended to let the meeting unfold naturally and allow the relationship to develop into something each would crave, but now found himself fighting rising irritation.

He'd spent time trying to locate Hallie, but the woman didn't even care he was in Mooreland. In fact, she was determined to rid herself of his presence.

Why was she denying their attraction? Had she no feelings for him? Or had he misread the shared kiss as just a flirtation?

He rubbed together his palms, feeling a chill in the air. This game could be played by two. The decision to stay in Mooreland was not based on Hallie, was it?

There was a sweetness and simplicity in this town, so unlike life with the Ancestrals, and he was in no hurry to return with the Heart Gem. When he left the other place to come here, certain gifts were surrendered, but the absence was acceptable. He'd lived most of his life without special abilities.

He tapped long fingers against the desk. How could he persuade Hallie to fall in love and wed without delay?

Some thought must be given about the

difference between undue duress and sweet persuasion.

The difference?

Perhaps it was seduction.

Chapter Ten

Hallie scrutinized the steady stream of well-heeled customers entering and exiting Tyler's Shop. Since last week, the renamed store had set Mooreland on its head with offerings of old and new curiosities and collectables.

"Excuse me," she apologized as she endeavored to get through the door but inadvertently trod on an elderly gentleman's toes.

"Hallie." Bremen motioned from a place at the back, a towering bronze-haired leviathan at his side. "May I introduce my…associate, Ruffian."

"The inestimable, Miss Hallie Pinefoy. I'm honored to meet you." The man dwarfed her hand.

Another exceptional male in Mooreland. Where *did* the mysterious Bremen and his cohorts hail from? "You know my name?"

"I've been listening to Bremen sing your praises for the past hour."

She shot a sharp look at Bremen who appeared pleased and unruffled. The man must have nerves of steel.

"Hallie, if you will excuse us, Ruffian and I were just concluding our business."

"Certainly." She inclined her head before stepping to the wall devoted to her dolls, and began to replenish and straighten the wares displayed on the shelves. She was just able to hear the men's furtive whispers.

"I've heard the Gem is back in England."

"Made it out of France, then? I have contacts in and around London and will spread out the net. And you?" Bremen asked.

"Word is placing my object in Wales, so that's where I'm off to next."

"I'll take the advice provided under consideration. Good luck, Ruffian, my friend."

The men moved out of earshot as Bremen escorted the visitor to the door. "Miss Pinefoy." The bearded man tipped his hat.

She gave a small wave with a gloved hand and continued working as Bremen moved to the front of the shop to answer a question presented by a customer.

Hallie placed seven new dolls on the shelf, posing them and fluffing the garments to best advantage. The past week had gone better than expected, and the dolls had become popular items in both Tyler's Shop and the toy store in town. Over a dozen of the children's dolls had already sold, and she had sent word to the London vendors to procure more supplies. So far, the custom-made dolls had not garnered any interest, but this would come in time.

Bremen was trying to make his way over to her, but the distance presented a mixture of relief and disappointment. While enjoying the success in placing the dolls with Bremen was rewarding, being alone in a room with him could pose some difficulties. So far their meetings were quick and professional with just an exchange of goods and money.

However their attraction grew with each meeting. She knew the man wanted to speak privately, but for some reason held back. She vowed to fight her burgeoning feelings as mixing a business proposition with any type of other proposition would make things complicated. And it appeared he was interested in an "other" proposition. Such a mistake could make conducting any sort of commerce together quite difficult.

Ignoring a tinge of regret at being unable to speak with Bremen, Hallie gave a cool smile and departed.

\*\*\*\*

Bremen ushered the last customer out of the shop and locked the door with a loud snap. Dammit that fate dictated he was never alone with Hallie. He must be the only shopkeeper in town who wished the patrons kept out so she could be kept in.

He glanced around at the merchandise hastily placed back into the glass cases and wall displays. In truth he originally hadn't the intention of keeping the store open except for Hallie's merchandise. In fact, *he'd* buy the dolls if doing so would keep her coming in each and every day. Luckily they'd become a popular item or by now there would be a whole collection in the back apartment. He frowned at the uncomfortable picture.

But what would he say if they were alone? He needed and wanted her? In spite of their short acquaintance she was meant to be his bride? Soon things would come to a head, as it was impossible to just look at the woman without touching and kissing. Those kisses in Wrightsville were electric, and he was aching for more.

He would have to swallow thick pride and beg the woman to give a second chance even if she rejected his advances as before. The next time fate allowed them to be alone, he would offer a suggestion to put the past behind. But now he, of all people, felt a bit nervous.

However, an apology could be made if his kisses had offended, and forgiveness would be granted to Hallie for not keeping a meeting, or at least saying goodbye with even the shortest of notes.

Bremen went into the apartment kitchen to pour a cup of cold black coffee and took a large swallow of the bitter brew before gazing to the paper lying on the table.

Ruffian's lead should be followed, and the search for the Heart Gem resumed in earnest. Waiting for numerous contacts to do the initial inquiries had not been productive; however, the idea of being away from Hallie kept him in Mooreland. He should be concentrating more on regaining the object. The Ancestrals were not known for their patience.

Chapter Eleven

Taking a too-quick sip of hot tea, Hallie scalded the tip of her tongue as Clay prattled on about economics and finances. "And that, my dear woman, is how to avoid the downfall that comes with debt," he concluded.

She waved her hand over the teacup to indicate to the waiter not to replenish the hot water. "Interesting, my friend, but there are inherent risks which must be assumed in investment. If nothing is risked, nothing can be gained."

"My dear, when you think so seriously, you get a little crease between your eyebrows. That can become quite unattractive as you get older."

She glowered until he lowered his eyes. "I don't think my aging needs to be a concern of yours."

"Ahh... But I hope to age with you."

For an intelligent man, he was not well versed in tact. She moved the chair from the table. "Thank you for the tea, but I must retreat and complete my banking."

Clay swallowed the remainder of the wine in one hearty swig. "I'll escort you."

"No need. My errand will be quick. Afterward I'll spend the remainder of the afternoon looking at fripperies and doodads. Perhaps I'll contemplate the merits of various yarns for an hour or two, then expand to pretty ribbons."

Clay's face blanched. "If you're sure, I'll leave you to those errands."

She smiled. She'd have to remember these ploys whenever he became intrusive.

First, there were monies to pick up from Bremen and deposit at the bank. So far a little nest egg was building, although she was not sure what to do with the funds besides purchase more supplies.

Hurrying around the corner of the teashop, she was at Bremen's in a few short minutes. Surprised to find the shop room empty, she advanced toward the curtained area that led to Bremen's apartment.

The divider opened abruptly. "Good afternoon, Hallie." Bremen looked delicious, his thick mane appearing tousled as if he'd just risen from bed.

She took two slow breaths, determined not to let him sense the feelings he elicited. Close proximity to the man did strange things.

"Hallie, I'd like to suggest a new start. Our first meeting in Wrightsville was…unusual, and I understand you think I took advantage of the situation. If so, my sincere apologies. We now reside in the same city and conduct business together. Let's never mention Wrightsville again and put the past behind. A fresh beginning?"

"An excellent idea, Mr. Tyler. My thoughts exactly. Friends." She stepped closer to shake his hand.

"Friends." He took her hand. "Or more than friends?"

Hallie remembered the moment at the Wrightsville Inn bedchamber door and tried to pull away but couldn't, unsure whether her arm wouldn't move or Bremen wouldn't release.

As he did that night, he lifted her hand and kissed it, then turned the palm over and placed another warm kiss. Her knees swayed. She shivered, shocked at the intense reaction.

With a measured movement, as though allowing her to call a stop, Bremen reached out an arm and pulled her waist nearer to press against his frame. Hallie's eyes fluttered closed as he leaned down for a kiss.

His mouth was warm and hard, and hers soft. Her desire for Bremen rose, forcing away unwanted thoughts for propriety. Now was a time to act not to think. Unmindful of the consequences, she relaxed into his body and as if by instinct raised her arms to encircle the strong corded neck. His hands roamed her hips and buttocks, making her gasp with want at the maleness of him.

She ran her palms over his wide shoulders moving in even closer, body and mouth.

"Hallie." His voice was ragged. "My darling, what we are gifted with is amazing. Let's not waste more time. I love you and want you to—"

The shop bell rang and she jumped. Grabbing a book from the shelf, she pretended to be absorbed in the pages as an older well-dressed gentleman came through the door. "Mr. Tyler, I must apologize for being late for our meeting. I'm glad you contacted me regarding the item sought."

Bremen unenthusiastically greeted the visitor. "I was just finishing my business."

"Yes, we are done, Mr. Tyler." Hallie shoved the tome into place.

"Thank you for coming, Miss Pinefoy. We'll finish our discussion at the nearest opportunity."

Chapter Twelve

The courtship had begun. Or perhaps the better word was *courtships*?

Bremen made small gestures to win Hallie's affection. Wildflowers left on a favorite garden bench, and a tiny box of perfect chocolates slipped into the doll basket. A simple note of "I love you - B" was delivered just yesterday. And she was not sure if he was keeping his half of the doll sales.

Clay had also been making efforts to win her attention. He played escort to the finest, most expensive restaurants in Mooreland and the surrounding cities. He wrote elaborate poems lauding her beauty, and listened attentively when she spoke about the doll creations.

There were advantages and flaws to be weighed for both men.

Bremen was the mysterious suitor, charming but with motives hard to decipher. The fresh start two days ago was pivotal, and although they had not been alone since then, their attraction had intensified into a maelstrom of lust. They held back in public, but what she really wanted to do was to ignore everyone in the room, jump into Bremen's arms and kiss. And more.

The "more" had occupied a great deal of heated thoughts lately. Just yesterday they came close to losing control in the shop and poor Mrs. Fulton, looking for a unique anniversary gift for her husband the Reverend, would have been shocked to witness "more."

Hallie felt her forehead crinkle. Did she really

want the pure excitement of Bremen? There was no doubt he was passionate and interesting and those kisses were seductive, but what of the women in his past? In addition, he'd never explained the beauty in Wrightsville.

Clay, on the other hand, was stable and loyal. Although she enjoyed his brotherly companionship, there was no thrill around him. However, Clay's family and hers were good neighbors, and father had made frequent remarks to show favor toward an announced engagement.

She knew what life would be like with Clay, and in some ways that appealed in spite of the lack of excitement. He was a proponent of living a quiet life, her continuing the doll business before raising children. Clay was...predictable.

Most importantly, did she have to settle on either man? The time in Boston as a single, independent woman had been supremely interesting. Aunt Agnes had participated in the suffragette meetings and lauded her own personal choice of a life answering to no man. A successful businesswoman, her money and time were her own.

Hallie fastened on teal slippers and gave a small spin enjoying the feel of the wide dress twirling about.

If her intuition was correct, tonight would be interesting. It was the evening of the annual town ball at the mayor's mansion and both men would attend.

She'd chosen a short-sleeved silk aquamarine dress in a shade that accentuated both hair color and eyes, and fastened on her mother's jewelry for the special occasion: small emerald drop earrings which matched the sparkle in her mood.

The smooth ride on the upholstered seat of the large carriage was soothing. Her father was already at the ball, having ventured ahead to take care of some business with the elder Mr. Nash. The drive alone was preferable; the expectant looks father dispensed after a companionable dinner with Clay had started to grate on her nerves.

The mayor's mansion overlooked the river that meandered through the county. It was the biggest building in Mooreland, and the mayor and his wife hosted the gala every spring. Hallie alighted and followed the crowd to the entry hall and through to the ballroom. Women dressed in new gowns preened as pressed and combed gentlemen paid attention. A quartet of musicians played in the back of a large room which smelled of a light mix of spring blossoms and tobacco smoke. The murmur of voices spun around as she tried to find the three people she was hoping to see tonight.

Hallie smiled hello to a number of friends and acquaintances before taking a place at the French doors.

First, she felt Bremen from across the room. Now, he was gazing with those deep brown eyes which reminded her of the melted chocolate drops at the sweet table. Then, he was standing so close she could see the striking silver flecks in dark irises and notice the curl at the very tip of coal-black lashes. The cologne was clean with a note of light musk, and the dark suit accentuated his slightly foreign looks. So much taller, she needed to look up.

"Mr. Tyler."

There was so much else she wanted to say, but her feelings could be frightening. Now the intensity of the nearness of him was overwhelming, and she held back from staring. What was it about him that both hypnotized and frightened her?

****

The only person Bremen wanted to see tonight was Hallie. Having overheard the Pinefoy's plan to be at the ball, he intended to claim every dance.

More than just a dance or two, he needed to set down future plans and obtain an answer from the woman. While the kisses and innuendos were exciting, she was his Heart Match. It wasn't as though he had all the time in the world for a courtship as society demanded. Instead, it was high time to start a life together.

The crowd shifted, and a vision of Hallie took his breath away. The sparkling green of those lovely eyes like spring grass and the rosy-warm complexion was an arresting combination. Long locks were pinned up for the occasion, beautiful, but he would much prefer to see the tresses loose around soft bare shoulders. Bare shoulders and bare everything would be the preference.

He strode over and smiled in appreciation. "Miss Pinefoy, a great pleasure to see you here. You are beautiful."

"Thank you." She gazed into his eyes in a way which made him want to slip her out of that dress and into his arms. Surely there was an unoccupied bedroom upstairs to escape to?

"Shall we advance to the less crowded foyer for punch?"

She nodded and allowed him to lead the way out of the dance room. He moved to the table and accepted two heavy crystal glasses. Then he guided Hallie to the edge of the chamber to keep them in full view of the matrons—at least until he could convince the woman to slip away. The Ancestrals' prohibition against a bit of "duress" was not making the situation easier.

"Lovely party." Her beauty intoxicated his brain and left him addled.

"Yes, it is."

His brain finally expelled an intelligent thought. "I'd meant to send word. I've had an inquiry in the custom dolls. A patron has asked for three, each one to resemble a daughter."

"Yes of course. Perhaps I can come to the shop tomorrow to discuss the details?

"It would be my pleasure. I'll stay closed until after our meeting." Clay Nash was approaching. Hell. "Hallie, before we are joined by unwelcome company..."

"My dear, I was hoping for a dance." Clay's voice was loud and high.

"Yes, of course, Clay. Mr. Tyler, thank you for the punch."

"Before we were interrupted, I was offering my own request for a dance." Damn Nash.

Clay stiffened and clenched both fists, his bulging eyes watching Hallie's response.

"Perhaps after supper, Mr. Tyler?"

"I will await that moment."

Clay led Hallie onto the dance floor. A waltz was playing, and a possessive hand was placed on Hallie's waist.

Bremen was furious. That should be him dancing, holding her, whispering into her ear. Tonight she would have to make a decision. Enough of this gentlemanly behavior.

****

At the sound of the supper bell, Hallie was quickly ushered from the ballroom. With a backward glance, she saw Bremen detained by a gentleman who appeared to wish to discuss business during dinner, and before she could hesitate, Clay moved to an area where only two chairs were available.

She took a seat at the table. In the past Clay had not been an enthusiastic dancer, but tonight seemed full of energy begging to dance each "favorite" tune together. Glad to sit, she accepted a beverage and plate from the waiter and began to enjoy the meal.

Clay patted the sweat from a high forehead and

refolded a silk handkerchief with precision. He cleared his throat. "Hallie, do me the honor of becoming my wife."

She looked over in mid-bite of the roast chicken. His face was flushed and round eyes looked forward without blinking.

"This is not the time to discuss something like this." The only answer could be no, but there was no need to spoil the evening. It was obvious he was having a famous time dancing and thoroughly enjoying the plentiful libations.

Clay gulped a third glass of wine. "This is precisely the time. What better memorable setting than the Mooreland Ball? We can tell our children how you accepted my proposal at the supper. Hallie, what is holding you back? You are not a teenager anymore. Most women your age are already married. It is proper."

"Thank you for your astute observation."

"Well, you know what I mean. You are wasting time."

"Hmmm. My dear Clay, I'm not in love with you. I do care for you as a dear friend, however."

"That friendship is a wonderful start. Once we are man and wife, the affection will grow."

She put down the fork. Why was this evening so complicated? Just a few years ago she and Viola had taken turns dancing with Clay, laughing in easy friendship and enjoying the ball. This year, Viola was nowhere to be found, Clay was acting like a jealous lover, and Bremen was distracting her to confusion.

"Why?" Clay whined. "Is it Bremen Tyler? Has he made any promises?"

Belying a desire to project a cool façade, she could feel her face coloring, and hoped Clay would attribute the blush to the heat and dance. "It has nothing to do with Mr. Tyler."

Mollified, Clay nodded. "Hallie, you look flushed. Perhaps I'll take you home. I'm afraid you are overexerted." A self-satisfied expression settled on his features.

Exasperated, she hurried from the table. "I'm not ready to leave; however I believe some air would be pleasant. Please excuse me."

"I'll escort you out." Clay started to rise.

"There is no need. In fact I insist." Would he stop? She could see his thoughts as though plainly written on the shiny forehead.

She moved toward the door to the gardens, feeling inordinately cranky. Her feet hurt, she was hungry and thirsty, and Clay's company left much to be desired.

Without a look at any of the guests, she rushed through the French doors and into the garden where, in spite of the lovely breeze, very few guests were strolling during the dinner break. The grounds were exquisite, especially at the hidden bench in a quiet corner near the oak trees. The sun had set, birds were singing and lightning bugs lit the greenery. Night-blooming jasmine scent filled the air and the crisp coolness of the breeze cleared out all irritation.

There was a sound of walking on the gravel path that led toward the bench. Had Clay followed? No, it was not him; now she could sense Bremen. In such a romantic setting things could get out of hand. Perhaps "out of hand" for him, she thought wickedly as her mouth turned up at the corners.

"Such a delicious smile, Hallie; I do wish to know what you are thinking. May I sit with you as you share those thoughts?"

She moved to the end of the bench. "I felt the need for some air. And you?"

"I, of course, desired your company, but also wanted to ascertain you were safe."

"Were you recalling the time I partook of a walk in Wrightsville?"

"Now that you remind me, perhaps it is safer if I'm here."

*I'm not sure how safe we'll be together.* "Perhaps."

"Are you enjoying the ball?" His eyes shown in the dark air.

"I think I enjoyed myself more last time. I believe being outside now is the most pleasant part of the evening."

"It is for me." He took her hand. "Hallie, I love you. Marry me."

*Dear Lord, what is in the punch tonight?*

"Darling, there is no reason to waste time. The reverend is attending tonight's event, and we can set an immediate date."

"I'm flattered by your proposal. However, our acquaintance has been short and our feelings are not of the proper depth to consider the prospect of marriage." In the back of her mind flashed some romantic images of the two of them enjoying the prospect of married life. She sighed. Was it becoming warmer in the garden?

His hand reached to shift her chin closer to his lips. "The feelings and attraction we share are unparalleled. You'll have everything my heart and body can give. I will love you with every ounce of my soul, and will give you the freedom in your pursuits you desire while protecting and providing for you our entire lives. My goal will be to make you happy. Say you will agree to be my wife."

She was transfixed by those beautiful words. Life with Bremen could be exciting and purposeful. And to actually live as man and wife together was also tantalizing.

He moved in closer, brushing her mouth. "Am I so disagreeable and unattractive, my love, you can not imagine a life together?"

"I have plans..."

"Your plans will become mine." Bremen whispered in her ear, "Can you imagine us as spouses and lovers? I can."

His mouth moved to her perfect fit, and the excitement was shattering. It was as though he was able to take away all inhibitions and reduce the moment to pure desire: just a woman and man alone in the night garden, the moon and stars as witnesses to raw need. She let down her guard, this felt too good to fight, and gave up to his mouth and touches.

She moved onto his lap, hard thighs beneath, strong arms wrapping her in his spell, mouth moving from lips to neck to lips. The gown slipped off the right shoulder, his lips following the strong hand which had swept away the intrusive silk.

"Want you," he rasped, the roughness of his voice melting her body.

She was unable to form any words, not wanting to think but to feel and continue to feel. She ran both hands over the hard planes of Bremen's face, the roughness at the edge of his jaw, then back to black thick hair.

Hallie's bottom shifted from Bremen's lap onto the cold stone garden bench. Why was he stopping just when the moment was getting interesting? Then she heard the footsteps in the distance, rustling along the path. Her head still blissfully dazed, Bremen's possessive hands moved to straighten the aquamarine gown's bodice, which had drawn away completely from her breasts.

Clay stepped into sight. His face was an angry red, even in the dark night. She jumped at the intrusion and attempted to yank her hand out of Bremen's, but his firm palm held on without releasing.

"Bremen Tyler, how dare you encroach on our

relationship? Hallie and I have a long-established agreement between our families. You must honor this arrangement and withdraw your presence." The shrillness of Clay's voice reverberated through the grounds.

"I haven't been informed of a promise or understanding. In fact, I have heard from the lady she is uncommitted. A state I'm determined to reverse." Bremen's deep voice was low and controlled.

"She would be committed to me if it were not for you. You are confusing her; she loves me but you are filling her head with promises and nonsense."

"I have given Hallie neither false promises nor nonsense. She knows my true feelings."

"She also knows my feelings and has said she will consider my offer of marriage."

Both men stared, waiting for a decision.

She stood from the bench, exasperated with both males. "I don't appreciate your speaking about me as if I were a child. My answer is no to both of you. And please do not think all I have on my mind are you two gentlemen. I have other pursuits." As gracefully as possible she flounced away.

Chapter Thirteen

Alone with Bremen.

A morning without interruptions could spell either bliss or disaster. Maybe both. No wonder she felt nervous.

Her brain reasoned that this was a business meeting, requiring the necessity to be at her best. Attired in an ensemble consisting of a favorite cream-colored satin blouse with violet sprigs paired with a linen lavender skirt, the look was soft yet polished. Her hair was up in a loose chignon and threaded through with a spring-green ribbon.

After last night, it was a miracle she had fallen asleep and was up so early. Nonetheless, she planned to arrive at Bremen's immediately after breakfast to not delay opening the business. One final glance in the mirror, and she packed the basket with the loveliest examples of custom dolls and set off in the small buggy.

She and her father had left soon after the "garden incident." While still dazed at Bremen's proposal and promises, there was a need to conduct the meeting this morning in a professional manner. She occasionally had a difficult time with decisions, but would not let either of the two men force a choice. Bremen could be persuasive, but Hallie would muster every shred of self-control and formality a proper English upbringing had been able to breed.

The city was quiet now, most of the residents sleeping in after last night's festivities. All the better. She and Bremen could discuss business without patron visits.

As promised, the Closed sign was visible at the front window, guaranteeing time alone. Bremen sat at the counter desk, reading a ledger and notes, a few newspapers spread out on the table. "Good morning, my love." He was cleanly shaved and wearing a crisp white shirt with a standing collar framing his strong square jaw.

"Good morning, Mr. Tyler." Being alone in a room with the man did something to her. He was just too exciting.

Bremen sauntered to the entrance and locked the door. "So we have no interruptions."

She swallowed hard. "You are up early." She tried to offer some additional meaningful words but failed.

"As are you."

"I suppose business is on our minds."

"Yes. Something is on our minds." He said the words, but the man's eyes spoke of being occupied with other less professional matters.

*Business, business, business,* she repeated. "I've brought my custom doll samples."

Bremen gestured to the open table, and she removed the dolls from the basket. Feeling more assured when the items were displayed, Hallie launched into the prepared words practiced back in Boston at Pinefoy's Playthings. "As you can see, this is the basic doll." She swept her hand over the assemblage. "Depending on the style selected by the customer, I can create variations in the composition and body. In this example, I've used an entire cloth body. Here, there is a combination cloth body with wooden limbs. Countless elements are available immediately or may be ordered. I then tint the wax to produce the skin tone required, and only use the best German-made glass eyes. Also, the head and face are shaped to a certain degree for the custom dolls. Regarding the hair, my figures may be adorned with any type of locks the customer desires—curly or straight, in whatever color or style needed."

"These are beautiful. Wonderful work." Bremen moved to stand closer.

"Thank you." She drew a few relaxing breaths. "I enjoy the work immensely."

"The customer I spoke about has an order for three dolls. Let me get my notes." Bremen disappeared into the backroom connected with the small living apartment and returned with a handwritten sheet.

"The patron indicated an interest in the best materials available for this set. For the features, one doll is to have blue eyes and braided straight brown hair. The second with brown eyes and curly brown hair, and the third with blue eyes and straight brown hair."

"I can have these completed by the end of the week. Do you think he would want each doll dressed in cloth from his daughters' own wardrobes? I can sew the garments too."

"I hadn't thought of asking. I'll check tomorrow if material may be supplied. Perhaps I'll get back to you then?"

"Perfect." Hallie glanced away from the product on the table and was surprised at how close Bremen was. They were almost touching along the length of their arms, and she felt the warmth emanating from the man's body. The fresh scent of soap and shaving cream wafted near her nose.

She tried to speak but before words could form on an addled tongue, Bremen leaned down and kissed her lips. The kiss was a question. Should he move forward or stop? The response was hers.

*Yes.*

Bremen turned her toward him with a smooth

motion and put his arms around her waist. Those beautiful eyes peered intently, sending messages of desire and persuasion. By reflex, she reached and put her arms around his neck. Now Bremen kissed wildly, building up the passion kiss by kiss not letting her think. She wanted the closeness, not knowing why or how she could be acting in such a crazed manner. She should retreat, but her body refused to take a step away.

Bremen touched his tongue to hers. She had never felt such bliss, and her core reacted with a warm tightening in the hips. His thighs shifted next to hers and she felt his male hardness press. She should step away, but these feelings were so exciting there was no possible way to stop even though her backside was pressed along the table. She liked the feel of his tongue, and tested his mouth with hers.

He bent and kissed her neck, drawing shivers. Her blouse was modestly cut, but for some reason it gaped open as he kissed lower around her collarbone and the top curve of the breast. She felt an urge to push the restricting bodice away but her hands would not leave Bremen's hair; they were too busy enjoying a run through the thick locks.

In one smooth stroke, Bremen lifted her bottom onto the edge of the table and fit in tighter. He moved, her knees spreading to give close access between her legs. He was very near her now, just a few pieces of fabric away from joining together. He ran his hand down over her breasts and then to the buttocks, drawing her up hard against the strong male hips. Bremen moved against her a few times and groaned. Or maybe that was her groan?

His large hands wound around her waist then under her blouse, pressing her breasts across both palms. She could feel her resolve dissolving. *Just one more touch and she would pull away*, she promised.

"Do you know what you do to me? Every time I

see you I want this and more. I want you near me every moment." He stayed hip to hip.

She kept her eyes closed to savor the moment, but breathed a delicious sigh. "Bremen," was all she could say.

"Hallie, tell me you will be my wife." His voice was impatient.

She didn't answer but placed another kiss on his lips.

"It serves no purpose to wait. In fact waiting delays our enjoyment of each other."

"I would say we are delaying very little at the moment."

"I would disagree with that assumption. Tell me you'll marry me."

She tried to shift away, but he wouldn't let her go. "I'm not ready to marry. I've just returned to Mooreland and have plans which don't include a husband."

"We are only delaying the inevitable, my love."

"I'm not sure we would be suited as husband and wife. After all, we don't know each other." She knew it was an awkward statement in such close physical proximity.

"I could prove we are meant for each other."

She reached to run her finger along that strong jaw. "How could you prove we are meant for each other?"

His mind was working, deciding on how to reply. The words he spoke didn't seem to be a first choice, "You are hiding your feelings, but you know we both want the same thing."

"My plans don't include a husband."

"That excuse is not valid. I've told you all I have it yours, including the shop. What is preventing you from saying yes?"

What was holding her back? Maybe that he had never offered an explanation for the abrupt

Wrightsville departure? Could she trust his words and promises? "I—"

A loud knock hit the door; the locked handle rattled. "Hallie, are you in there?" Clay's voice called from outside.

"Ignore him." Bremen bent to kiss her bare shoulder.

She swayed while he licked the collarbone.

"Hallie, are you all right in there? Do you need any assistance?"

"Annoying pest, tell him you are fine and I'll allay all your reservations." He placed a nibble on the left ear lobe.

She was tempted, but...strong resolve had been tested today and almost failed. She was ready to leave. "No, please unlock the door."

The skeptical lift of his eyebrow joined a disappointed expression. "Just a few more moments?"

"Just a minute, Clay. The door must have locked." Hallie repaired the disorder of her clothing and slid off the table.

Bremen unenthusiastically unlocked the door while she grabbed the closest doll and pretended to fix its clothing also.

Clay entered the room with a frown. "Just the two of you?"

"Yes, how observant." Bremen stood in the entryway with crossed arms.

The comment was ignored. "Hallie, I thought I saw your buggy."

"Did you need transport? I was leaving."

"What are you doing here?"

"She doesn't answer to you." Bremen's tone was sharp.

"Neither to you. I was making sure Hallie was safe."

"Are you insinuating she is not safe with me?"

"Is she safe from you in all respects?"

Hallie took a step between the squabblers. "Gentlemen, your banter is tiresome. Clay, if you must know, Bremen wanted to see my dolls about a special order."

"Bremen did." Clay emphasized the use of the first name. "Well, if your errand is done, we could have coffee together. I have a few messages to deliver from the merchant friends I introduced a few days ago."

"Of course, I was just finishing."

Bremen was looking cool. "Miss Pinefoy. I'll let you know about the dress material for the customer."

"Yes, please do. I can do the preliminary work until then."

"I look forward to continuing our interrupted conversation."

Chapter Fourteen

A final chest of drawers remained. Once inspected, Bremen could be assured no mention of the Ancestrals existed in Uncle Roman's personal effects. One by one each key on the large chain was tested until the correct key fit the lock. The tumblers turned; they eased open with a creaky protest.

A lone manila envelope sat in the bottom of the drawer. It was labeled: *To be opened in the Law Offices of Morse & Morse.*

Bremen was familiar with the solicitors having been provided copies of legal documents and keys for the shop. If that was his uncle's wish, then so be it. The envelope would be an easy delivery as Morse & Morse was located at the end of the street.

He put on a black coat and placed the envelope in the front pocket, then locked the building. Crossing the cobblestone street, he went into the office, a brightly lit room stacked with books. The twin brothers at their respective desks looked in unison.

"Good afternoon, Gentlemen. I trust you have a few moments?"

"Of course Mr. Tyler." Abraham Morse, the stockier of the two, swept the papers from the leather chair. "Please take a seat."

Bremen reached out and shook the men's hands. "I've found an envelope in the last of my uncle's things. The inscription directs the note be opened in this office."

The brothers exchanged curious looks. Abraham put on thin wire spectacles, took the envelope and slit it open as Jacob stood looking over his shoulder. "Hmm." Jacob held the document up to the light.

"Well?" Bremen tapped a hand on the desk.

Abraham scratched his head. "Before the letter's contents may be divulged, we must request Miss Hallie Pinefoy's presence at a joint meeting. I'll send the lady a note to join us."

"Miss Pinefoy is mentioned in the paper?"

"Yes. Are you available tomorrow morning at eleven?"

"Of course."

"We are afraid the letter stipulates that both you and Miss Pinefoy are here together when the document is read."

"Well, I suppose if that was Roman's wish. Tomorrow then."

"Very good, sir.

****

Hallie re-read the short message before entering: *We respectfully request the presence of Miss Hallie Pinefoy at a meeting tomorrow, June 3, at eleven to discuss a matter of utmost importance.*

What could this be about? A niggling of discomfort crossed her mind. Although not having required the services of the law office for the business, the solicitor's reputation was sterling in Mooreland.

The group seated around the desks included not only Messieurs Morse & Morse but Mr. Bremen Tyler. The three gentlemen stood, first Abraham then Jacob shaking her hand. "Good morning, gentleman."

Bremen held out a hand, causing her face to warm. Really she must learn to be more casual around the man.

"Miss Pinefoy, a great pleasure as always."

The look from him caused her already nervous breathing to come a little quicker. "Mr. Tyler." She was pleased at least her voice was calm.

Abraham Morse started the meeting. "We appreciate your coming on such short notice, Miss Pinefoy, so this will be brief. The matter is regarding the estate of the late Mr. Roman Tyler. Mr. Bremen Tyler will be hearing the news for the first time also. Jacob, will you do the honors?"

Jacob unfolded the paper and cleared his throat. "The last will and testament reads, in essence: 'I, Roman Tyler, being of sound mind and body do bequeath my business in Mooreland and its contents to be split in equal proportion to both my nephew, Bremen Tyler, and my dear friend, Miss Hallie Pinefoy.'" Jacob looked up to meet first her eyes, then Bremen's. "Abraham and I have determined the document appears to be duly signed and witnessed and is dated subsequent to the first document maintained in our office. Congratulations Miss Pinefoy on the inheritance."

Bremen was unfazed by the shocking revelation, and in fact, a smug smile settled upon those handsome lips.

"I must refuse."

The three men wore surprised expressions. "Why is that?" Bremen's body tensed.

"I hadn't expected such a gift."

"Obviously, my dear Hallie, Uncle Roman thought well of you. I'm pleased by the meeting's outcome."

"Then, I ask you, Mr. Tyler. Sell your half of the business so I can own the enterprise outright."

"Again, I say to you, Miss Pinefoy. I have no interest in selling. Moreover, the prospect of running a business appeals even more now."

"Sirs, have I any recourse to own the entire shop?"

"Well," Jacob leaned in the leather chair. "If Mr. Tyler isn't amiable to divesting half, you cannot force his hand. Therefore, forgive the directness, only through circumstances such as marriage or death would you own the entirety."

Neither was appealing at the moment.

"And if I may add to my brother's statement, Miss Pinefoy, your diligent dedication to your new enterprise would be greatly served in a half ownership."

Bremen's eyes twinkled wickedly. "The former prospect mentioned by Jacob would give you full ownership."

She frowned. "Perhaps the latter would be more easily attainable? May I rely on your assistance, Mr. Tyler?"

The lawyers watched the verbal exchange with great interest. "All legal, Miss Pinefoy. Our congratulations again. We will commence filing the transfer documents."

"I'll provide you with a copy of the extra keys today." Bremen really was enjoying the outcome, and instead of being upset at the half-loss of the shop, the man seemed content.

"Then I will accept Mr. Roman's endowment with gratitude." Hallie folded her hands.

"Accompany me to the shop for a full tour."

"I suppose that would be correct," she conceded.

"I know how important it is for you to be correct." Bremen stood and extended a hand to the lawyers. "Thank you both for assistance in this matter. Shall we leave, my dear?"

They walked the short distance in silence. He unlocked the door leaving the Closed sign showing.

"I think this will work out well."

She wished to wipe the self-satisfied expression from Bremen's face. "I think it will be awkward."

"Awkward for whom?"

"For us. Uncomfortable."

"I don't feel uncomfortable. On the contrary, I'm

very comfortable right now." He moved closer. "Do I make you feel uncomfortable? Is it because I'm standing so close?" He placed a strong hand on her breastbone, just beneath the neck. "I can feel your heart racing." Bremen bent to kiss the spot. "Your heart is pounding, my love. Why is that?"

She needed to step back, but her reluctant feet wouldn't go. "I'm comfortable. Perhaps a wrong choice of words. This is a small shop; there may not be room for both."

He kissed the side of her neck. "I like being in close immediacy. Don't you?"

"What I mean is we may find it difficult to remain professional."

"Why is it so important to remain professional? Perhaps unprofessional would be preferable. Yes, that may work better." He kissed the side of her mouth.

Why did her breasts feel so heated and full all of a sudden? And why did she lean closer? *Traitorous body* was her last thought as he kissed her full on the mouth. They fit well, just like puzzle pieces, then Bremen unpinned the prim hat, running his fingers through the luxurious tresses.

"Hallie," he breathed. "Why do you hesitate? Everything I have is yours, body and possessions. Marry me, my love."

She shook her head. "Are you certain you did not orchestrate the reading of the will, Bremen? How very convenient it would be for you to give me half the business to press your case."

A frightening coldness crept into his eyes. "You assume a great deal, Miss Pinefoy. Your distrust is striking. I can assure you I did not forge a legal document and in fact had no hand in this matter."

"Do you see how incompatible we are? One moment kissing, the next arguing. What sort of life would that bode?"

"An exciting one."

"Show me the shop, Bremen, please."

"As you wish, my love."

First there was the kitchen, neat and utilitarian. On the stove was a simmering cauldron of fragrant stew, and she sniffed the tasty aroma of bay leaves and tomatoes emanating from the black iron pot.

"Did you prepare this, Bremen?"

"A bachelor must learn to cook, my sweetheart. Will you join me for lunch to discuss the arrangement?"

Was he wearing her away or winning her over? Possibly a little of both, but for now Hallie would just enjoy the moment.

"As you can see, the apartment contains the kitchen here. The bathroom there. And through these doors is the bedroom area." Bremen whispered, "I can give a thorough tour of that room, if you wish."

"I...don't think so. But thank you for the kind offer." She cringed a bit as the words came out, even to her ears too prim.

His loud laugh rang out. "Really, darling, who is it you don't trust, yourself or me?"

She stepped back into the safety of the kitchen. "You are cooking something."

"Beef stew. Lunch, my love." He pulled out a chair and set two bowls, forks and napkins before ladling servings of the fragrant meat and vegetables. He cut up the bread, still warm from the bakery, and served the meal.

"Now that you are part owner, my dove, I can expect you daily?"

"I must think this through, but yes, I suppose each day. How do you feel about that? You would not sell me half the business a short time ago."

"I do believe now that part owners will suit us

well as nothing could make me happier than to have you here during the day. Except, however, to also have you here during the night."

She decided to let the comment pass, lifted the fork and took a bite, savoring the flavor. A handsome man who could cook, quite interesting.

He took her hand and kissed each finger.

"Have you ever been in love, Bremen?" she blurted. Flustered and blushing, Hallie rephrased the question, "Have you had many women in your life?"

"We can feel affection toward many people, but that true and pure love comes once in a lifetime." He leaned over. "Either we take love when it comes and grab hold, or move on to other people and just feel a shadow of that kind of real love."

His one true love. Was it she? "Have you ever been engaged? Any beautiful women in your life?"

His face hardened. "There is no one you need be jealous about." He paused to add, "At one time there were certain obligations which were thrust upon me. None that will be fulfilled."

"So you've been engaged?"

"It depends on what you call engaged. Have *you* been in love, Hallie?" Bremen parried.

"I'm not sure what true love is. I think love frightens me as this emotion seems so all-consuming. As though one could not be a separate person."

"Not the love we will have. It grows and enriches and enlivens."

"You are expert in this?"

"My parents demonstrated such deep unconditional affection. Others too. We can have this."

The clock struck, jolting them both.

"I must go now."

"I can take you back."

"No, I think the air would do me good. I haven't far to travel to an appointment." She stood to leave.

Bremen reached to a nail over the kitchen work counter and removed a set of keys. "To a growing partnership in all respects." His lips moved to her mouth, innocent at first then more heated. She stood on her toes to reach him, until pulled off the ground and off her feet.

"Come to the bedroom."

She felt indecision unlike anything before. How far could they go, and must she always do the right and ladylike thing?

"I'm a virgin, Bremen."

"I know you are and can stay one. If you want to remain so, that is."

She saw the promise in his eyes of going to the edge and sensed the need of his body. Bremen held out his hand. She took it.

As if not to allow a moment's thought, he led her through the bedroom door. In a haze Hallie saw a comfortable bed in the middle of the room and was lifted and lowered onto the mattress. The smooth waves of loose hair fell around her shoulders when the chignon was unpinned. Slow kisses were pressed on both eyelids and the tip of her nose, and the bed shifted as Bremen descended down. His fingers moved to the top buttons of the pin-striped blouse and undid each fastening one by one.

Now the kisses were harder and more passionate as his tongue slipped into her mouth and explored. Distracted, Hallie didn't notice that the silk blouse was now completely undone and the chemise was ready to follow. As kisses moved down, her neck received attention until, even lower, Bremen put her breast in his mouth and sucked greedily.

He looked into her eyes, and drew a large palm under the skirt and up the leg until touching the skin at the top of her thighs.

She should probably slow what was happening, but this felt so good. Running her hands over his muscled back and hard buttocks, Hallie knew the man was being pushed toward a precipice. But that could not be first concern; her own precipice loomed. The velvet skirt was up and the lower half of her body was exposed when he stood and started removing shirt and slacks.

She rose on both elbows and watched. The broad chest was gorgeous. Toned and with just the right amount of hair, strong and sleek. The trousers and undergarments came off in two bold strokes.

She gasped. The museums in Boston exhibited statues of nude men, but none as well endowed as Bremen.

"Touch me."

Her fingers came out in wonder to touch the steel-silk of his manhood hanging heavy between his legs. The grimace of pleasure on his face awoke an answering throb in her loins.

Bremen moved back onto the bed and loosened her skirt off and pushed the offending fabric to the floor. She should feel shy, but the power coursing through her feminine blood felt emboldened by the touches.

"You are sure you want to remain a virgin?" he coaxed.

Was it possible to give in to the pleasure without giving in to the ties? "Convince me otherwise," she whispered.

His look took all breath away. She was held transfixed in those flashing eyes while one male hand moved on and into her, the sensations making her want to weep with pleasure.

"Hello!" A woman's voice called from the gate. "Is anyone there?"

"It's Viola!"

Bremen groaned when she jerked away.

"Just stay here, no one needs to stop us." His fingers moved again.

"Hallie? It's Viola. Are you there?"

The moment was gone.

After throwing Bremen an apologetic look, Hallie attempted to put tangled hair back in order and fasten clothing into place. Sprinting from the bedroom, she advanced into the courtyard while endeavoring to appear cool and relaxed.

Viola looked embarrassed as if sensing what had been going on. "I'm sorry to interrupt. Your buggy was down the street, and I thought we could meet for tea. There was something important I wished to speak about."

"Speaking with you is always a pleasure, Viola, but I was just leaving for an appointment. Can you call tomorrow for tea? I'm free in the afternoon."

"Yes, lovely."

Bremen stepped outside the door, giving Viola a tight nod.

"Mr. Tyler, I'll visit tomorrow morning," Hallie suggested.

"Yes, Hallie. Tomorrow. We'll finish what was started today," he promised.

Chapter Fifteen

Bremen heard the light tap on the back door. As usual, the woman was punctual. Dressed in simple clothing, a preference when wanting to avoid attention, Tilda waited at the courtyard door. "Bremen. How wonderful to see you."

"You are well?" He led to the table and chairs in the main room.

"As well as possible in light of the circumstances. And life has been good to you, my dear cousin? It appears you have fulfilled the dream of the simple life. Have you fulfilled your dream of love too?"

"The love, Tilda, must still be convinced. Therein lies the difficulty."

"You, of all people, can't get your way?" she teased.

"I would be more forceful; however, the directions of the council hold me back."

"Then perhaps when successful in the search for the Heart Gem, you could prove to Hallie your perfect match?"

"That wouldn't be necessary. My own heart speaks the truth."

"There is calm assurance in your eyes. I wish you great success then, in both endeavors."

"What of your own search?" He poured white wine into gold-rimmed crystal goblets.

She sighed and played with the fringe edging the shawl, "Fruitless for now, but in Ireland, there have been some clues both for Malone and the Heart Compass. But what I heard two days ago may be of interest to you."

"You have heard this from whom?"

"The lady's maid. What better source than household staff when deciphering the inner workings of society? It was whispered in confidence that a Mr. and Mrs. Fairchild of Dublin are to employ the use of an unusual object to help make a decision in the choice of spouse for the eldest son, Percy."

"Promising. The best news I've heard so far."

"I thought you'd be pleased. The least I can do is assist with the search for the Heart Gem. After all, you would not be in this predicament if not for Malone's attempt at ensuring he and I would be able to wed. Now, let me share the secrets from Dublin."

****

The oval cast-iron mirror reflected a slim woman dressed in flimsy black tissue-silk lingerie and stockings. She also had over-eager eyes, glowing skin, and a nervous expression. Satisfied, Hallie pulled the low-cut amethyst gown over the undergarments.

Earlier that day, she had purchased the finest sheer unmentionables available in town, blushing as the discreet French shop clerk wrapped the lacey items. Wearing the garments now underneath the satin dress made her feel wicked at the calculated plan.

And the gown, while stylish in Boston, displayed more cleavage than was decent in the less cosmopolitan English city of Mooreland. But as Bremen had earlier today seen the skin below the dress, what harm could come of it?

She lifted a thick curl and placed it charmingly over the left shoulder. She'd taken pains with the locks, wearing them loosely as he liked. An additional dab of hibiscus perfume behind the ear lobes should provide even more enticement.

The illicit plans had fallen beautifully into place; even her father was out of town on business and couldn't comment on a late night return. Or even a late morning return.

Bremen had promised to finish what had been started earlier that afternoon, and this evening he would get an opportunity to show just what that meant. She pulled a black silk shawl over her décolletage, enjoying the sensuous feel of the cool gossamer on warm skin. How far would things go tonight? She was not sure. This afternoon Bremen had given assurance she could have returned home a virgin after spending time together, but her lustful attraction for the man was so strong his own reputation might be in jeopardy tonight.

She'd made a decision after those delicious moments shared, even if a husband was undesirable at this time, it did not mean she needed to remain pure and untouched. Perhaps, in fact, enjoying the pleasures of the flesh with this delectable, willing man would cure her of a constant state of excitement and preoccupation.

****

Bremen completed his copious notes. "I'll need to travel within the next few days, Tilda."

"I've other serious news to share."

"Yes?"

"The Ancestrals are growing impatient. There are whispers some do not want to continue to wait for the return of the Heart Gem. They want it back now."

The side of his neck started to work. He placed the wine glass down to avoid the urge to snap the stem. "Now? What has caused this urgency?"

Tilda bit her lip and considered her words. "There are those who don't believe you are as faultless as the council originally determined. Some believe you took the Artifact and have hidden the object away."

"That's absurd. You know that."

"Yes, but I'm not on the council. May I suggest you find the Heart Gem as quickly as possible?"

"I've been preoccupied with other matters."

"But those other matters may be lost if the Artifact is not returned without haste."

"I realize the risk in staying in town, but couldn't leave Hallie." He picked up the goblet again and swirled the liquid creating a small whirlwind. "Even my journey now to Dublin will be difficult, albeit necessary."

"I of all people understand separation. I long for Malone every moment, with every bone in my body. Let me suggest then, the separation will sweeten the reunion."

"You understand if I find the Gem before being able to convince Hallie of being my Heart Match, I can be called back to the Ancestral Stronghold. Permanently. That is the reason I've focused on winning her love first. And the love could have been more easily won without the limitation of not using coercion or duress."

Tilda gave an all-knowing smile which made him feel very naive. "Do you believe that?"

He was silent.

"Dear Bremen, perhaps you need to take the risk of showing her a view with the Heart Gem. If the impatience of the council continues to grow, you will be forced to return and all shall be for naught. The worse for having known what you will have lost."

"You've given much to consider, Tilda." He raised the glass of wine and tapped the edge of her goblet.

Tilda stood. "I must leave now for the Mooreland Arms. Tomorrow evening I am setting off for Spain." She held out both arms to embrace him. "Be careful."

"You also, Tilda. Keep safe."

****

Hallie knew it was fruitless to try to calm the panic and erratic breathing which had almost made her want to turn back home. Fortunately Viola did not ask any questions during the two-mile long drive.

Without making any specific explanations to her friend, Hallie had asked for transport from home to town. It would have been impossible not to incite gossip by leaving the Pinefoy buggy at Tyler's shop into the wee hours.

"Shall I wait a few moments, Hallie?"

"No need, I see the lights are on. Please leave me here, and I'll walk to the end of the block. Thank you."

"I wish you a good night, then." Viola winked and urged the horse forward.

Drawing nearer, Hallie adjusted the gown's bodice and licked her lips. Usually she was skilled with intuition, but for some reason, her thoughts were murky this evening. After passing the last darkened neighboring building, she was close enough to peer into the well-lit windows of Tyler's shop. With a smile ready to catch Bremen's eye, she peered into the room.

The smile faded with shock of seeing Bremen at the table with the most stunning woman in the world. All the exquisite, sophisticated women in Boston could not compare with this beauty. Bremen hung on every word coming from that lovely mouth.

He raised a glass of wine and toasted the lady. The woman clinked her goblet, and they drank, then the beauty stood up and held out her arms to Bremen and they embraced.

Chapter Sixteen

Hallie tore off the silk undergarments and ripped them to pieces before tossing the scraps into the bedroom fireplace. The insufferable bastard. Flattering and seducing, while playing with another woman later the very same day.

The black cloth curled and glowed; she resisted the urge to climb in and disappear along with the lingerie. As tears rolled down her cheeks and dripped onto the collar of the old nightdress, she ran cold fingers over the sleeves of the rough fabric. The prickliness was comforting after the smooth chemise. Smooth fabric was a reminder of that snake's smooth words.

She pictured Bremen's handsome face in the flames. He was a cad, and she an idiot for trusting and believing the false words spoken. So unlike good, faithful Clay, who had not even looked at another woman while she was away in Boston. Hallie wiped her eyes again and vowed to sleep away the last few hours of this horrendous day. Pulling the covers up under her chin and squeezing her eyes shut, she begged for sleep to come.

Instead she tossed and turned unable to fall asleep even in the early morning hours. Each time during the night, in the moment of drifting off, thoughts of Bremen poked into her head pushing away all tiredness and substituting fury in its stead.

When the sun climbed out signaling a new day, she jumped out of bed, splashed cold water on her face and determined to never let Bremen know how horrible and disappointing yesterday had been. And today, when she would have preferred to have time to simmer in discontent, Clay had requested to come in the morning to walk in the gardens.

Hallie looked into the mirror. As expected, there were tired shadows under her eyes and the usually rosy skin was pale. From the armoire, she chose the least offensive walking dress in an effort to redeem the day, which promised to be as horrible as the last. No doubt the elegant amethyst gown was completely ruined by last night's long trek home across meadow and mud.

She padded down to the hallway at the appointed time and tapped a foot impatiently. Clay was approaching the door, and for a moment she battled an urge of ignoring the knock, then diving back into bed for a prolonged crying jag.

"My dear, you look lovely." Clay reached out to take her hands and leaned forward through the doorway to peck both cheeks. "I've been looking forward to our time together all week."

Aware of being ungracious, she ignored the comment but took the proffered arm.

"The gardens are lovely here. Do you remember, dear Hallie, how we used to race on the grounds, you, me and Viola? I hope to see my children race here one day."

She cringed, feeling a tightening in her chest. "Good luck." This was not a day for niceties.

Undeterred, he continued, "Do you remember our childhood exploits? Remember stealing a pie from Cook? 'Where is my pie?' she kept saying. Do you recall how we convinced the woman she hadn't baked a dessert, even cleaning up the kitchen to prove nothing had been prepared?"

She burst out laughing. "The poor woman. But I think the pie tasted all the sweeter for our exploits."

Clay was charming and funny, entertaining with stories and reminiscences of their childhood.

She laughed at his jokes and imitations, and missed the uncomplicated relationship the three of them had shared before leaving for Boston.

Moving through the hedge maze, they took a seat on the park bench at the center, surrounded by bougainvillea and hemlock. Butterflies flitted about as the sun shone down, and Clay moved an arm around her, laying her tired head on his narrow shoulder. Warm and sleepy, Hallie let her eyes close for a moment.

Clay patted her hair. "Our future life together will be so wonderful. Not only do I love you, but my family loves you as a daughter. I have spoken to your father and he has given us a wholehearted blessing."

She yawned. A nap would be so nice right now.

"I have given your interests some thought. You can make those dolls and things. I know you find the toys important, and playing with the different pieces gives you happiness." He leaned to kiss the top of her head. "Say you'll marry me."

Her sleepy mind rolled the words around in her brain. There were no complications here. Did it matter that there was no attraction for Clay? Attraction had only caused trouble with Bremen. He could have his beautiful woman—she could move on too.

"Yes, Clay, I will marry you."

"Hallie, my love, you'll not regret it. We'll be content, settled and devoted. I look forward to many years of marriage as we grow old together."

His mouth descended. She was repulsed by the attempted embrace, wanting to bolt just like a deer in the forest pursued by prey. His lips were cool and a strong smell of wine emanated from Clay's breath. She pushed. "Please."

"Of course, it would be unseemly for you to feel passion as I do. Your reserve is commendable, my dear."

Images of her wantonness with Bremen warmed her face.

"I have shocked you with my ardor. I must confess to find modesty attractive in a lady."

She squirmed. Just yesterday she'd bought a seductive ensemble to seduce and be seduced in with that other now-hated man. "Perhaps you can walk me back home, I feel exhausted."

"Of course, we can make our plans when you are rested and your father has returned. I have a few of my own plans to take care of today."

****

Bremen watched Clay Nash move about the shop. About five minutes ago, the younger man had pushed open the door of the building, a smug expression gracing his plain face. The self-satisfied look was a bit disconcerting.

Interrupting his thoughts, the sole customer regained Bremen's attention once more, "I'm not sure if this is the birthday gift to give, Mr. Tyler. Reverend Fulton can be so particular. This mask is from Africa, you say?"

"Of the best mahogany, hand carved by the Tutli tribe of East Africa. The paints are produced from native plants, and each mask is a unique work of art, ma'am." He'd already explained the item to Mrs. Fulton three times.

Her high brow furrowed in thought while stubby fingers twisted in indecision. "Or perhaps this item, Mr. Tyler. Tell me again what it is."

He fought the urge to snap, ready to hand both items over and ask the lady to leave so he could remove Nash from the premises. "This is a ceremonial dagger, used by the Aztecs in ritual sacrifice. The handle is of silver, made by the finest craftsman."

"Where you do find these items is beyond me."

Mrs. Fulton shook her bonneted head while glancing between the two items. "Reverend Fulton does like something different, but he may think the 'ritual sacrifice' is a bit heathen."

"What do you think, Mr. Nash?"

Clay stepped forward and bowed to the lady. Bremen's stomach twisted at Nash's exaggerated showmanship.

"I'm not quite sure which of the items would be preferred, however, I desire to speak with the reverend today about officiating in a joyous occasion. Perhaps I can ask if he has any preferences at that time."

Bremen's hand itched, ready to thrust the Aztec knife into Clay's chest, grab the man's collar and throw him out on his ass. Instead he wrapped the items in newspaper and handed them to the lady. "I will tell you what, Mrs. Fulton. Why don't you take both? One will be from me as a gift, the other from you."

The woman seemed to only be able to think of one thing at one time. "Shall I tell the reverend you'll be calling today?"

"My fiancée and I will be calling. To speak about our wedding preparations."

Acid churned in Bremen's gut. She could not have agreed to marry Clay. There must be a mistake. This man was an idiot.

"Good news, Tyler." Clay paused for effect. "It looks as though the best man *has* won in the end."

"What do you mean to say, Nash?" he snapped, causing Mrs. Fulton to let out a startled noise.

Clay ignored the question and spoke to the confused woman. "Hallie Pinefoy has granted me the immense honor of agreeing to be my wife."

Mrs. Fulton beamed and clapped her hands together in joy. "How wonderful! I know the reverend will also be happy to hear the news."

Bremen couldn't speak for a moment. His anger stood in his throat blocking out the air from his lungs and the life from his soul. "You are mistaken."

"This morning Hallie accepted my marriage proposal," Clay repeated the information, emphasizing each syllable. "We're to wed as soon as my fiancée decides on a date. You'll forgive us if you are not invited to the nuptials?"

"I don't believe you."

"I don't care if you believe me or not. It's the truth. Let me add, gypsy, I never want to see you around my wife again."

A look of bewilderment appeared on Mrs. Fulton's face. "Gentlemen, please lower your voices. A marriage is a blessed event."

"Not when it's to the wrong man," Bremen asserted.

"I am the right man. Therefore, she has chosen me."

"She's not in love with you."

"Has she agreed to marry you? She has agreed to marry me, and rightly so."

"You arrogant fop. She can't have."

Clay sneered a challenge at Bremen. "Then ask her yourself."

His self-control broke as he stretched out his fist right into Clay's nose. The man grabbed his bloodied face, a stunned expression behind both hands.

He waited for Clay to retaliate. It would be enjoyable to beat the life out of the bastard.

Mrs. Fulton stepped between the two. "Now, gentlemen. I suggest a little reserve, please."

"I didn't throw the first blow, ma'am." Clay reached for a handkerchief to sop the flowing blood.

"I apologize for fighting in your presence, Mrs. Fulton. I'll make sure there are no bystanders next time. Leave now, Nash."

"With pleasure. This will be the last time I step

into this place of business."

"But Hallie will step into this place of business again. She is half owner, you know."

"This has just been an amusement. Once we are married she'll have other matters occupying her time. Like amusing me."

He threw another punch at Clay's mouth bloodying a second part of the man. "This is your last warning. Get the hell out of here or I'll kill you."

"Sir! Do not use that language," Mrs. Fulton scolded.

"My apologies to you again, ma'am."

"Gentlemen, the decision who to marry is at the lady's discretion." She turned to him with a compassionate look. "Mr. Tyler, if Miss Pinefoy perceives she will have a happier married life with Mr. Nash you must accept those wishes. There is no way to...see the future. We ladies must make our decisions based on the facts before us."

"We'll see about that."

****

Hallie countered the twinges of regret forcing their obnoxious ways into her head by determining to get back to work. After luncheon, she would make a delivery to the toy store, but would avoid Tyler's shop today. She had not determined how to continue conducting business with Bremen. However, the latter of the two conditions ensuring her sole curiosity shop ownership, which Mr. Morse mentioned, was swiftly gaining favor.

Vaughan's Toys had been a good partner. Not of the custom dolls, as Mr. Vaughan preferred not to work with those orders, but of the baby dolls and clothing. She completed new stock to replenish the items sold last week. No personal concerns would prevent her from important obligations today.

Vaughan's was small and compact, the interior packed floor to ceiling with all manner of children's toys. Three shelves were allotted to the dolls. She'd made the best use of them by prominently displaying items to their best advantage.

After smiling at the boisterous young boys playing in front of the entrance with their hoops and spinning tops, she went through the toy shop doors. Her feet froze in place. Standing by the children's books was the stunning woman she'd had the misfortune to find at Bremen's last night. Hallie flipped around on her heel to retreat, but before being able to take a second step a beaming Mr. Vaughan waved.

"Ahh, Miss Pinefoy." The short rotund man wove to her side. "This lady was just commenting on the craftsmanship of the dolls."

"They are exquisite. I've never seen anything like them," the beautiful woman responded in a perfect cultured voice.

Vaughan proceeded to introduce them, "Hallie Pinefoy, Tilda Tyler."

To her horror, the owner stepped away to help a customer. Hallie's head spun as the name Tyler screamed in her thoughts. Bremen's wife *was* in town.

"A pleasure, Miss Pinefoy. I'm pleased to finally meet."

"You know about me?"

"Oh yes. Bremen has spoken of you often."

"He has? This doesn't concern you?"

"Of course not. He spoke so fondly of you last night I feel as though we know each other already." The woman's warm voice was like honey.

"Bastard."

"I beg your pardon?" A crease formed between Tilda's perfect eyebrows.

"How well do you know your Mr. Tyler?"

The woman's smooth arms crossed over a perfect bosom. "Quite well."

"Do you trust him?"

"With my life."

"I'll have you know, he tried to seduce me yesterday." As she spit out the words, righteous indignation flowed. There may be children involved.

The woman gave a quizzical look. "My cousin loves you."

Her stomach felt sick as fingers and toes turned ice cold, and her heart started to beat a panicky staccato. "C-cousin?"

"Yes, our fathers were brothers. I paid Bremen a visit yesterday. We haven't seen each other in weeks."

"I-I did not know he had a cousin," she stammered like a babbling idiot to the breathtaking creature."

"I assure you, we are cousins, Miss Pinefoy. Are you feeling well? You appear pale."

"Yes, I'm well. I did not know Bremen had a cousin." She felt the need to repeat the stupid words.

Tilda's face took on a look of alarm. "Yes. Miss Pinefoy, may I get you some water or a chair? The sun is exceptionally strong this afternoon. Perhaps I should call Bremen?"

She was going to faint. Regaining some composure, she tried to exit as gracefully as possible. "It was a pleasure meeting you, Miss Tyler."

The warm air hit her face hard as though a blow. How could she have made such a mess of the situation? Usually thoughtful and methodical, impulsiveness did not come naturally. As the ever-responsible one, she should have known better.

What was she to tell Clay? *I must retract my vengeful acceptance of your impossible proposal because I misinterpreted a situation.* Or was this the way things were meant to be? Could she just change her mind in order to "think" about things?

What was she to tell Bremen? Whatever the

explanation, she must speak with the man now, before he heard the news of the engagement from anyone else. She rounded the corner, dreading their conversation as each dragged step brought her closer to the shop. The empty room stood eerily quiet. "Hello?" She peered into the darkened area of the living apartment.

Bremen came out carrying the black leather travel bag. She was shocked by his terrible appearance. Pale of skin and shadowed, there was none of the sparkle in his gaze. Her heart contracted knowing she had caused the suffering.

He tossed the bag across the floor and closed the space, grabbing her arms and demanding, "Tell me it isn't true."

"You've heard already."

Disgusted, he pushed away. "You would discard what we have? Why? Why, Hallie? You don't love me? You don't believe I love you? What is it?" He moved up less than an inch from her face. "What is it you find in Clay which I'm lacking? Tell me. Is it this?" With a rough hold he pulled her against him, forcing his tongue into her mouth, kissing and biting her lips, running greedy hands against her breasts.

She opened her mouth to kiss back just as violently, needing to stop the thinking.

"I feel your desire, Hallie. I smell it. I could take you right now and have you begging not to stop until you've taken your full pleasure."

He took her face in his hands, gazing in until she felt swallowed up. The flecks of silver in his irises flashed in an otherworldly fashion. "Tell me you don't want me. Say it."

"I don't want to wed, but instead…"

"So, good enough to bed, but not wed?" His voice was tight.

She gazed at the floor unable to explain complete thoughts.

"No. I want it all. Every part of you, every bit of your being. I want your body and soul all in one package. That or nothing. Forever in this life and the next." He moved to the other side of the room. "Why didn't you leave me your address in Wrightsville?"

"Why weren't you waiting at the Wrightsville Inn?"

"I was called away, but left a note." He gripped the edge of the table. "The clerk misplaced it."

"The clerk at Mooreland Lodge said you left in the middle of the night with a beautiful woman."

"The woman was my cousin who came to see me on an urgent family matter concerning our departed Uncle Roman. She was traveling with her betrothed."

Hallie stared for a few moments, shocked by the difference in their lives if they'd met the morning of her departure to Mooreland.

Bremen knelt, cradling her, his heat warming away the coldness which had crept into every bone. He kissed her belly. "Why have you promised yourself to Clay when it's me you crave? The love we share is nothing we'll ever have with anyone else. We are each other's fit, for life, my love. You will exist with Clay, but with me you will live. Tell him you'll not have him. I'll tell him if you wish, but he must know you are mine and I'm yours."

She closed her eyes, the tears slipping out. "I'm not sure. My emotions are so difficult to understand. What if what we are feeling doesn't last? What experience do we have with love, how do we know this is real?"

"What we have *is* real. You, with your intuitions should know. I don't know how to be better to you, Hallie. I'm only a man. But if what you want is a man who will love you with his entire body and soul for the rest of eternity, then I'm him. Whether you say yes or no to me, I'll continue to love you. Love is all I can promise. I can't pledge riches, or society or the best of anything. My heart has to be enough."

"I don't know what to do."

"I can't try any harder." His voice held a note of finality.

"I must think, Bremen."

"Yes, you must think. I can't persuade. But you must decide soon. I am leaving to give you a day or two to be certain."

"Yes, I'll decide." Her body was numb.

Bremen took up the bag, leaving without a backward glance.

She watched the closed door for a long time until the evening shadows took over the room, and the darkness matched the gloom in her heart.

****

The dream was so real. Hallie held an unusual flat stone on her palm. It was warm to the touch and glowed around the edges with an almost haunting beauty. She was unable to look away from the object or let go.

Then an image shimmered, stopped and started, finally producing a fuzzy reflection on the stone's surface which appeared to be of two figures. She sensed the image of the woman shown there was her, but the identity of the man was unclear. In her dream she strained to make out the man's face but the features were impossible to ascertain.

Before she could discover the person's identity, the stone rose and a foggy veil surrounded and slipped over her body. She reached into the opaqueness, trying to grasp the object, but it was elusive. A few times her fingers skimmed the edge of the stone but when she stepped forward to grab, the mist enveloped tighter, almost suffocating the breath from her lungs. She started crying, was this dream or reality?

133

Two figures of men stood just outside the muted light. From their outlines, it was clear that one was Bremen and the other Clay. She took a step forward, but one melted away. Her vision clouded, and wouldn't reveal who was left standing there. But his arm reached forward.

She took the hand and woke.

Chapter Seventeen

As crisp sea air filled his nostrils, Bremen stepped onto the ferry, which was to travel from England to Dublin. He ignored the food and drink sellers; it was unlikely he'd have an appetite during the next day or two. Staying hungry physically as well as mentally would be best.

He showed the ticket and followed the porter down the narrow hallway. He'd paid extra for a private room for the short voyage across the Irish Sea.

The porter opened the door to the cabin, sparse and plain but clean. Only a lonely cot was set up against the wall. Bremen passed over a coin and closed the door to the tight space for the next few hours. He placed the travel case on the floor and lay on the bed, putting an aching head down on the pillow. In all likelihood, the task could be completed and a return to Mooreland would be made in two days. What awaited back home he couldn't be certain for he had no gift for prescience.

He rolled over toward the thin wall and drew a deep breath in and out to expel the pent-up tension. Although astonished by her decision, Hallie would be provided with time to think. He'd come to her without reservations about their love and future, and needed her to do the same without any doubts.

There were two paths. His first choice had been that she would marry willingly, without any indecision or proof they were meant to be together. That hadn't happened.

Now, the second plan of action was to find the

Heart Gem and use the object to prove they were each other's Heart Match. Less than ideal as the decision to knowingly use the Gem before they were wed came with its perils. By using the Heart Gem this way, the Ancestrals could decide what his future would be, which could mean a life with or without Hallie's love.

Adding to the urgency was the news of the council becoming impatient at the prolonged wait for the return of the Gem. The members could summon him at any time of their choosing by using methods which could not be ignored or fought against. Including the manner used on Malone to cause him to forget Tilda's existence.

The ship rocked as the vessel left the dock. Tilda had given good reason to travel to Dublin. A marriage was to be settled in unusual circumstances, and if rumors were correct, the parents would use the Heart Gem to determine the spouse of their eldest son.

Closing his eyes, he hoped some restful sleep would finally drive away the troubling thoughts. The darkened space helped his throbbing skull, and the rhythmic creaking of the vessel filled the room.

Now there was more urgency to the search, and he had to hurry. Time was running out. He didn't need prescience to realize the obstacles in his path.

****

Bremen's uniform fit tightly, particularly across his privates. Although successful in bribing the Fairchild's footman for the use of a uniform, he and the man were obviously of different proportions.

He mulled over the mission. This was the closest he'd gotten to retrieve the Heart Gem since leaving France. He cursed having neglected the search for so long. While courting Hallie was a great pleasure, he hadn't won the woman's heart. If found, the Heart Gem could give Hallie a view, assuring of a happy life together.

The hansom cab turned through a posh neighborhood, but while focused inward, Bremen paid no attention to the stately residences. Now was the time to do *anything* to secure the Artifact. Whatever it took, whatever the price, he had the will and the funds to secure the object.

"Here, sir." The cabbie stopped at the requested location, about a quarter mile from the Fairchild's Dublin residence.

He walked the last steps with a determined gait until coming to the large white-stoned mansion looming at the end of the drive. According to the information received, the family was old money looking for an infusion of new funds. The lady of the house gambled and the gentleman whored, but the family was welcomed into the best homes on the East Coast of America and throughout Europe.

From Tilda's source, Bremen heard that the son, Percy, was of marriageable age and the parents were set upon a match to place the lineage securely into the most elite circle of the wealthiest families in the world. From the information gleaned, there were three young ladies Percy had an interest in courting. The Fairchild's plentiful money and determination to procure even more money would make the family of great interest to the current holder of the Heart Gem. Bremen was determined not to walk away from the house without information on the Gem's whereabouts.

Although a clandestine questioning of the servants might provide information, the preferable approach was the most direct and best source of knowledge: Mr. and Mrs. Fairchild. Employing the Heart Gem would be done in secret, and although most staff knew the private details transpired in a household, using the Gem would be so secret a view would be done in privacy with no outsiders present.

He pulled the red cap down further and slipped through the back door, nodding at the bored footman stationed at the place. Going about the house, Bremen took care not to be discovered by looking out of place.

The riches adorning the mansion were impressive, and treasures displayed matched some of the magnificence of the Ancestrals' Stronghold. In fact, most museums could not boast such grandeur. The furniture was crafted by master woodworkers, and the artwork was priceless. Limoges vases and royal porcelain stood on display, and the finest oriental carpets splayed across the floors.

A footman was escorting a man—probably a merchant—from the back of the house. The man appeared upset about something. Bremen stopped at the rosewood marble-top table and pretended to inspect the mirror for smudges as the irate salesman was guided into the main drawing room.

****

George Iberville fumed. Though summoned to bring the Heart Gem, one of the great Artifacts in this world, he was directed to use the back-door entrance. If not in a position of desperately needing money at this time, he would stand at the front door making a scene in protest for being insulted. The snobby Fairchilds should consider him a revered guest in thanks for the service he was prepared to provide. Now, seeing the opulence in the mansion, he felt the fool for not having asked thrice what was bargained.

The footman led him toward the drawing room. A hidden pistol lay reassuringly across Iberville's hip. There had been previous clients who wanted not just a view, but possession of the Gem.

Once ushered in, Iberville bristled under the scrutiny of Mr. and Mrs. Fairchild. The couple sat on separate blue-striped settees looking bored as the son Percy, an unattractive gangly youth, sat on a leather chair between them.

"You may leave now," Maximilian Fairchild said, dismissing the staff. A cold gaze scrutinized imperiously down a too-thin nose. "To the point— your services are requested. We have the three items required."

Iberville had practiced containing his emotions since childhood. He would not be put off by this pointed statement of being deemed unworthy of an introduction to the family gathered there. He inclined his head and brought out the Heart Gem from the secret pocket in his vest using a flourish practiced many times. The young Mr. Percy Fairchild stepped forward indicating a small table set to the side. The youth produced three white linen handkerchiefs and placed the set on the table.

Iberville opened the first handkerchief. A small golden lock of shiny hair was curled on the cloth. He motioned to the prospective groom. "Put the lock itself into one hand and hold the Gem in the other."

Percy glanced over at his mother, who nodded. He did as directed.

The Heart Gem began to glow green around the edges. Then to the amazement of the three jaded observers, an image formed in the middle. It showed Percy Fairchild older now, with a richly dressed woman coifed in golden curls arranged elegantly upon her head. The couple sat across each other in a large room, a setting of pure extravagance. The chamber was filled with fabulous artwork and other valuables excelling those in the Fairchild's Dublin home.

The golden-haired woman was drunk and gulped out of a crystal goblet rimmed in heavy gold and adorned with jewels. A young maid entered with a chalice for Percy Fairchild, and he gave the girl a look from top to bottom. He pinched her posterior and elicited shrill giggles. The golden-haired woman flung the wine-filled glass at Percy. He countered by standing and reaching to slap her face.

The image on the Heart Gem blurred and turned clear.

The three Fairchilds exchanged surprised looks.

Iberville removed the lock of golden hair and replaced it with a coiled red curl from the second handkerchief. Again the Gem on Percy Fairchild's palm glowed, this time a deep blue at the edges. The surface revealed young Fairchild as a middle-aged man walking with a red-headed pretty woman in the gardens of a country home. The couple laughed while walking, her arm tucked affectionately under his. He guided the woman to a seat on one of the benches and held her hand, exchanging kisses and smiles. The gardens, however, did not appear in order. The grass was unkempt and the bushes looked as though not trimmed in a long time. The couple's clothes were plain and worn, patches sewed at Percy's jacket elbows, the young woman's gloves smudged.

Again the image shimmered and blurred, then disappeared.

Without a word Iberville replaced the red curl on Percy's palm with a straight ebony lock from the third handkerchief. The Heart Gem glowed black as a third image appeared. Young Mr. Fairchild was an old man, sitting napping by the fireplace in a dingy room. An old woman entered and tucked a blanket around his legs, leaving a small plate of bread and beans on the table. She kissed his forehead before leaving the room.

For the third time, the Gem's image shimmered and disappeared.

Iberville was relieved, as always, at the effectiveness of the Gem. "Have you seen what you wanted?" He fixed a smile upon his lips. "Does this help you arrive at a decision on a spouse, young man?"

The three observers stared without responding until the elder Fairchild reached into a breast pocket and produced an envelope containing a number of bills. The man handed over the paper without touching Iberville's fingers. Maximilian Fairchild reached to the bell and rang for the footman to return.

"Our business is completed. Direct him out."

Dismissed again, Iberville's anger simmered. He would not lose his temper; the Fairchilds could direct other business his way. He bowed a farewell and turned before following the footman out the servant door once again.

****

Feeling the pistol tucked under the jacket, Bremen was ready to complete the mission of locating the Heart Gem this day. He'd debated about bringing the gun. One of the few edicts the seekers had to follow in retrieving the Artifacts was not to kill to secure any of the objects. However, he'd been grateful in a few situations in the past to have the deterrent Remington revolver with him to serve its useful purpose.

As the footman escorted the unhappy salesman out onto the stoop, Bremen moved just beyond the open drawing room and was able to hear snatches of conversation by the Fairchilds. Fortunately there were so many servants he was able to blend into the household without being perceived as out of place. He was aware the upper crust of society didn't take an interest in the menial staff. He paused at the entrance to observe the couple inside and waited for an opportunity.

After dismissing a young man from the room, the older man stood and spoke down to the seated woman, "I believe the decision is clear, Mrs.

Fairchild. The family will prosper from an assignation with the Webster family."

She gave a questioning tilt and returned the same frigid regard.

"If our son is to marry, Noelle, it should be beneficial to all involved. The greatest riches can be attained through marriage with this girl. The other two chits have been proven useless." The man's tone was detached and impervious.

"As in our marriage," Noelle answered in kind, "wedding for anything other than money and social status would not be advantageous, would it?"

"You wish him to marry for emotion?"

"You wish a marriage such as ours on our son?"

"As in our marriage, emotional attachments are better sought elsewhere."

"Then we both subscribe to a similar philosophy."

A look of displeasure crossed the man's face before he left the room.

Bremen caught the woman's eye when she glanced toward the doorway. This might be the one chance to appeal to the lady of the house in private.

He slipped into the room. "Ma'am, I know you've used the powers of the Heart Gem. I'm here to tell you the man who has the object is a thief, and I'm seeking the Artifact's return to the rightful owners."

Her eyes scrutinized, first over his thick ink-black hair, pausing at the shoulders, then concentrating on snug pants, until finally moving to muscular legs encased in footman's stockings.

"Please lock the door." Her smile was open and friendly.

He crossed over and turned the key in the lock, returning to stand before the woman. "Mrs. Fairchild, my name is Bremen Tyler. I've been searching for the Heart Gem for the past month. Can you tell me the name of the man who brought it here, when it was used, and how he was contacted?"

She was quiet for a moment, seeming to think over the request. "Mr. Tyler, to what length would you go to procure this information?"

"Any length, Mrs. Fairchild. I have funds available at my disposal. What sum were you considering?"

She reached out delicately manicured hands dressed in heavy rings. She placed his fingers on the opal buttons at the top of her couture dress. "I have needs other than monetary, Mr. Tyler. Fulfill those, and I'll answer all your questions."

He was stunned. Was she serious? Meeting her eyes, he knew she was. He pondered how far it was possible to go to retrieve the Heart Gem. He could be done with the task and return home with the Gem. He had no feelings for this woman, and it would be a purely physical act. And if done as asked, he could give Hallie real proof their lives would be happy together.

He kept his hands in place at the opening of the gown. No one needed to know. This woman meant nothing but was a more than willing means to an end.

Noelle appeared to notice the hesitation and unbuttoned the top button of the dress, a look of great concession upon the smooth face.

He stared, running through the alternatives once again. It made sense. This could solve his dilemma.

"Well, Mr. Tyler? Or are you interested in begging and pleading as an aphrodisiac?"

His body responded to the request—physically, the act could be completed, as the long period of self-imposed abstinence was not natural for an Ancestral. He moved forward to touch the woman's thin glossed lips while his fingers reached out to open the second button of the gown. He closed his eyes, not wanting to see the woman's face.

He stopped and pulled away.

No. He loved Hallie. There could be no other woman, no matter how great the reward, and even if the reward brought Hallie, knowing this was how he obtained the Heart Gem would sully true love forever. While his people enjoyed sensual pleasures, once they met their Heart Match, there was and could be no other. He lowered both hands to the sides and responded gently, "You are a beautiful woman and I'm flattered, Mrs. Fairchild, however I am not able to accommodate you."

A gleam appeared in the blue eyes as if accepting a challenge. She placed a hand on his manhood. "I could accommodate you."

He moved back a step. He had no time for games. "Mrs. Fairchild, I have available a sum of 100,000 pounds, ready to be delivered within hours. No one needs to know we spoke. Tell me the name of the man who brought the Heart Gem and when it was used."

She closed the dress's buttons. "This is your decision?"

"I am in love." He could offer no other reason except this simple statement.

The woman breathed out an irritated breath, then reached over to ring the bell. In a moment, the footman knocked on the door. "Mrs. Fairchild is there anything you need?" a booming voice called from outside.

Noelle looked at Bremen and smiled. "You are a fool."

Bremen knew what she intended to do, but his response wouldn't have been different.

"Help, Johnson! The assailant won't open the door! Help me!"

He stepped toward the door intending to unlock the entrance, but the footman launched the aperture open. The man grappled him, but Bremen ducked and propelled the servant aside. The burly man clutched him by the shoulders, but he broke the hold, and kicked out at the man's knees. The footman staggered and rolled to the ground as they continued to fight.

While brawling, Bremen saw an enthralled Noelle Fairchild watching the fight. His shoulders strained the fabric of the jacket, and his large fists were controlled and direct. Johnson was a rough sort with a husky build, large flailing fists connecting wherever possible during the scuffle.

He reached to the cherry wood side table to grab a Wedgewood vase, broke it over the footman's head, and yanked out his pistol to aim directly at Noelle Fairchild. "There appears to have been a misunderstanding, Johnson. I'm leaving this house—now, without any trouble."

Noting his upper hand, Noelle signaled to the footman to step away, allowing Bremen to back out of the room, the gun still pointed. He could see the footman looking to the lady of the house for further direction, but she shook her head at the question on whether to follow. A moment after Bremen left the room, the door locked once again.

Chapter Eighteen

The splendid feel of a thick wad of pound notes in his pocket, Iberville settled back on the seat of the first ferry to England. In spite of the condescension encountered at the Fairchild's, the payment had been made as agreed upon, and the trip to Ireland had been as fruitful as anticipated.

Now to return to the small house he'd rented in a nondescript town in Cheshire County called Wrightsville. There he planned to take up temporary residence, once again using the name of George Smith in business dealings.

Last month, using some of the wealth accumulated from other discreet customers needing his services, he'd discovered parts of the story behind the Heart Gem. Apparently there was a man named Bremen Tyler who searched for the Artifact. This man—or one his associates—had been following, sometimes just steps behind.

Obviously his pursuers weren't aware he was an expert in evasion. Avoidance had been practiced his whole life. He wiped both hands against the pant legs. A few of Bremen Tyler's associates had been made to disappear, either through bribes or more harsh methods. The harsh methods were preferable and used more often since significantly cheaper and simpler.

But this Tyler fellow stood in his way, keeping him from using the Gem freely. To earn the riches and power desired, a plan must be devised to eliminate Tyler's interference permanently. Nothing obvious which could be linked to Iberville, of course.

He closed both eyes and drew in a breath of cool sea air to clear his head from the bouts of black thoughts which had been clouding his mind since the time of leaving France for England. Those dark episodes stirred never-imagined anger and hate.

The bench seat moved. A young woman sat across the aisle, dressed in maid's clothing and carrying a heavy bound package tied in thick twine. He smiled a charming grin and stood in a courtly gesture to acknowledge her presence. Flattered, she responded with a flirtatious look. He wondered what the respectable miss would do if he pulled out his wad of cash and waved the money under the pert nose.

She removed a white bonnet to uncover her head and Iberville stared. The maid had lovely golden hair, just like Louise's. The lightest of blondes, silky—almost white. The young woman smoothed out the black dress, pulling the fabric tightly over large breasts, pretending to not notice his interest.

Perhaps *this* woman was his Heart Match? He'd become obsessed lately with finding the woman.

He slid toward the maid, extending a hand. "George Smith, Miss. May I interest you in a light supper?"

****

He slapped the woman's rump and drew a giggle. Iberville led the woman from the ferry up the staircase of the Wrightsville house, to his room and over to the bed.

"Lovely house, George. Me, I live with my parents and seven brothers and sisters. Too many in one place, there are."

He ran his fingers over the blonde hair. She could ramble; it mattered not as long as she was his Heart Match.

"You do need a woman's touch here. Looks like the place hasn't been cleaned in months and there's

147

a bit of a sweet, musky odor that begs for a good airing."

"You're very pretty." Not as pretty as Louise, but there was that same hair. And in the darkened room, Jenny looked younger. He stepped to the dresser, poured two portions of liquor and lifted a glass. "To Jenny: the lovely lady who walked onto the ferry and changed my life."

With a pleased smile she took the glass and then flicked a fallen lock of hair behind a shoulder. She tapped his glass and downed the strong cordial in one gulp.

"Let down your hair." His voice was gruff as the madness ebbed at the edges of his consciousness.

"You are quite the one that likes the hair." Jenny took out the pins, letting the silky curtain fall.

Aroused, his eyes fixed on the voluptuous body, and a growing lust stirred. "Do something for me."

She waited, a knowing look on her face.

"Hold my hand."

Her light brow creased in confusion, but she took the hand. He removed the Heart Gem from its secret pocket and held the object forward. There was wonder in the woman's eyes.

"What is that, George?"

"Look."

The stone started to glow, and the outer edges blackened. He held her firm, keeping the hand close. An image shimmered and formed on the surface of the stone. The view showed them in a violent argument. Jenny was crying as he was beating and slapping her. Heavy in pregnancy, she attempted to hide her stomach from the blows. He turned away for a moment to grab a cane, and she tried to run. "Not my child," his Image screamed. Her Image tried to reach the door, but he restrained her.

Jenny yanked her hand away and broke the connection with the Gem. "I want to go."

He was furious. Another betrayal. He tried to speak but words wouldn't come.

"You're insane. I'm going now." She edged toward the door.

"Oh, no. You'll not leave. Not after what you've done."

She shoved and made him lose his balance momentarily. He slipped onto the floor, but grabbed her ankle causing her to fall to the rug. The woman screamed at a high pitch, the noise causing his head to want to pop open. He had to stop the noise. He crawled over to her, straddling her body and moving to encircle her neck and tighten. Jenny started screaming again, making the pain in his head unbearable. When his hands loosened, she rolled to the side. Iberville grasped and caught a handful of hair, but she pulled away and sped down the stairs and out the house.

He waited until the darkness stopped, now taking more time to clear than usual.

He opened both eyes and stared at the clump of long hair in his hand, reveling in the softness. Reverently, he placed the mass of silky blonde on one of the pillows of the bed. He was right. It was just like Louise's.

Anxiety flooded his body. Where was his Heart Match? When would they meet? Each time he found a woman, the Heart Gem showed another tragic picture.

He went to pour a second drink, took the glass over to the bed, and stretched out. Bremen Tyler must be interfering. Maybe Tyler was keeping his Heart Match from him. Maybe Tyler even had his Heart Match *with* him?

Chapter Nineteen

The crowd at the pier wound around Bremen, the passengers pushing and shoving to enter the last ferry of the day scheduled to sail back to England. Tired in both body and mind, he pulled the collar up to keep out the chilly sea air. He would be glad to settle into the ship's cabin for a rest before heading back home.

Bremen felt a jostle, and a small hand brushed against the right side of his coat laying something of weight there. He reached into the pocket and pulled out a well-worn billfold, tips of paper money notes peeking out from the corner of the leather pack.

"Thief!" a familiar booming voice accused. The crowd stopped their march toward the gangplank, halting in confusion while looking around to seek the offender in their midst. "Thief!" the man in the street shouted louder, this time moving over to stand on a raised stairway to point a finger.

One word sounded in Bremen's head—*trapped.* The crowd opened, harsh voices buzzed as wagging digits pointed to the wallet in his hand.

The Fairchild's footman stood on the stairs, Johnson's bruised face and swelling black eye grotesquely marring the rugged features.

"He accosted me and stole my wallet." Johnson waved over a constable standing at the doorway of the ticket stand. "Officer McManus, arrest this man."

Bremen's hopes of making the last ferry started to fade away but he walked to the two men, and tossed the billfold to Johnson. "Here is your property. Admit you planted it in my coat pocket and you won't be accused of bearing false witness."

The officer administered a speculative look before turning to speak to the footman, "Mr. Johnson, can you identify the wallet just returned?"

"My initials are engraved in the leather, and there are exactly three pounds there."

Officer McManus took the leather piece and gave a cursory examination. "It appears you are correct, Mr. Johnson. Sir, I'm placing you under arrest for assault and robbery."

He'd had enough. Hunger gnawed in an empty stomach and muscles ached. "No." Frustrated, Bremen raised his voice to a loud roar, "I'm getting on that boat and forgetting everything about this godforsaken place. If you really are a true officer, you'll step aside."

"Are you saying you didn't accost this man?" McManus countered.

"Let's say there was an altercation about a lady and leave it at that."

Officer McManus and Johnson exchanged glances. The officer placed a hand on the wooden baton at his waist before making a menacing step. "It's the jailhouse for you. These London troublemakers travel in everyday to rob our good, hard-working folk and we'll not stand for it any more."

Bremen watched the ship pull away from the dock, a number of curious passengers observing the heated exchange from the deck. *Damn. Another impediment.*

There would be no justice in this situation. He needed to escape, and if able to get to the warehouse area, there would be an opportunity to either blend in or hide. He slid to the left. McManus anticipated the move and responded with a left hook. Bremen ducked and spun out of range, ready to defend.

McManus pulled out the baton, raising the object.

Bremen pulled out his gun to use as a last resort, then pushed an odorous fruit cart into the pursuers' way before racing toward the emptying street. He cursed the late hour that had thinned the crowd to a disadvantage.

He wove with the people, ducking and moving as the heavy McManus made an effort to catch up, his portly frame preventing a close follow. Johnson was moving too, but the sore knee delivered earlier in the day slowed the man's pace.

Bremen was sprinting, trying to get to the other side of the street but on this avenue there were suddenly too many people about making it difficult to get through. A cab moved in front. The startled horse raised its front hooves in alarm just inches from his chest. Bremen backed up trying to regain balance.

WHACK! McManus' baton came down hard causing him to double over and drop to the ground. *Click.* The handcuffs snapped shut around Bremen's wrists.

****

"Are you sure you haven't seen him?" Hallie persisted.

Mr. Vaughan sighed. "No, Miss Pinefoy, not a glimpse."

She pressed further, "And you do not know where he went?"

Mr. Vaughan was growing irritated with the insistence. "Just as I told you yesterday, and the day before, and the days before that, I don't know where Mr. Tyler went off to. If I see him, Miss Pinefoy, I assure you I'll give word."

Her throat was tight. "Thank you, Mr. Vaughan."

There had been no additional help from the neighboring businesses, and now the owners were avoiding her unending questions.

Outside Tyler's Shop, she went through the set of keys to unlock the door. Except for a little more dust settling on the furniture and floor, the room was unchanged and nothing had moved. Bremen had not come home.

He'd promised to give two days to think, but now it was two weeks.

Every day she came here to look for him. Every evening she returned home with a greater fear of never seeing the man again.

Seated at his desk, she lifted the favorite gold pen and caressed it between her fingers. His beautiful, elegant hands held this pen. This was the pen he used to write her love notes. She tossed the implement down on the desk. Infuriating man. Couldn't he keep his word? It seemed since they'd met the man was appearing and disappearing. Bastard.

She jumped as the bell rang and the door opened, her heart starting to pound.

"Good morning, Miss Pinefoy," Jacob greeted with a tip of his hat.

"Mr. Morse." Her voice sounded dull. As dull as her life was without Bremen.

"I was wondering if Mr. Tyler has returned. There was an item which was to be ordered for the office."

"He isn't here." Much to her horror her eyes threatened to spill tears.

The man's expression was a mixture of pity and unease. "Oh. When do you expect him back?"

"I don't know." She sniffed hard.

"But he is coming back?"

"I...I hope so."

He adjusted the banded collar and took a step backward as though terrified to be confronted by an emotional weeping woman. "Well, then. I'll check back tomorrow."

She ordered herself to stop the incessant crying and whining. "I hope I have good news tomorrow."

He snapped a bow and made a hasty retreat.

She rose and locked the door. There was no one worthwhile to talk to today. However, it might be uplifting to keep busy during Bremen's absence.

In the kitchen, she heated the beeswax mixture prepared the day before. Going over to one of the doll parts boxes, she picked up a piece then dipped the hardened papier-mâché doll head in the thick solution on the stove. After pausing to let the wax drip off, a metal tool was used to roughly shape the wax to reflect eye sockets and cheekbones. Again she dipped the head in the wax and allowed the excess to flow off. The tool shaped the facial features further with more definition.

Distracted for a moment, Hallie pressed with excessive force and the wax split to the composition, an ugly gash forming in the drying substance. It was no use. She couldn't concentrate on tasks—all creativity had left along with Bremen.

Rising, she took a last glance to the front of the shop and was surprised to see a fair-haired stranger standing outside the locked door. She debated over letting the man in but instead decided now was the perfect time to take a few well-deserved moments to wallow in her distress.

Hallie went into the bedroom, laid on Bremen's bed, and curled up on the pillow. While smelling his wonderful scent upon the sheets, she closed her eyes and drifted off to a deep sleep, the built-up exhaustion of the last two weeks finally taking over.

****

Iberville crept up to the small mercantile displaying a shiny new sign: Tyler's Shop.

It had cost a pretty penny to track down the city where Bremen Tyler lived. He tested the handle on the door, and with long-practiced experience, attempted to open it without making a sound. Locked. Very unfortunate. He could have picked it, but stood in a busy area in the town center.

Making sure not to meet any of the passersby's eyes, he glanced around the sidewalk. A number of walkers stared for a moment before going past, but no one offered to help. That was good. In a town smaller than this one, residents might be more inquisitive about a stranger's appearance.

Iberville couldn't spend more time loitering at the front without attracting attention so he perused the length of the building, observing a shared courtyard of sorts just beyond his vision. Presumably there would be another door.

With a purposeful step, he headed into the back in the search for an open aperture that would afford easy admittance. He peered through one of the windows in the rear and saw there was an apartment behind the shop—a small kitchen and few other rooms. He reached to touch the door handle. Also locked, but in this private area he could break in. A sound startled him, and he met the questioning eyes of a middle-aged washerwoman working in the back courtyard.

"May I help you, sir?"

"Good afternoon, madam. I'm here for Mr. Bremen Tyler."

"He's not here at the moment. By the way the public entrance is at the front."

"Oh yes, I saw the front was closed, so decided to go around back." He offered an obsequious bow and appreciative perusal.

"Well, the back is private."

"Mr. Tyler and I have important business dealings. I'm sure he wouldn't object to my waiting inside."

"Do you think I'm an idiot? Off with you or I'll

call the authorities."

He could remove the woman but doing so would draw attention to his plan, an undesirable outcome. "I do thank you for the excellent advice. I'll return on another day, hoping to find Mr. Tyler."

She exchanged glances with the hefty blacksmith who stepped into the courtyard to work at the forge. The giant was ready to assist. "Hester, need anything?"

The woman stared at Iberville, a question in the brown eyes.

"Good day, ma'am." He tipped the hat before leaving.

****

Hallie awoke to murmured voices in the back square, followed by the new blacksmith hammering at the forge. It was time to get up. It was time to get on. Enough of this moping and crying.

She stretched every tight muscle as she prepared for what needed to be done next. She must officially break the impulsive engagement with Clay. He would be hurt, but to allow the implied commitment any longer was unfair. She had avoided her friend's company these past two weeks, but the time to talk had come.

She gathered a wrap before making the walk to Clay's home. Even if Bremen, God forbid, didn't return, she couldn't marry Clay. Her heart was Bremen's. How stupid of her not to realize so earlier.

She took the path through the edge of the woods and was at the Nash residence within a short time. She let the knocker fall twice and waited. "Is Mr. Nash in?"

The maid smiled in a welcoming manner. "He's in the study, Miss Pinefoy. Shall I escort you there?"

"No need." The door to the library was open; Clay sat on the cushioned chair reading and sipping on a large brandy poured from a crystal decanter placed nearby. "My darling!" Clay stood when she entered the room.

"I must apologize for coming unannounced."

"We don't have to stand on ceremony here, especially given our upcoming union."

"Yes. Well that's something we need to speak about." She slid away to sit on the chair across from the desk, seeking to put some distance between them.

Clay's features hardened. "You can be assured I will go along with whatever plans you want. Food, music, it matters naught. Whatever you want is acceptable."

He wasn't making the conversation any easier. She paced to the fireplace and examined the figurines displayed on the mantel. "Clay, I've given a great deal of thought to this matter. We must break things off. I don't love you as a wife should love her husband. You are a dear friend, however, I can't reciprocate the same feelings as you." Her speech was spoken too fast, but the words needed to be uttered before he could interrupt.

Clay grimaced, a frown settling on the small mouth. "I know your reason for wanting to break the engagement. I tell you Tyler isn't what he appears. Rumor has it he even has gypsy blood. He came to this town out of nowhere and charmed himself into your life. Where is he now? I hear he's disappeared without a word. Did he tell you where he was going?"

She bit her lip. Nothing said would change this decision.

"Don't worry, I'll send him away. I love you and have always loved you. You know me, my character, and my intentions. What do you know about him?"

"I've made this choice because marriage is not meant for the two of us."

Clay guided her to the couch and took her hand. "Your love for me will grow. Once we are man and wife, we'll grow deeper in love as we raise children and grow old together. I'll be faithful and steady."

She squeezed his hand before pulling away. "No. I'm sorry."

"Remember when I was your friend and confidant? When our mothers died within months of each other, I was the only one who understood your feelings. We clung to each other and sobbed. No one could ever be closer to me than you. We can go back to that time of intimacy."

"The episode we shared was a different sort of intimacy and occurred many years ago. We are now adults."

"What can I change to make you want me? I'll try harder to show my love. I'll write poems and court you more. Whatever you need, just tell me, and I'll do it."

"It's not that."

His nostrils flared. "If Tyler wasn't persuading you, you wouldn't feel this indecision. Think of what we can have."

"I'm sorry," she repeated.

He stepped to the table and drank the rest of the brandy, then threw the glass to the wall. "I'll show you real love. There's no reason for modesty anymore."

Clay grabbed her and pinned her against the wall.

The struggling seemed to excite him, and his eyes fixed on hers as he plunged his mouth down and kissed.

She winced with pain but was able to knee him in the nether regions.

Clay gasped and moved.

"I'll forgive you this unfortunate incident this one time. However, if you ever make a move like this again, you'll regret those actions. I promise."

She spoke in measured tones, making her voice

as cold as possible.

"You'll regret this, I promise *you*." He didn't make a move to follow, but added the threat in a barely audible voice.

## Chapter Twenty

Two damn weeks in this hellhole. Two more left, if lucky, and then he might go to trial. Bremen knew there'd be no fairness from a judge who'd already refused requests for a speedy hearing, or even the passage of a letter back to Mooreland. He now cursed this place: its cold, damp walls, wretched excuse for a cot, mealy blanket and food not fit for a dog.

Arrested for thievery, of all things, when he was chasing a thief. Bremen laughed out loud, hearing the hard sound echo against the walls.

Again he tested the bars, disappointed in the cell's sturdiness. If he ever got his hands on Johnson, the man would never be able to lie again. He turned toward the stone firmament and stared at the etching he'd made of her face. The crude, sharp stone couldn't capture one bit of her sweetness. He'd told Hallie he'd be away for only two days. God knows what she would be thinking by now. Maybe she'd even have wed that dim-witted ass Clay Nash thinking she'd been deserted.

He sat on the edge of the wooden bed frame, putting dirty hands over his face while attempting to think of a plan of escape. The promise of a bribe to the jailer had not met with any success as his wallet had been taken away at the beginning of the incarceration. The broken nose bestowed on Officer McManus with a head butt just after being shackled no doubt was the reason he was branded a dangerous criminal. Someone who warranted an isolated area of the jail away from any influence on the other prisoners.

Even being taken out of here by the Ancestrals was almost preferential to being stuck in this miserable place. He lifted his head and listened. Small, heeled steps pattered down the dank prison hallway. He focused his sight far into the dimmed light until a petite, fur-caped woman walked to the cell, face covered. His spirits fell. It wasn't Hallie. Of course not. She had no idea of his location.

"She must be a very special girl," a feminine voice projected into the cell. "Has she been worth it?" The woman pulled the hood and let the covering fall elegantly around her shoulders.

He felt a faint glimmer of hope, tempered by what the lady might request to extract his freedom. "Yes, Mrs. Fairchild, she is my life."

A few fleeting creases marred the china-doll forehead. "In spite of the nauseating affection you have for this girl, I've arranged for a release."

"Have you? Why?"

Noelle didn't answer for a few moments but swept a gaze to the floor. "Redemption, I suppose," she whispered.

Bremen pressed against to the iron bars of the cell.

"At least someone will have love in their life. I didn't have it. Yesterday I assisted in an arrangement for my son to never experience this emotion. Percy could have been happy, but I was complicit with Max's plans for money over love for the child." A pitiful expression moved over the smooth features. "Now, perhaps I can redeem myself by contributing to your happiness. Perhaps this will be my one selfless act in this lifetime."

Noelle Fairchild eased the hood back onto her head. "I know who you are. My grandmother was from Scotland and spoke of the Ancestrals and the Artifacts in their safekeeping."

"Then tell me, who was the man who brought the Heart Gem to Dublin?"

"I can't help you. I never could as the man dealt exclusively with my husband. Maximilian wouldn't tell me who the man was even if I asked. Especially if I asked."

The heavy jailer clinked down the hallway toward the cell, giving an interested glance at the woman covered head to toe. "Free to leave, mister."

Bremen stepped out and kissed Noelle's hand. "Thank you."

He watched as she retraced her steps along the empty corridor, and the woman's slim outline disappeared from sight.

Chapter Twenty-One

Bremen's body jolted at the rough stop of the train as it pulled into the Mooreland station. Outside the window, sheets of rain plastered against the glass. No doubt he'd have a miserable walk to Tyler's Shop.

As he made his way, the rain started to let up the incessant pounding against his body, but not enough to lighten the black mood he'd settled into. Hearing the sound of loud splashes, he turned in time to see a carriage drive past, the wheels bouncing off a muddy hole in the ground the size of a large watermelon and dashing dirty water over him from the neck down.

"Sorry," yelled the driver.

Dripping, Bremen shook off the water. The wet grey buildings matched the dismal sky. The clouds were darkening, but hadn't yet become as black as his disposition.

He was incensed at having returned without possessing the Heart Gem. Adding to his worries were possible actions by the Ancestrals. If the council decided to call him back, there was nothing in this world or the next which could be done to prevent such an action. The council could force him to leave everything and everyone behind.

In the back courtyard Bremen pulled out the hidden key and went into the empty shop. He peeled off the dirty sodden clothes and washed the remaining filth from his skin.

He set some coffee on to boil. Not having any idea what had transpired during the past couple of

163

weeks was frustrating. Killing Nash *could* solve his problem, but that wouldn't bode well for a number of reasons, including being the waste of a good bullet. He paused giving the option of murder more thought than necessary. Anyway, killing Hallie's "fiancé" might fall under the context of "undue coercion." He allowed a lighthearted laugh.

But Nash wasn't his biggest obstacle. It was the obstinate, independent, beautiful woman he'd fallen in love with back in Wrightsville.

****

The rain pierced down while Hallie drove the buggy at breakneck speed through the sudden storm. Cold water soaked through every layer of clothing but she didn't care. At this moment, her only mission was getting to Bremen as soon as possible. She'd gotten word the man had returned and not even a violent storm could deter her.

The rain softened as she parked the buggy under the roof and jumped out from the seat. She bolted to the front door of the shop, meeting the resistance of the locked door when turning the handle to enter. "Stupid door." She groaned and kicked the bottom of the wooden panel. In her haste, she'd forgotten to take the keys.

She dashed around the courtyard to the apartment door and pounded. "Bremen, please open the door! It's Hallie! Bremen, I've come to tell you I've ended with Clay. I love you, only you." There was loud movement in the house, and the door flung open.

Her eyes teared in joy. It didn't matter that his hair looked as though it hadn't been combed in a very long time, or that he sported a beard and his clothes were wrinkled. He was delicious.

He grabbed and pulled her into the house. "Repeat what you said."

She held Bremen's hands to her heart, "I said, I

love you and can't live without you." His bone-crushing embrace almost melted her body to his to become one.

"I'll make you the happiest woman in the world. I can't tell you in words how much I love you."

"You are the only one for me. I know that now. I was frightened of my feelings but no longer."

"And you need no proof? You're certain you love me and will be my wife?"

"Silly man. Who has proof?"

His tight clasp enveloped her again, squeezing frigid rain onto the floor.

"Take off your clothes, Hallie."

"Your eagerness is flattering," she sighed.

"While I *am* eager, my darling, what I meant was you are soaking wet and will become sick with cold. You need to change into something dry."

She was beginning to feel an uncomfortable chill and followed his lead to the bedroom. Bremen handed over a pair of trouser pants and shirt, then winked when he left her to change. She put on the clothes, reveling in the smell of the manly warmth. Being dressed in his apparel was as though his whole body was wrapped around hers.

She came to the kitchen feeling shy, but Bremen took the wet things and hung them in a discreet place in the courtyard to dry in the sun that had started to peek out.

Bremen poured some hot coffee and sat, taking her hands in his as he rubbed the fingers warm. "What was it that changed your mind, my dove?"

She basked in the heat. "When you left I was afraid you wouldn't return. I knew if you did, hopefully when you did, I'd be there. I couldn't be happy without you in my life. I just hoped it wasn't too late."

"I wouldn't have stayed in Mooreland if you'd married Clay. But I wouldn't have given up until the last moment."

She leaned forward for a kiss.

Somehow they moved into the bedroom. Bremen felt Hallie lie upon his chest, the trousers against long limbs outlining every feminine curve. The boldness, the lack of inhibitions in going this far, was almost too much to bear. Every touch and kiss aroused.

Power coursed through him, knowing these breasts, these buttocks, would soon belong to him as her husband. He couldn't wait much longer. But would. "We must wait until we are married." He despised having to say the words.

She stopped unbuttoning the silk blouse. "What? Why?"

If Hallie were to become pregnant before the wedding and the Ancestrals forced his return, the woman would be left alone and expecting. "Now. Let's go see Reverend Fulton at this moment. We can be wed today."

"At this moment? But the town will talk."

"What do we care what people say? We'll be man and wife. Together from this day forward."

"I'm not in favor of a long engagement either, but I do need a few months to plan. It may even be best to delay the wedding until next spring."

He froze in shock. "The marriage will not be delayed until spring."

She toyed with the swath of hair falling over his eyes. "Not an indefinite postponement, but to plan and set up a household quickly might be difficult."

He moved the fingers away. "The marriage will not be deferred." His tone was deliberately final. This was non-negotiable.

"The urgency is admirable, but what is the hurry to wed? Is there some other reason?" The released hands began to re-button the clothing.

Bremen brushed the hair from his forehead and

needed to avert both eyes. "Yes, there is urgency. That's all I can say. Just trust me. You've agreed to marry, and I'll hold you to that vow."

A stubborn look crossed Hallie's face and she sat up. "You'll hold me to that? This isn't a business contract to be entered into. And I don't like to be directed so."

"I've promised you may pursue whatever interests and business you desire. I will support you in every choice, and am prepared to relent in every other respect, but a ceremony must be held as soon as possible."

"Isn't it the woman who rushes a man into marriage?"

Her words terrified him. Each morning he woke wondering if the day would be the last in Mooreland. "I'm an anxious bridegroom. Surely you can't find fault in that?" He attempted a flirtatious cajole.

"You're being evasive, and I don't appreciate that behavior. After all our misunderstandings, I want the truth. What if I say I want to delay the wedding until next spring?"

"I won't force you to wed or cause duress."

"That's an extremely unromantic answer, Bremen."

He needed the assurance a wedding would provide. Even the Ancestrals would acknowledge such a ceremony and hesitate before parting them. "I love you. Is it so important to wait for the sake of the townspeople? Please, my darling."

The stiffness of his body relaxed when Hallie leaned full against him. He began to kiss her in the way she loved: power and gentleness, but this time with restrained passion.

He would have to count down the days. And pray the Ancestrals wouldn't call him before the marriage was consummated.

Chapter Twenty-Two

"This surprise will reassure me as to the wisdom of agreeing to a wedding just two weeks hence?" Hallie relished the kisses Bremen nibbled along her neck.

He lifted his mouth a fraction away. "Most definitely. And I'll have you know it's a great concession on my part to agree to a two-week wait. I don't like it."

"You are a mystery man. I'm not sure whether to be alarmed or not. It's as though you have no past, and your life began at the moment of our meeting in Wrightsville."

His gaze was possessive and sensual. "It did."

She felt lightheaded when Bremen spoke in such a manner and gazed into her eyes the way he was now. "So, what sort of curiosity am I to see?"

Bremen kissed the tip of her nose and laughed. "Not divulging something is the essence of a surprise. Come and see; that is the way to discover."

He urged the horse forward, and took them from the city toward the lush summer fields and wide meadows painted with wildflowers.

"Is it far?" What could the man be so excited about?

"Not far but far enough." His tone was teasing as he lifted her hand and kissed the palm.

"Will I like it?" She ran a couple of fingers through Bremen's hair as the warm breeze blew a few locks over those scrumptious dark eyes.

"I think you will."

She fell into the flirtatious mood. "Is it bigger

than a loaf of bread?"

"Considerably so, my love." Bremen put his warm palm on her left knee, and little jolts of pleasure burst against her skin.

"Is it bigger than the moon?" she countered by placing her own hand on the square knee and seeing with satisfaction how the man tensed with excitement.

"Not quite so, love."

"Hmmm....are you sure this is for me?"

"It is for you, but I hope you'll allow me to share. There is much I look forward to sharing with you." A slow hand moved from knee to the inside of her thigh. "Soon."

He stopped the buggy in a shady spot and swung the reins over a branch to anchor the horse. "We'll walk from here."

She gazed around the clearing rimming a trail into the green woods. She loved the feeling of the thick forest, but hadn't wandered there during the past few weeks as work and now wedding preparations engaged so much time.

They crossed the narrow path through the trees until the area opened to reveal a large-framed house. There was a flurry of activity all around as men sawed, hammered and worked at various tasks inside and out.

"What is this?"

"It's your wedding gift. My Uncle Roman initiated the building of the structure a while ago, but wasn't able to complete the house. I directed the work to be finished as soon as possible."

Bremen greeted the men, and led her to the large wooden door inlaid with ornate prisms of glass. "The furnishings are not all here, as I believe you would desire to pick most of the accouterments. What do you think?"

"The house is spectacular. You are doing this for

me?"

"Yes, for you, only you. Come see inside."

She stepped into the large entry hall and across the stone floor before turning around in the large drawing room. There were a few odd pieces in the room now, but the remainder of the trappings still needed to be chosen.

She followed into the kitchen where a new large wooden table was set, and a fireplace cooking pit in addition to a new stove. To the left were two shelved rooms; one could be used for a large pantry.

"Come upstairs." They moved up the grand stairway of knotted pine into a large hallway.

The washroom was of the latest style, with running water in the house and a flush toilet; a large claw-foot tub stood against the wall.

Speechless, she followed in a daze.

A small bedroom was first. "Perhaps a nursery one day." He brushed lips against her hair.

"Perhaps we'll be so blessed."

Second, third and fourth bedrooms followed of a good size. The fifth bedroom was to be their chamber with two dressing rooms built on each side, one for the lady and one for the gentleman.

An enormous marble-manteled fireplace stood across from a brass frame. "What a large bed." In truth, she had never seen a mattress so great.

"Necessary as most of our time will be spent there."

Luscious heat moved across her skin.

"Come and sit." There was a new emerald velvet settee placed against the wide wall. Bremen drew her to sit close, thigh to thigh.

She was overwhelmed by the beauty of the house, and the reality of living a life with Bremen here was sinking in. This was to be their home together.

"So?" She heard the trepidation in his deep

voice. "Hallie, do you like it? Will you make your home here?"

"Of course I love it. I'm just," she groped for a word, "flabbergasted."

"I am elated it appeals. We can go into town now to pick the furniture and lamps and all the other things you would like to have here."

The made their way back to the buggy and turned toward the larger town of Rutherford, which boasted numerous mercantiles specializing in furniture and housewares.

"What are you thinking?" Bremen looked at her as they started to drive.

"I'm thinking how magically happy I am. I had never thought I would be so in love and so loved. Is this a dream? Will we wake, alone and unhappy?"

"This is real and will be so for us. We have found each other and will live a long life together. I vow to you, you will become my life and my purpose is to make you happy each day. I'll wait at the gates of Heaven for you, because it will not be Heaven without you."

"You should not talk that way. You will tempt the fates."

"I'll not, this is how I feel." Bremen stopped the wagon and tipped the attendant to water the horse and mind the property.

"So, my dove, what do you want to look at first?"

"I believe we need a couch and lamps, then dishes and pots, and linens too."

"We will take care of it all, and stop for supper before heading back."

They spent the next hours shopping. She was careful in the choices, believing Bremen was a man of comfortable means but not independently wealthy.

They picked items to be packed and taken today, and arranged for larger pieces to be delivered the next week. As promised, Bremen left the choices to her. She tried to keep the man's taste in mind, but was unable to resist the flowered curtains and embroidered sheets admired at the linen shop.

Tiring of shopping, they went into the café in town and took a seat at the outdoor table and sat in companionable silence while watching the busy people walking by.

"Less than two weeks, Hallie."

"You are counting down the days? Have you a fear of my bolting?" she teased. "Do you worry of my leaving you standing at the altar?"

"Every day I worry we are one day too late. If you agreed, we'd go now to the reverend and say the marriage vows."

She found the seriousness in his voice alarming. "We are in enough of a hurry. I'm sure everyone is counting nine months forward, and there are already the sly glances at my waistline."

"Forgive me for any discomfort you feel, but I want us wed without delay."

"You are sure you don't want to wait until spring?"

"Too long."

She took a sip of tea. "Bremen, you speak nothing of your family, and there are no guests from the Tyler family attending the wedding. Was there a falling out between you and your kin?"

"Yes, numerous instances of strife over many years. As an adult, I decided to go my own way for a time, wanting a different life. The things I'll tell may sound amazing, but swear they are true despite how difficult to believe. I spent my teenage years in a different place. The large group I lived with had certain abilities which are not readily found here. I had a few proficiencies too, but divested the gifts when deciding to make my own way in this world."

She watched the flash in his eyes. "I had no

doubt you were different."

"My people, the Ancestrals, are the keepers of mystical objects collectively called the Artifacts of Love. No one knows the true origins of these Artifacts. Some say the Ancestrals created them; others swear the Ancestrals were only the caretakers. Long ago, great battles were fought and lives were lost in order to possess the powerful Artifacts until finally all four objects were secured in the Ancestrals' Stronghold. From that moment forward the Artifacts were not openly spoken of in the outside world, but became legends, curious possibilities. Each of the Artifacts of Love can lead the holder to their one true Heart Match."

Bremen gazed forward as if seeing a different vista. "The complete truth would probably frighten you right now. While I won't lie, some of the details are unimportant at this time and may be omitted. My parents died years ago. My younger sister, Bremma, still lives with our extended family in the Highlands of Scotland, but most family members live in the Ancestral Stronghold. I decided neither of those lives was for me. However, there were some responsibilities difficult to break from.

"These Artifacts of Love were stolen recently from the Ancestral people. I promised to find one of them and return it. I'm still searching. There are those I commission to assist in locating this object and sometimes, as done in the past, I may have to leave for a while to follow information which may lead me to recover it."

She was fascinated by the tale. "What sort of item?"

"It's called the Heart Gem." He paused again searching for the correct words. "I have seen it employed. This Artifact will show the future life of a couple. If two people, or even the substitution of a close belonging of one of the people, share a connection with the Heart Gem at the same moment, the Gem's surface will reflect an accurate picture of the essence of their union. The Heart Gem is used by my Ancestral people to help select the best marriage matches."

"It is like a crystal ball?"

"No, not quite that. The Gem shows the future but in a different way. It does not show exactly what will happen in the future, but the essence of what would happen if two people joined together."

"Do you think you'll be able to find the object?

"I have come close. It was spotted in France, London and Dublin; however, the Heart Gem is never used out in the open. Also complicating matters is the fact that the illegitimate holder of any of the stolen Artifacts is never in possession of it for a long time. The curse of the Artifacts is the madness the magic brings to those humans who should not have them."

"Then you will return the Heart Gem to your people once found?"

"No, I will destroy it."

Chapter Twenty-Three

Life was going to be extraordinary, now that all impediments were removed. Love, work, home—everything had fallen into place. Even now Bremen was at their future home supervising the final delivery of furnishings.

She dusted the shelves with a light step and a soft hum as a handful of customers in the shop perused the antique books.

The door opened to admit a dapper blond man of average height with piercing blue eyes. She'd seen the gentleman before—in fact, on one of the days Bremen had been gone. He was the customer at the front shop entrance she had decided to ignore in order to wallow in distress at Bremen's absence.

"May I help you, sir?"

"Yes, I believe you may. Can you direct me to Mr. Bremen Tyler?"

"I'm sorry. Mr. Tyler is out at the moment."

"Have you any idea of his return?"

"I'm not certain. Your name, sir?"

The man's smile didn't reach the cold eyes. "We've never been officially introduced, so my name will mean nothing."

"What message would you like me to convey?"

"No message. May I ask if you are his lovely fiancée?"

She resented the appreciative perusal. "I'm both his fiancée and business partner. So if you have anything to discuss with him, you may speak freely." She was aware of his penetrating eyes. It was as though he was weighing her worth.

"Actually, I'd like to surprise him."

Her mind sharpened and focused on the man standing there. Something was false here. "Surprises aren't always pleasant. What is it you want to tell him?"

"He'll know soon enough." He tipped his hat. "Good day, Miss Pinefoy."

"You are sure you do not want to leave a message?" She felt a desperate unease.

"He'll hear from me shortly. I promise."

Two customers called for attention, and she turned for a moment. When she looked back, the blonde gentleman had left without a sound.

Hallie shivered in spite of the warm room. The man had known her name.

\*\*\*\*

"Mr. Tyler, you are in agreement with Miss Pinefoy of omitting the word 'obey' from her vows?" Reverend Fulton's bushy brows shook in disbelief.

She gave Bremen a saucy look. How she enjoyed seeing the self-assured man squirm at times. She turned an angelically innocent look at Mrs. Fulton while waiting for her fiancée's response.

"That would be an interesting word to keep. However, if my future wife would like to substitute something else, I am agreeable to those wishes. Perhaps the word 'mind'?" Bremen responded with exaggerated sincerity.

"Oh." The reverend shook a finger. "I do believe that is very similar."

Mrs. Abigail Fulton bobbed her head in agreement.

"I did mention our desire for a quick ceremony, didn't I?" Bremen put down the fork at the side of the plate.

"I believe you have a number of times, Mr. Tyler. I will do my best to speak as quickly as possible."

Mrs. Fulton dabbed her mouth, "I must say, sir, you are already rushing the nuptials. A lady needs time to prepare for the rigors of marriage."

Hallie's womb tightened in anticipation at the expression on Bremen's face. She was sure her future husband would provide a rigorous marriage, and even the word "obey" might not even be such a bad choice after all.

As if reading her thoughts Bremen added, "Then 'cleave' would be a good substitution."

Reverend Fulton gave a conciliatory look, "I'm afraid 'cleave' is assumed in a marriage."

"Good." Bremen slipped a hand under the table and onto her thigh.

She shifted, checking that the older couple remained interested in their dessert plates while Bremen's fingers played concentric circles on her thigh, moving up slowly toward her center.

"Yes," Mrs. Fulton chimed in as she directed her attention from the berry pie, "it is your obligation, my dear Hallie. If you are concerned about performing your wifely duties, I would be happy to advise in the place of your dear departed mother."

"Thank you for the offer, ma'am, but I will try to manage as best I can."

A flood of relief swept over Abigail's face as though released from an irksome responsibility. "That is well, my dear."

"And the marriage license." The reverend pushed his large belly from the table.

"Everything is ready."

"Mr. Tyler, I do believe you are the most enthusiastic bridegroom I've encountered in thirty years." The reverend offered an apologetic look to Mrs. Fulton. "Of course, after myself, my dear."

Mrs. Fulton tittered and blushed like a teenage girl. Hallie smiled at Bremen. She hoped they were so after thirty years.

He squeezed her hand under the table. "Hallie and I thank you for a wonderful evening. I believe we'll depart as we've walked here this evening and the hour is getting late."

"You may use my buggy," offered Reverend Fulton.

Bremen pulled out her chair. "Are you tired or will we walk home?"

"Let's walk. Fresh air sounds wonderful." She moved to embrace Mrs. Fulton. "Thank you, ma'am, for the wonderful meal and hospitality. Bremen and I look forward to hosting you and the reverend once we're settled."

The men shook hands, and Bremen helped her into the wrap. "There is a shortcut to your father's house."

They set out a path toward the house, and the evening was cool and comfortable. She felt carefree at first, but after alighting on the almost invisible trail looked about apprehensively, hesitant at taking the path through the woods.

Bremen must have noticed the pause in her steps. "Are you all right?"

"Just nerves, I suppose."

He gave her a curious look and continued walking.

The forest stood as a hub between a number of properties, including her father's and their future home. In the past the woods had felt welcoming. Before, it was as though she was at home among the trees, but Hallie now sensed some evil present.

Fear moved slowly through her body as they crossed in deeper, a growing terror now rising and warning to run away. This was not a delicious, exciting fear of the unknown, but a premonition of something terrible. She set the pace quicker and noticed Bremen was quiet too. She started to imagine things. What if something happened to them here? Would anyone find them?

There were no night sounds in the forest, as if an expectant silence surrounded and waited for the next move to be made.

Bremen leaned over and whispered, "Someone is following us."

"What?"

"There is someone behind us." His grip on her hand tightened, "Just keep walking. We need to get out in the open. Let's go toward our house instead of your father's. It's closer." Bremen changed the direction at the central path of the woods and led west.

True fear coursed in every inch of her body. Hallie had the urge to dash from the trees and race for the safety of the house, but Bremen held back, keeping their pace sedate. She heard the footsteps behind, placed with care, muffled by the brush and with planned movements.

"I've no weapon and am not sure what our pursuer has. Keep walking unless you hear running, then hurry to the house. Lock the door and I'll do what must be done."

Bremen reached into a pocket and palmed the house key to her hand. "Hold this."

"Who do you think it is?" She responded with a calmness she didn't feel.

"I think it's one person. Could be a vagrant or poacher. Whoever it is, you'll be all right."

He didn't say, "*We'll* be all right." She was shaking now.

Bremen broke their deliberate stride. "Who's there?"

The steps froze.

"Who is there? Speak out now!" Bremen insisted.

Not a sound or movement rose out of the woods: no insect, no scurrying creature, no bird. Even the trees seemed frozen in time. Just the full moon drifted in and out from behind the wispy clouds.

They marched out of the forest.

"I heard the footfalls soon after entering the trees. I believe it is one person, probably a man."

"We are near now, Bremen, aren't we?"

"Yes." An angry grimace cut across his forehead. "What possessed me to take you out in the middle of the night? I should have brought you home to bed. And joined you there."

They passed into the clearing and the house was visible. She strode with him, conscious of foreign eyes watching as they left the trees.

"Do not look back. Just go on, Hallie."

Her mind was screaming to dash, but her body moved calmly to the front door. He took the key from her sweating hand and opened the door, then locked it behind. He turned on the electric lights, drew the curtains, and went to the parlor fireplace to pull out the poker. "I need to explore the house to ascertain we are alone. Take this, go into the pantry and bar the door."

She refused to take the iron poker. "No, I'm accompanying you." She grounded her feet.

He seemed to weigh the words. "Once again, you won't listen, my love."

Room by room, poker in hand, they went through the house and checked every place and corner until confident the house was unoccupied.

"Bremen, do you think he's gone?"

"Must have been a poacher."

She moved the edge of the curtain aside an inch to survey the lawn. "You must be right."

"We can't return to your father's house tonight, but we'll be safe here until morning."

She agreed it was the best option, but out loud said, "What will the staff think about my not coming home until morning?"

"We are promised, and our wedding date is set. What will they say? Besides, your father is out of town and won't be back tonight. The servants will believe we stole away for the night."

Bremen pulled the length of her against his body, and bent down to take her mouth while strong hands moved down over her buttocks.

"Mr. Tyler, I believe you are attempting to distract me." She moved into the safety of muscled arms again and stayed there until all fear ebbed away.

"Since we'll spend the night here, we should see to our comforts. There are some of my personal things here from the shop apartment, and also blankets in the linen closet along with some food in the pantry."

Bremen stoked a crackling blaze in the parlor and spread out a number of quilts along the planked floor while she made tea and cut some cake from the pantry. He gathered candles to illuminate the room, and they sat on the floor toasting each other with mugs of chamomile as the night grew dark and long.

Those unusual dark eyes sparkled and his hair was like black coal. He gestured with long and elegant fingers, and she thought of the soon-to-be moments when this would be her home.

As though reading her thoughts, Bremen remarked, "You can take the bedroom tonight, Hallie. I'll sleep down here and keep watch." Although his words were straightforward, he looked as though ready to pounce on her right there on the quilt. She imagined them making love here before the fireplace. Or was that a premonition of the future?

"I would feel safer with you."

"Are you sure you trust me?"

"I trust you with everything."

Looking through the muted light he countered,

"Do you think you should trust me so? I'm only a man, weak and very wanting right now."

Her loins began that familiar tightening. "Can you trust me?"

"Sometimes I wonder." He shifted closer and ran a finger over her soft lips. "Perhaps it's my virtue that is at stake. Perhaps you should test my virtue and see if I can withstand the temptation."

"Perhaps I should." She responded in the most serious voice she could muster before leaning over. Bremen lowered her down to the floor, laying her atop him.

After a few moments, he half-heartedly murmured, "Perhaps I should stay downstairs?"

"I'll not bite much." She placed a nip on the man's neck, "but I would feel safer with you near me."

"Then I'll be strong for you, love."

It was late by now—past midnight, when they decided to go to bed. She put her hair into a loose braid and washed her face and hands, then donned the pair of baggy pants and soft shirt Bremen provided.

There in the bedroom, Bremen looked so delicious. His stomach was taut and the broad shoulders well defined, and Hallie caught a glimpse of some unusual black tattoos spread across his upper shoulders.

"Good night." Her throat was dry as she slipped under the thick covers.

"You don't need to be nervous, sweetheart. We've waited this long, we will wait another week. Let me hold you, though. I want to fall asleep with you in my arms." He drew her near.

He smelled wonderful. Soap and clean clothes and male, and all hers. She reached and put her arm over his stomach to rest in contented bliss. He turned to his side and looked through the semi-darkness of the fire-lit room. She couldn't resist turning and reaching out to kiss his firm mouth.

"My love, I'm already having a hard enough time waiting."

She'd never heard his voice so strained. "I'm also."

"I think it's different for a man."

"I have no knowledge of how it is for a man, but it is hard for me too."

He offered a wicked smile. "Very hard?"

"Of course."

He took a deep breath. "If I touch you now, I haven't the strength to stop."

"Just touch me a little then."

Permission granted, Bremen reached and pulled her full length against his body, demonstrating just how hard it was for him to wait.

"Oh." That one word was sufficient to deliver a message.

"Perhaps I should go back downstairs?" His tone held no conviction.

"No, I want you here."

"What do you want me to do?" His rough voice became mesmerizing.

She stretched out, touching every inch of his body. "I just want to feel you."

He pulled close, naked chest against soft body, manhood pressed against her hips. "What I want to do is roll you underneath and take you quickly." He whispered, "This close? Much closer and I'll be making love to you. Do you want me closer?"

"This is perfect." The moment was intoxicating. The room sizzled as their bodies molded in a perfect fit—hard to soft, pushing to yielding.

She memorized the feel of his rough chest hairs against the smooth skin where her loose shirt had fallen open. His hand slipped over her leg from knee up to the curve of the round hip. He rolled the waistband down over her tummy, and put his hand between her legs. The moist heat diffused against the thin fabric.

Her breasts ached to be touched too but her mind focused on that hand sweeping over and around, scorching everywhere it touched. She couldn't stir, even to kiss, she was so intent on what that magical hand was doing. One shift and Bremen might not be able to hold back in spite of his desire to wait.

"Hallie," Bremen breathed into her ear while sucking on the lobe. "Give me just one inch. Will you?"

"Yes," she moaned.

He moved his mouth to her lips, kissing her as he rolled the waistband over hips, legs, and feet. It was amazing how quickly she was naked from the waist down.

He lay between her legs, kissing and exploring her mouth. Her hands went to his waist then to the buttocks. She was a bit shocked that somehow his pants were already off. He moved her legs wide open and she heard a deep groan of pleasure. Then he was sliding around her entrance, wetting, readying. The room was dark, but she sensed his size. A ping of nervousness entered her mind: certainly one single inch would not be a problem? Then Bremen lifted himself over her, poised to enter that one promised inch...

A loud noise clanged from outside in the direction of the barn. Then came the sound of a man's voice swearing.

Bremen tensed.

"Is someone there?" she asked in a daze.

"There must be." In one frustrated movement, he rose out of bed and hurried to the window to focus his vision on the back area. "I can't see in the dark."

She felt a sharp, fearful pain in her insides, as

though a knife was twisting and turning.

"Are you all right?" Bremen came to her side in concern. "You are white as a sheet."

"Please don't go out there. You don't know what to expect. I have those strong intuitions and know something horrific would happen if you departed now."

"I will be careful and only gone a few minutes."

She started to cry. "Please, Bremen, please don't go. If you trust me and love me, don't leave."

He looked at her, weighing the decision.

"I know it is against your instincts. But you will be defenseless against whatever the intruder has. Please."

He went back into the bed and held her tightly, his fireplace poker within reach next to the bed. They lay in each others arms and she fell asleep.

****

Scurrying from the barn, Iberville crouched in the hideout made in the woods. Finding Bremen Tyler and his fiancée was easier than he'd thought.

The pretty pigeon would have been easy to trap, but he would bide his time. First it would be best to decide how to move his enemy out of the way, then take the woman. And if the woman was his own Heart Match as he believed, the view could be seen with her at their leisure. If she wasn't the one, she could be as easily disposed of.

Bremen Tyler had gotten close a few times, and was becoming a nuisance with his inquiries and spies.

His fiancée, Miss Hallie Pinefoy, was lovely. Not his usual type but one could not have everything.

If only Tyler would have come down out of the house, he could have knocked the man unconscious and taken the woman. Now it would be more difficult to take Hallie Pinefoy from Tyler. It was unfortunate that just as Iberville moved to enter the house, he tripped over the tools laid about the barn.

He put his head on the pillow of soft leaves waiting for the swirling black episode in his head to pass. With the help of his Heart Match, the periods of roaring madness and terror in his mind should be soothed away.

Soon things would be better since he knew exactly where his enemy lived.

****

She awoke with Bremen's arms wrapped tightly, warming her skin in the cool morning air. The fireplace had extinguished but the bed was toasty and comfortable. She stretched and rolled to the edge yawning, but he reached and kissed an exposed shoulder. "Good morning, sweetheart."

"Good morning. Should I make coffee? Are you hungry?"

"Very hungry." His grin was wolfish as he swept the blanket off.

She pulled the gaping clothes together and threw a smile, escaping his arm as it shot out trying to capture her again.

"Spoilsport."

She went into the modern bathroom to wash and put on her clothing from the day before, glad of not having had to sleep in the dress. She fixed coffee and bread with honey for breakfast.

It was unimportant if anyone gossiped about them spending the night together. She'd made a decision to be Bremen's wife and had no reservations. If not for the intruder, she would have become a wife in body last night. And she was not sure if they could have stopped at the one inch asked for.

After a short while Bremen came down freshly washed and shaved. "I like having you with me when I wake." He pressed against her back, holding close. He kissed the side of her neck, nipped there, then slipped the dress down over her shoulder to caress.

"And to make your breakfast and coffee?"

"Of course, that too, among other things. But I don't think I'll give you much time for cooking once we are married."

"Will we wait then, Bremen? One week?"

"Yes. Will you wait?"

"Just one week."

She sat down next to him on the kitchen bench. After eating for a few moments, she asked," Do you think we'll be safe going through the woods?"

"We will be. It was probably a poacher last night. If they wanted to do us harm, they could have."

"You're most likely right."

"I'll take you back when we are finished. Will you be all right with any gossip?"

"I will. And you?"

"Yes, darling. The only gossip will be jealous. Ready to go?"

They opened the door, and she watched as Bremen peered forward into the forest while examining the landscape. His piercing eyesight could spot anything within a few miles in the daylight.

"We can go."

He escorted her back to her home, and while the servants exchanged glances over their story of the poacher in the woods, nothing was said. The wedding was to take place one week from that day.

## Chapter Twenty-Four

Hallie pulled the final stitch of pink thread through the exquisite little dress. She wove the needle through the costume's hem and hid the knot, then held up the doll's gown to admire the work.

One of her best efforts, in spite of completing the task against the noise the workmen had been making today. She smoothed the outfit, pink and lacy with mother-of-pearl buttons and an embroidered collar. She unwrapped the tiny handcrafted leather shoes and carefully dressed the doll in the new clothes.

She and Bremen had decided on her taking the downstairs workroom off the kitchen as a doll-crafting space and office. Slowly she'd moved the supplies from her father's house to the new home, which she would share in a few days. A new roll-top desk for her paperwork was delivered yesterday, and when she was ready, most of Tyler's Shop would be allotted for her wares. The majority of Bremen's work, the process of putting client together with merchandise, would be handled through correspondence and contacts.

A timid knock tapped on the front door. She didn't expect any visitors or customers today. Did the workmen need a question answered? She rose and moved to the small window set into the wooden panel. Viola stood in the entry. When she opened the door and let her in, the girl reached out and clung to her while sobbing.

She was shocked at the change in Viola, but held tight. Their friendship had been somewhat distant since her return, and something seemed to be preoccupying her friend.

"Come in and sit, Viola. I have some tea." She led her through the drawing room into the kitchen to the bench seat. "What is it that has upset you so?"

"I've made a terrible mistake and come to ask your forgiveness."

She paused for a moment in pouring the tea. "My forgiveness?"

Viola blew her nose into a lacy handkerchief. "I must tell you a story." She looked down at the table, tracing a finger against the grain. "When the three of us were growing up, I had always thought of Clay as the best a man could be. You and he seemed to have understanding; certainly your fathers did, so I never interfered. Then you went to Boston. You didn't seem to care if he waited, and I believed he was lonely. While you were gone, I also believed Clay was falling in love with me as I imagined I was in love with him. We met and over time things became...intimate."

Viola glanced up to meet her eyes, before gazing away. "I gave myself to him in love and thought he realized it was so. I believed we would marry. But when you returned to Mooreland, Clay only wanted to be with you. I was hurt, and ashamed I lied to you, my dearest friend. Now I come to ask for forgiveness for the deception."

Hallie was speechless. "I had no clue you had an interest in him, or he for you. If you would have told me your feelings, I wouldn't have even considered his courtship."

"He isn't the man we both thought he was."

"Obviously not."

"I'm expecting his child."

She understood the implications of the situation now. "Are you sure?"

"I'm sure." Viola nodded. "He is avoiding me in

public. I should have forced him to make a choice in the beginning, but even this little time was better than none, and I still hoped he would realize he loved me too. I left a note for Clay at the Nash house informing him of my need to speak about something important and to meet after luncheon in the clearing." Viola's voice cracked as tears started to fill her eyes.

"He must take responsibility."

"When I speak with him today I'll tell him that," Viola replied without conviction.

"And if not? What will you do?"

"My grandmother has family in the next county. I must tell her my news and ask if I can go there to live. If I stay here the town gossips will brand me a loose woman and make my life miserable. I think people are already suspecting. I've been slowly loosening my dresses this month."

Hallie's mind started to plan. "Let's wait before you make a decision to leave."

"I don't have much time left. Will you go with me to speak with Clay today?"

After the altercation at Clay's home a few weeks ago, her being in the same area with him might not be for the best, however, Viola needed her support. "If you wish it. We can leave whenever you are ready. I'll tell you, though; I believe he's been drinking too much."

"You're right. I've noticed his frequent inebriation also."

She was afraid of leaving Viola alone. In his condition he might do her and the baby harm. "Yes, of course I'll go with you."

It was warm and the smell of the summer flowers was strong and sharp. They went toward the clearing, no more than a short walk from the house.

Hallie sat on one of the old tree stumps feeling the strong wood beneath her, running fingers along the rough bark. Things were so simple just a few years ago.

Viola eased down and plucked a fern, pulling off each leaf one by one as they waited for Clay.

There was a rustling and the noise of snapping twigs through the woods. With a prominent frown on his face, Clay entered the clearing, stopping in confusion when he saw the two women sitting there. "What is this?"

Viola took the lead, "I must I tell you something important." The woman reached out to take his hand, but he ignored it. "I'm expecting our baby."

Clay glanced over at Hallie. "What is that to me? I had nothing to do with it."

"You can stop pretending."

"You are going to be a father," Viola continued.

"It can't be! Why did you let that happen?"

"You let it happen too. I couldn't have done this myself."

"But I thought you would prevent this."

"What do I know of that? You are the only man I've ever been with." Viola began to cry. "What is there to think about? I thought you loved me. That is the only reason I gave myself. Did you think of me a strumpet you could use and throw away? We can be wed right away. Let our child be born in wedlock. You don't want to punish an innocent."

"It's not as easy as that." He gazed at Hallie as if seeking help.

She swept her eyes away in disgust.

"It is as easy as that." Viola's voice was more assured.

"I must think about this. What I really want now is something to help me forget this terrible evening and news."

"Well, you don't have much time to think. This winter I'll be having your child. I want to be married before the birth."

"I never promised you marriage." A vein started to pulse on the side of his forehead. "Keep your mouth shut. Everyone will think you are a whore. I'll even deny we were together. "

He straightened his back as if regaining some boldness. "Get away from me now, woman. I never want to see you or the brat. If you spread any rumors about my part in your unfortunate situation, I'll deny it. Or worse, I'll tell everyone I was just one of the many men you were whoring with."

He turned toward Hallie, "This is your fault. If you would have given me some encouragement, answered my many letters to you while you were gone, I wouldn't have turned to another woman. One word from you, and I would have remained faithful to your memory. Instead you went off to start a new life and came back without a serious thought for me."

"We were friends."

"Friends, but with an understanding. Our families had that understanding too. Why do you think our fathers conducted business together over these many years?"

"I don't love you. Not like that. I never did."

"You never gave me a chance. But damn me, I still want that chance." He turned away from both of them before heading back into the woods.

Later that evening Hallie went back to her sewing. The next clothing she would stitch would be for Viola's baby.

Chapter Twenty-Five

Iberville curled his body down as small as possible, the combination of tall grass and leaves adding to his camouflage. Bremen Tyler stood across the field, near the oak trees, poised to cross into the open area. Once that man made a few more steps he'd have clear aim. No doubt the authorities would think he was killed by an errant shot from a hunter. Case closed.

Iberville started to pull the trigger, his finger enjoying the feel of hard metal ready to spring. He winced. A throb of the black madness flowed in his head clouding all concentration for a moment. Distracted, he blinked hard, and then watched in amazement as Bremen Tyler disappeared, shimmering out of view.

****

Bremen had never felt the move back to the Ancestral world without the use of the veil, but knew it could be done with a concerted effort by the entire council. He grounded his body and waited until the moving stopped.

It was a rebuke to be brought back this way instead of being sent for by one of his kind. A show of mistrust. Already a bad start.

His vision cleared when the spinning slowed, and he was in the outer chamber of the Ancestral's Stronghold fortress. The cold air blew against his face and neck.

Scarpello stood with a smirk. "Called back, I see. Must be something important. Enter, Bremen Tyler, into the council chamber. They're waiting."

The muscles across his back tightened as he followed the scribe into the room. Tilda stood at the platform; the hard eyes of the council members moved in unison to look from the woman's face to his.

His cousin acknowledged him with a weak smile before addressing the council, "As I have said, neither Bremen nor I had anything to do with the actual theft of the Artifacts."

"So you said," replied the Head Council in a skeptical voice. "Tyler, you've had ample time to retrieve the Artifact. We have grown impatient for its return."

He would modulate his voice, removing the anger and frustration from his tone as much as possible. Those attributes would work to his detriment in front of this audience. "Council, can you understand the difficulty in retrieving the Heart Gem? I know none of the other Artifact Hunters have returned with their objects."

"This is true, but none of the Hunters, except you both, knew Malone."

Tilda clasped her hands together before replying, "Council, Malone made a terrible mistake. The mistake was his alone, but we have paid dearly for the error. Neither Bremen nor I encouraged Malone to take the Artifacts."

"As you say. And you, Bremen Tyler, of your search for the Heart Gem. How close are you to recovering it?"

"My associates and I continue searching. Although there've been a number of leads, no concrete information has passed to allow me to regain the object."

"And you have concentrated on only this task?"

He knew this was part of being called back. "Not only my task. I'll admit I've searched and found my Heart Match during my absence from the Ancestral world."

"It appears you have spent more time acquiring your Match, not the Gem."

"It has taken me an inordinate amount of time to win the woman. You've set difficult restrictions that have impeded my progress. However, we are promised and are to be wed in one day."

"Regarding the apparent diligence in acquiring her love—has this attentiveness been due to the promise you extracted to allow you to remain in the outer world, shirking your responsibilities in this one?"

"It has not."

The Head Council swept his arm in a circular motion. "We are not sure. You have been determined to live in the outside world, away from here. How convenient that once the Artifacts were," he paused, "*stolen*, you promised to return the Heart Gem if we gave permission to live outside the Stronghold. There are those of us here who believe you orchestrated the theft of the Artifacts of Love in order to gain freedom from our world. How do you answer to that charge?"

His palms began to sweat, a cold feeling of panic moving through his blood. "I have told you the truth. I tell you again. I had no part in the theft and have made a concerted effort to retrieve the object assigned." He heard the voices chattering and murmuring, discussing his purported guilt.

"Does she know of our kind?"

"She knows a few bits of information of the Ancestrals and my search. Council," he addressed the crowd, "She and I are to be wed tomorrow. Return me there."

"The return will be on our time, not as you dictate. We must discuss. You are both dismissed until your presence is required again. We shall advise when a decision has been made."

He and Tilda were ushered into the outer chamber once again. "This is maddening," he said when they were alone.

"I agree. Unfortunately for me, I was called back unaware as you were, and in a moment of discussion with a man who'd seen the Heart Compass. The last thing I saw was the look of fear on his face as I faded from sight. I'm afraid when I return the man won't come near me."

Bremen rubbed his jaw hard, the sharp ache helping to clear his thoughts. "The council wishes us to search the entire outside world, to find an object which is held in secret by a human who is falling into madness. And if we take too long, our actions are suspect."

"I want to know why they came to question our loyalty." Tilda tilted her head.

"That's interesting, isn't it? Let's speak somewhere privately. We can't be sure who is listening."

He guided her back to his chamber and ushered her in. He poured two glasses of wine. "Who is working against us? Have you any idea?"

"I don't think it can be one person. The entire council seems to be moving in unison. First to retrieve us, then to question us. No one spoke in our favor."

"I noticed that. But who would gain by our being brought back to the Stronghold? An enemy should be pleased to have us away from here." He paced back and forth. "Tomorrow is my wedding day."

"Did Hallie see you disappear?"

"No, but it would have been better if she did. I can't imagine what the woman will think if I don't return." He downed the remainder of the wine. "Tilda, are you any closer to finding the Heart Compass and Malone?"

A swift knock rang on the door. Scarpello's voice

spoke from outside, "You are directed to return now."

They followed and again took a place on the platform.

The Head Council addressed the crowd, "We are considering allowing you to return, if as you say you are to wed within one day. We are keepers and preservers of the Artifacts of Love, sworn to promote Heart-Matched couples. Our dilemma is: how will we know this woman is your Match without the proof the Gem would provide?"

"You've my word Hallie Pinefoy is my Heart Match. I know it in my heart and soul."

"In light of the circumstances, your affirmation is not enough."

Bremen was at a loss for words and looked at the eyes around him, boring in as though trying to read his mind. He could feel the roar of the expectant silence booming in the chamber.

"I will verify the woman with Bremen Tyler is his Heart Match." The eyes of the council members turned to stare at the Seer who had risen from a seat to announce the promise.

"You will vouch for them, then? Without the proof the Heart Gem would provide?" The Head Council's expression was shocked.

The Seer's iridescent grey eyes glowed, meeting the look each council member gave, one by one. "Yes, I will vouch for them." The words were said in utmost confidence.

He was astounded. He knew what a risk this was, even for the Seer. If it was discovered she was wrong the very foundation of the Ancestral world would be shaken.

The Head Council shook his head. "I believe those are foolish words, but in light of the circumstances, we agree. However, Bremen Tyler, once you obtain the Heart Gem you must give your woman a choice. A choice her own. You must offer her a view into the Heart Gem. If she accepts it, and the view shows you are not both each others Heart Match, you must leave her and return to our world permanently."

\*\*\*\*

"My future son-in-law is missing the day before the wedding? Where is he?"

Hallie felt reduced to the status of an errant child. The situation was stressful enough. "I'm afraid I don't know, Father." She squirmed, uncomfortable with the suspecting inquisition doled out by her parent. She needed to control her emotions as no doubt this was a situation out of Bremen's control. "I do know something is wrong. Something has happened which isn't of his making, I'm sure."

"You haven't argued? Or do you think he's acquired cold feet?"

"Neither of those. However, there was an incident in the woods a few days ago. I pray he hasn't fallen into any danger."

He father was a man of action. "Take a few of my men and search. I don't feel comfortable with you going alone." As an afterthought he added, "I don't think this would have happened with Clay, my dear."

"I can assure you it's time to let go of that notion. It was your plan, not mine." Her voice rose to an unpleasant pitch, but he deserved the shrewish tone.

"You are independent, just like your mother." He bent forward to kiss her forehead. "She would have been proud of you. As am I. Go get a wrap and wait out front. I'll direct a few of my men to provide escort."

She hurried to her room to grab the paisley shawl and the set of keys for the shop, returning a few minutes later to join Hank and Donald waiting at the larger buggy. Both men were armed.

"Where to first, Miss Hallie?"

"To the shop."

Her fear rose with each clip-clop of the horses' hooves. Something was wrong. In spite of her hope of finding Bremen at the shop ready to explain away the absence as one of having to complete an unexpected errand before they would close up the business for a week to enjoy a private, undisturbed honeymoon, she didn't expect to find a sign of him at the business.

Her fears were fanned by the abrupt emptiness of the place. She entered and saw the kitchen still had food out, not put away for the day. Bremen was meticulously neat and would not have left bread on the table without planning to return to town the same day.

"We'll check the house now." She averted her gaze, not sure if the two men were alarmed by Bremen's absence or believed she'd been abandoned just before the wedding day.

It was a longer ride than usual to her future home. The workmen were gone, having completed the final tasks earlier. Bremen had rewarded them handsomely for having the work accomplished before the wedding day.

Hank and Donald followed as she eased the key into the lock and pushed open the door. There was emptiness in the atmosphere, but she didn't sense danger. She scanned the room for any signs of struggle but found nothing out of place. No broken lamps or furnishings.

"Gentlemen, I'd appreciate your assistance in examining each room."

She was correct in not expecting to find Bremen there. In particular Hallie searched for his traveling bag. Finding it was still stored in the extra bedroom gave some ease. If that was gone she wouldn't have known what to think; however, the unsettling situation was now open to more nefarious possibilities.

"I thank you both for accompanying me, but I believe we'll return now and wait at my father's house."

Still hopeful, she prepared for bed at the late hour. If he did turn up—when he did, she corrected herself—she would be well rested for the next day. Her wedding day.

The fireplace crackled as she lay in bed, the aroma of the vase of country wildflowers wafting through the room, familiar things set about the chamber. The blue washbasin and pitcher with its chipped handle, which had been hers since childhood sat on the cherry-wood stand. The copper brush and comb set from mother was laid on the dressing table, waiting for one more use. Next to the bedroom door were two large travel trunks filled with new and old clothes, favorite books, and various drawing tablets to be transported tomorrow morning to the new home to be shared with her new husband. Everything was ready for the wedding that was to take place tomorrow. Today, she corrected as a nervous sweat coated her skin.

All the plans were set, except for the missing groom. Less than twelve hours from their wedding ceremony and once again, Bremen Tyler, had disappeared from her life.

She threw back the duvet, unable to rest. She should be awake with blissful anticipation, not fearful expectation. Either he was in danger, or he had gotten cold feet. She felt guilty to admit the preference at the moment was the danger. If it was hesitation on his part, she would put him in danger herself.

Whichever it was, she needed to know now and was determined not to be standing at the altar waiting for an errant groom.

She froze, her hearing tuned to a distant sound. She pushed the thick braid away from her ears. Then closer, the neighing of a horse outside the house. She ran to the window.

"Bremen!" She waved and ran over to the chair to grab wrap and slippers and drew on the articles as she hurried down the stairs almost tripping in haste. Flinging open the door she jumped into his arms, placing kisses on his face and neck. "Where were you?"

"Come outside so we can talk. I don't want to wake the household."

She took his hand and followed to the small greenhouse on the side of the house. The heady scent of blooms filled the small dim space.

"Bremen, tell me where you were. I was so worried."

"I'm back, although I can't promise this won't happen again."

"I was afraid for your safety and even afraid you had changed your mind."

"Of the latter, my love, you need have no concerns. I was called away without my permission and held without my consent. Get some rest now. Go to church in the afternoon. I'll be there at the appointed time."

"First tell me what happened." Did the man really believe she wouldn't ask?

"I was taken to the Ancestrals to report on why the Heart Gem hadn't been returned. There was also an inquest into if you and I were really Heart Matched and a challenge of my motives."

"Your motives?"

Bremen paced the small conservatory. "The council levied accusations asserting I want to wed in order to be able to leave the Ancestral Stronghold permanently."

"And?" Some mystery into his background was

acceptable, but evasiveness was another matter.

The pacing stopped and his full attention rested on her. "And what?" There was the cold voice again, but hers could match as well.

"Is that true?" She enunciated every word as the time to be clear on this matter was upon them.

"Is that what you believe?" His voice was quiet, but with a steel edge.

She blinked. "I don't suppose so."

"What? I have spent the past day worrying about you and our life together and you ask such a ridiculous question."

The glass shook from the yell, and Hallie imagined the panes shattering onto the wedding flowers lying on the tables. Such an omen would certainly be ominous. "No question is ridiculous."

"An answer shouldn't be required in this case."

Exhaustion slumped Bremen's shoulders, but she continued, "Why would they even think such a thing?"

He met her eyes unflinchingly. "If I wed my Heart Match, I don't have to return."

"That's what they offered you?"

He stepped away from her toward the southern windows. "That is what I negotiated."

She pulled the robe in tighter. "I knew we were rushing too much. We should have waited for a spring wedding."

"We won't wait for a spring wedding. We will be married today."

"Because you say so?"

"No. Because we love each other," he roared.

"From the moment we met, you have been a most intractable, domineering man. I won't be dictated to. Not now, not after we are married."

"If you would have just followed my request two weeks ago, we would have been wed by now, happy and without any fear of the Ancestrals' meddling."

"Must it be your way with this? Perhaps I wanted to plan an elaborate wedding as is every young girl's dream."

"As you would have done with that imbecile, Clay?"

"He was my friend and confidant for many years—unlike the short time I've known you."

"I don't like his possessive attitude."

"*You* don't have a possessive attitude?"

"You belong to me."

"You have no ownership of me."

"It is not a matter of ownership. It is a matter of your belonging to me."

She turned away, frustrated and angry. All her worry about his safety this past day and here they were arguing just hours before the wedding. "I need to think."

"To think about what?"

"Just to think. Is that acceptable to you?"

"Hallie, I'm going to be waiting at the church at 2 p.m."

"Please escort me home now."

He gave a curt bow, and they walked in silence back to the house. "I'll see you tomorrow."

She didn't answer.

Bremen turned her to make her face him. "All I can tell you is this. Come to the church if you feel in your heart of hearts we are meant for each other. The only one for each other. I need you, more than ever, to come stand beside me at that moment. But only if you are sure of our love because, believe me, anything less than that will have tragic consequences."

With those parting words, he leapt onto the horse and rode away.

****

As soon as Hallie heard the first chord of the wedding march, she took her father's arm and stepped forward into the church. She could hear the soft rustle of the wedding gown, a sheath of the finest lace adorned with the exquisite embroidery of tiny rosebuds upon the bodice. Resting about her neck was the glowing emerald necklace she'd received earlier, a gift from Aunt Agnes who traveled from Boston immediately upon hearing of the upcoming wedding.

The groom patiently waited at the front of the church, an eager expression on his face as Hallie swept closer. With warmth flowing from those dark eyes, he mouthed, "I love you," and she knew, in spite of their disagreements, there was no doubt they were well matched. Nothing had changed, nor ever would.

Reverend Fulton cleared his throat and began speaking, "Dear friends, we meet together here to join this couple, Bremen Tyler and Hallie Pinefoy."

She faced Bremen standing a hand's breadth apart and made the solemn vows, promising to love and honor until death parted them.

The reverend finished with the blessing, the abbreviated ceremony the groom had insisted on completed. "You may kiss the bride."

She felt Bremen's hand on the small of her back, and moved closer to meet their vow-sealing kiss, one unlike any other shared before. It was as though her soul and mind was joined to his at that moment by an unshakable, invisible thread.

She took her new husband's arm and proceeded out the rear doors of the church. Passing the last pew, she noticed a young petite woman with unusual grey eyes who seemed inordinately pleased to be at the ceremony. Hallie found it curious that when the guests filtered out to congratulate them in the receiving line, the woman was not there. It was though she disappeared into thin air.

Due to her father's congenial relationship with

the mayor, she and Bremen had use of the mayoral mansion for the wedding feast. Supping on the finest freshly-caught salmon and tender beef, they toasted each other before most of the town. Although Clay's parents attended the event, he didn't join the festivities. If there was any chance of a scene, however, she would not have wanted his attendance, but had hoped, if things were different, her long-time friend would have shared the day.

Hallie stared down a few of the frowning matrons who looked Viola over with disdain. Dressed in a lovely blue gown that emphasized her new curves but could not conceal the now-expanding waistline, the maid-of-honor shared in the new couple's joy.

Bremen led Hallie out to the first dance as man and wife and whispered against her ear, "Do you remember, I never did get my after-supper dance at the Spring Ball?"

"However, you always seemed certain we would dance the wedding dance together." His muscular arms wound tightly around her frame.

"How I wish at this moment to have you alone in our bed doing a different sort of dance. We will dance tonight, I promise."

She leaned in for a kiss.

"Hallie, my people have a strong belief in the concept of a Heart Match. Each soul has one other soul connected to them in a way that complements and fits the other to perfection. Sometimes, the Ancestral people can recognize their Match immediately, and when I met you, my love, I knew without a doubt you were my Match."

"I don't think you knew I was your Heart Match at once. I do believe you hated me."

He twirled her around as the melody ended, but didn't release his hold when the band began the next waltz. "Never hated you. I was furious at the danger you seemed inordinately fond of that evening."

She laughed. "I was afraid I was in deeper danger from you."

"My love, I would die for you. Your safety is paramount."

She was concerned at the seriousness of Bremen's tone. "Is there any danger I should be concerned about?"

"I don't believe there are any concerns at the moment as it's unlikely someone could locate me. However you know of the story of the Heart Gem and how it can drive a human to madness."

"I'm not worried." She didn't think anything could spoil the delicious mood.

"Good." He leaned down to place a quick kiss on her lips then vowed, "Perhaps a few more dances, wife, and I can show you how much I love you."

Before she could formulate a response, the mayor claimed the next dance, and from then on she and Bremen did their duty as host and hostess for the evening.

Finally needing a beverage to soothe her dry throat, Hallie joined Aunt Agnes and Viola speaking near the refreshments. "Do you know, dear Aunt, if it was not for my sojourn with you, I wouldn't have patronized the accommodations at the Wrightsville Inn and met Bremen?"

"My dear Hallie, I have a feeling you and Bremen were fated to meet."

Bremen's chest brushed against her back. "I think it's time we made our exit, Mrs. Tyler."

"Yes, I agree wholeheartedly."

They slipped out surreptitiously, not wanting to draw any ribald attention to their departure. Bremen lifted her onto the seat then bounded up with exuberant energy. His right hand clasped around hers as he guided the buggy carrying them toward their new home.

The night was warm and the moon lit their path, and there was clarity in the night air, as though all was right and in the correct place. All the indecision and turmoil of the past months floated away, and she was with the man more beloved than life itself.

Bremen opened the door and lifted her in his arms kissing her and crossing over the threshold. "I've wanted to do this since the moment you said yes. Do you remember when you came to the shop on that rainy day weeks ago and pledged your love? You stood there soaked to the bone telling me that it was me after all you wanted. That was the happiest day of my life. Until today when you became my wife."

She watched him speak, that beautiful mouth in a sensual smile, those usual flecks flashing in dark eyes. "How could I even doubt for a moment?"

"I've waited for you so long, longer than the past few months. My soul has waited from the beginning of time for you to come into my life," Bremen whispered in a rough voice. "Are you in agreement of our waiting long enough? Shall I give you a few moments?"

She nodded and went into the bedroom, already having left her nightgown and toiletries at the house. She was nervous. Although she had imagined being with Bremen, and had come close to consummating their union a few times, their actual wedding night was here. She sat on the edge of the bed waiting for Bremen in a blindingly white new silk nightdress.

She had created and sewed the gown during the past two weeks, an ankle-length creation boasting a few well-placed pearl buttons commencing from just under her chin and going down to the tips of her toes.

With a brief knock, Bremen strode into the room and stared. "You are beautiful, heart of my heart."

She felt his eyes ravishing, becoming almost animalistic in intensity. Having been stretched to the extent of his limits, he was done waiting.

"I swear, Hallie, if someone interrupts us tonight, I'll commit bloody murder."

She let out a throaty laugh in response.

"Let us toast our wedding, my love."

"Of course."

Sensing the nervousness, Bremen ran his fingers over her cheek then poured out two glasses of champagne from the bottle received as a wedding gift.

Her husband stood wearing only a pair of black trousers slung around lean sculpted hips, his chest bare and muscular. She could see the tattoos now, the strange symbols etched into broad shoulders, the characters indecipherable.

"My love, sit by the fire with me."

She followed to the settee and nestled close. He'd stoked the blaze red-hot, the light from the flames licking into every corner of the room in a wild dance. Bremen was her husband now; there was no need for modesty, was there? Every part of her body was now his, to do with as he pleased.

He was kissing the top of her hair, slowly hypnotizing the mood with the rhythmic back-and-forth motion. The cadence flowed through her body, until an answering ache in her loins begged for attention. She leaned forward to kiss the front of his strong neck, and he lifted her face, pressing a gentle then more passionate kiss on ready lips.

Bremen paused before slipping downward to the slim throat and the top button of the silk gown. He stopped and gazed into her eyes questioningly. She responded to the question by slowly unbuttoning the top button of the gown. He leaned forward and kissed the ivory skin the button uncovered there.

Each opened button received a kiss.

The button baring her throat. A kiss there.

The button baring her collarbone. A kiss there.

The button baring her breasts. A kiss there.

The button baring her stomach. A kiss there.

The button baring her waist. A kiss there.

The button baring her belly. A kiss there.

"You know I just want to break these damn buttons and rip off the gown?"

"Yes."

The button baring the juncture between her thighs opened. A long kiss there.

The button baring her thighs opened. A kiss there.

The button baring her knees. A kiss there.

The button baring her calves. A kiss there.

The button baring her feet. A kiss there.

Finally there were no buttons left, and Bremen lifted her from the seat and carried her to the large bed. Along with all modesty and inhibitions, the white gown fell away when she floated into the softness of the satin sheets. Reveling in the desire and craving coursing through every inch of skin, she wanted this man's body immediately. Why was he still dressed?

As if reading her mind, he divested the now-tight trousers and stood in stunning nakedness. Muscle and definition. Danger and tenderness. And the look of lust in black eyes took her breath away making it almost impossible to breathe. She looked down and allowed a moment's fleeting worry about his obvious endowment, but her hips responded in affirmation to the awaiting ecstasy.

"At last, you will be my wife in body." He lay alongside and kissed her mouth, slipping his tongue in.

She swept eager fingers over Bremen's body, exploring and touching every part of maleness that now belonged to her to do with as she wished for pure pleasure.

****

Bremen could kiss this way all night, but the time had come to satisfy them. He turned to Hallie's right breast and put the pink nipple into his mouth and sucked. He heard her groan with bliss, and soft fingers reached for him, sliding a hand along his length. He didn't want the raging intensity to stop, but if her palm continued its motion, things would be over too soon. He shifted atop her.

"Are you ready?" He'd planned to take a prolonged time to prepare her, all night if necessary, but now just wanted to be in.

"Now."

He spread those long legs and tightened up at the glorious sight before him, a place for pleasure.

She wriggled closer. "Put it in."

He stroked the entrance, pushing against her barrier. She was so tight; he was concerned about getting in. He pushed a little harder and Hallie tensed up.

"Are you sure it will fit?"

"I'll make it fit," he rasped, realizing right after the words were spoken a more calming declaration should have been offered.

He went back to concentrating on kissing her mouth and touching with fingers until feeling her relax underneath him again. It had to be now.

"Unclench your muscles," he directed, "and let me in."

She did as he asked and he slid.

He wanted to weep with the rapture of it. He moved over her, into her, his size big, stretching. The pleasure was intense and focused as Bremen held back from wanting to pound and finish, instead forcing the fervor to wait to prolong the magic for her sake.

He put hands on her hips tilting up. The

connection intensified.

"Yes," Hallie whispered.

He pushed harder, accelerating with a wave she started to match. The exhilaration built until his wife tightened and clenched. She screamed his name. Bremen groaned and released.

When his head cleared, he tried to heave off, but she held him down. "Not yet," she said kissing again. He hardened inside and continued their pleasure into the morning hours.

Bremen opened his eyes and bound both arms around Hallie's naked body. There were very gratifying advantages to married life.

He turned her around to face him, skin to skin. "Are you happy?" His voice was growly.

"Quite so. Why didn't you inform me of how this would be between us? We could have made use of one of the many empty rooms in the Wrightsville Inn that first night," she pretended to pout.

"I did try, my love, quite often in fact when we first met, to convince you of trying me out before we wed. Now I'm afraid you are stuck."

His hands caressed over the silky skin, each touch lingering and exploring. "I do believe, Mrs. Tyler, we've wasted enough time."

Chapter Twenty-Six

First, Hallie found the stepped-on daisies outside the kitchen window. Then came the distinct feeling of being watched. Something was amiss, and as much as she tried to ignore and reason away any uneasy awareness, it was as though the smooth surface of a pot of water was ready to bubble over and spill its scalding contents.

She took a look outside the door at the beautiful day but was unable to shake the apprehensiveness that began just before she and Bremen had married. It was as if someone was waiting for the right moment to...to what? She hadn't said anything to her husband yet not wanting to spoil any of their time together by unfounded fears and nervousness. Perhaps she must learn not to be so fanciful.

She closed the door and went to the side table and mirror. She put on white kid gloves and pinned on the elegant hat, then stretched and rolled her shoulders. She'd discovered unknown muscles during the first days of marital bliss.

Even now her body was still tingling and rosy from their lovemaking this morning—a session that started before the sun came up and continued quite a while after sunrise. Her limbs were not cooperating when it came time to get out of bed and join Bremen for the drive into town, so she'd promised to walk and meet him there at noon. But now she wished to have driven to the shop.

She heard a knock on the door. She warred for a moment, wondering if it was better to ignore and hide. Would she cower in her own home until

Bremen came back? No.

"Hallie." It was Clay. It had been over a month since seeing him, and she still held out hope the man would come back to be with Viola while awaiting the new baby.

She opened the door. "Clay."

He quickly moved forward to embrace.

She returned the clasp for a moment then pulled away to take a look, and was shocked by his appearance. He had aged considerably in the short month. Two bloodshot eyes were set in a now ruddy-skinned face. Usually meticulous with clothes, the pants he wore were dirty as though he had wiped muddy hands across the thighs. Even the splattered jacket was torn, and a filthy kerchief was wrapped around his sunburned neck. The unpleasant odor emitted made her take a step back, and she could feel the tremor in his hand. "What's wrong? You look so different."

"Just a little thirsty."

"Come in then. I'll make some tea."

He followed and sat at the kitchen table while she fixed the hot water and placed a few slices of raisin cake on a plate. He looked as though he hadn't eaten in a few days. "Are you unwell?"

"Much better now that we're together." His expression became serious, "Come away with me, Hallie. I'll help you escape from Tyler."

"I'm happy to see you but have no absolutely no intention of leaving my husband." She took an instinctive, subtle, step further.

"Don't be afraid of him. I'll protect you," he hissed while reaching for her arm.

She brushed off the dirty fingers and moved to the other side of the table to put some space between them. This wasn't the Clay she was familiar with, but this man was changed and delusional, even the look in the troubled eyes was alarming.

"Clay, come back tonight for some supper. I have no bad feelings and welcome you here."

"I would never sit at table with him. Hallie, don't you now see Tyler for what he is? Don't you see that he'll tire of you and break your heart? He's a drifter, unhappy staying in one place."

"Bremen is a wonderful husband."

"Then where does he get his money? Why is he evasive about his origins and never speaks of his childhood? Don't you see he is hiding something?"

"You must go on with your life now. What about Viola and the baby? Speak with her. The child will need its father, and you can have a wonderful family life together."

"What are Viola and the brat to me? I have no feelings for them. It is only you, my dearest. I'm on my way to speak with my father about an advance on the inheritance. Then we can leave. You don't need to bring anything with you, and I'll provide everything."

"As I said, I'm happy to see you again. However, I wish you the best, and Bremen and I will do whatever we can to help you."

Clay knocked the mug over and sped to her side.

She steeled herself. This was her home, and she would not be intimidated. "Let us help you. Your home is in Wrightsville. With your family and friends."

"I need something stronger. Do you have anything besides this damn tea?"

"No," she lied.

They looked at each other for a few moments, just a few hand spans apart.

"You have to come with me," he persuaded.

"No."

Expressions flitted across his features, ranging between begging and forcing.

"I'm going now." Clay finally said.

She walked him to the door and stood at the open aperture watching him walk in the direction of town. She wouldn't tell Bremen about this visit with Clay as he had enough on his mind with the Heart Gem.

Besides she hadn't really been afraid. She paused before closing the door when she noticed the roses at the front window were trampled at the edges. That was very strange; they had been perfect at the time she let Clay in.

****

Iberville sprang from his bed at the Mooreland Arms upon hearing the man in the room next door stumble. He hoped the bloke was sober enough to speak coherently this time. He slipped out of the room and stood before the neighboring chamber until the cot creaked under the man's weight.

Iberville tapped on the door and entered without waiting for an answer. He examined Clay from head to toe, finding much lacking. "Mr. Nash, I have a proposition which would benefit us both." He took a chair and pulled it near.

Clay's eyes were trying to focus. Iberville could read the interest there, but it was restrained by the inebriation. He was satisfied. The man was just sober enough to understand the plan, but tipsy enough to be open to questionable suggestions.

"My name is George Smith, my friend. It appears Bremen Tyler is keeping us both from what we want. With your most valuable help, we could work together to take Tyler permanently out of the picture. With him out of our way, you, my good man, could step in to console the lovely lonely widow."

"Hallie?"

"Yes, Mrs. Tyler." He observed the man attempting to concentrate on what he was saying, senses becoming more alert now.

"What are you looking to gain out of this?" Clay

slurred.

"Bremen Tyler is trying to steal an object which belongs to me. I wish to put a stop by whatever means necessary." He paused and looked at Clay directly. "And I have no reservations about using whatever means *are* necessary."

"I don't want Hallie hurt. I love her."

"Of course, I understand. She is faultless in this matter, but Tyler has bewitched and deluded the woman. You must free her, and she will turn to you."

Sense and sobriety filled Clay Nash's face. "What should I do?"

"You will help me. Your assistance is required, you know, as this is something neither of us can accomplish on our own."

"Yes, we'll help each other." The man nodded.

This was even easier than he had thought. "First, tell me about Hallie. Everything. Her interests. Where she goes and what she does."

Chapter Twenty-Seven

Hallie wiped both hands on the clean cotton cloth and handed Viola the doll across the kitchen table.

Voila turned the toy over to examine the detailing. "It's amazing how expensive these custom creations are."

"It's surprising Mr. Smith didn't balk at the prices, or try to negotiate a lesser cost. He must be a particularly wealthy man. Two weeks ago I received a letter from Wrightsville requesting a basic doll sample for inspection. Shortly after, Mr. Smith dispatched a second missive complimenting the model along with the enclosure of a generous cheque in advance for a custom order of four dolls. One for each of his young granddaughters."

"When is he coming to Mooreland to retrieve the toys?"

Hallie poured more tea from the silver service and placed a blue chintz plate of plain biscuits and cucumber sandwiches before Viola. "Mr. Smith requested a personal delivery in time for the girls' short visit to Wrightsville."

"Personal delivery?"

She took a sip of jasmine tisane and nodded. "Due to an infirmity, Mr. Smith is unable to travel to Mooreland. Moreover, at the time of our meeting, he's expressed a desire to discuss future orders. I'm excited by the prospect of a recommendation allowing an expansion of clientele outside of Mooreland and the surrounding villages."

"Bremen must be pleased."

"I've not mentioned this order. We try not to speak at length of business matters once home." She winked while taking out boxes and lids from the adjoining storage room. Those other non-business matters left little time for anything else. Sometimes finding the time to just eat and drink was difficult enough.

Viola laughed. "When will you and Bremen travel to Wrightsville?"

"That's something I wished to discuss this afternoon. Bremen has received sudden news requiring out-of-town travel. To...complete a task. Would you go with me to Wrightsville for an overnight trip, Viola?"

"Of course."

Placing the final touches on the ebony-haired doll, Hallie sat back to admire the figure's lovely face. Each was lifelike with a sweetness and translucence sometimes difficult to achieve in wax-coated dolls. The pure wax-molded dolls had a fine quality, but were time-consuming to make and too delicate for children. Her creations required numerous dips in the beeswax to produce a thicker-than-usual coating, combining the beauty of poured wax and the durability of composition dolls.

"Each one is so different," Viola noted.

"They must be lovely girls. See the distinctive features according to the instructions of Mr. Smith." Holding out the first one she explained, "This beauty was painted with sparkling aquamarine eyes and the lightest blonde hair I could find. Smith was particular about the color of the hair. "White wheat" was requested. The next figure was to have an ivory tone of skin, brown eyes, and red curls. The third, light brown locks and green eyes."

"The third is attractive. So similar to your coloring, Hallie."

She brushed away a warning feeling. Surely

brown hair and green eyes were not uncommon. "Finally here is the fourth doll topped with tight-bunned black hair and jet eyes."

"Lovely. For the attire just the plain shift?"

"Yes, Mr. Smith did not express an interest in the choice of clothing for the set here. However, the letter indicated the next order of dolls will include fabric so dresses matching his granddaughters' own apparel can be fashioned."

She wrapped the dolls individually in tissue paper before packing them in boxes for the next day's delivery. A blue ribbon fastened the lid over the box. The front door opened and closed as the last bandeau was knotted. "I do believe Bremen is home."

He came into the kitchen. Amazing how the man's presence made her heart race. "Hallie, my love. Viola. You are feeling well?"

"I have my good and bad days. Today is better. I must leave now and take advantage of today's energy to complete a number of errands." Viola stood with a sway and smoothed the loose pink gown.

"I'll walk you out."

She handed over the bonnet and parasol to Viola. "Tomorrow then? We will take the morning train to Wrightsville and arrive by noon."

"I will be ready," Viola assured with a wave.

Hallie could hear Bremen moving about upstairs and followed to the bedroom.

She plopped on the bed while watching her husband pack various articles of clothing in the black travel case. "How long will the trip take?" It would be difficult to sleep in the bed without him. It was fortunate her trip coincided with his.

"Hopefully no more than a day or so. Why don't you stay at your father's house? Or perhaps Viola can visit for a few nights?"

"Don't worry. There is a doll order I need to deliver to Wrightsville. I'll take the morning train, spend the night at the hotel after meeting with the client, then come back the next day."

"I'm not comfortable about your traveling alone. Wait for me; it should just be a few days delay."

She toed off the black kid-skin slippers before stretching out on the bed. "I can't. The order is promised for a special occasion. Besides, Viola will accompany me to Wrightsville to procure a few baby items not available in Mooreland."

"Is the client meeting you at the inn?" he queried after placing the case near the door.

She removed the pins from her hair and shook the locks loose. "Yes, and we are to speak of future orders for his granddaughters." The soft brown tresses cascaded and curled around her shoulders.

The bed moved, and she rolled toward Bremen sitting on the edge of the mattress. He placed his fingers under her chin and brought her lips up. "No walks around the town. Promise?" The smoldering look reminded her of their first kiss at the inn. Her limbs started to melt.

"Promise. I'll even take the little metal nail file along for protection." She shot him a flirty smile, then placed her hand against Bremen's stone-solid chest, feeling him breathe against her palm.

"Hallie, do you know what I wanted to do with you the moment we met?" His chest rumbled as he laughed.

She gazed into his eyes, lost in the silver flashes.

Another sensual kiss."Take off your clothes and see," he demanded.

Eagerly, she stood to unfasten the black glass buttons at the top of the prim jade gown then she peeled off the fitted dress. She eased out of the lacey ivory chemise and undergarments to stand before Bremen naked and open to his attentive gaze. "Like this?" Any shyness had ended on their wedding night. Nothing could stand in the way of the pleasure they gave and received.

"You are the most beautiful woman in the world." He watched with dark hungry eyes.

"And you have far too many clothes on, Mr. Tyler. Well?" She stretched out on the mattress again.

Bremen unbuttoned the white linen shirt and yanked it off. Sighing, she admired the strong chest sprinkled with just the perfect amount of hair, and the wide shoulders with the spread of tattoos etched across the top. She liked to run her fingers over the intricate imprints when he was on top of her.

He pulled off his trousers and proved he matched the wanton need. Bremen lay down next to her and touched her lips and face, then broad strong hands explored down breasts and belly. His lips were upon her neck and shoulders then lower whipping up embers of lust. She reached down to pull his mouth back on hers wanting him in her so badly, but delayed as his slow touches tantalized all her sensitive areas one by one.

He slipped a finger into her and she grasped around wanting more. She would never tire of his hot touch.

"Say you want me," his husky voice whispered.

"Please," she begged, "I want you."

He laughed wickedly before slipping in a second finger. She rode his hand until he moved away again, delaying the pleasure.

Evil man, he was making her wait, the familiar heat and tightening in her loins was driving her mad. She took his hips over hers. "Now, Bremen."

Instead of answering the desperate plea, he sucked her breasts in maddening slowness, building the tension more. He nipped on the bud, and she screamed in pleasure as she found divine release.

"You couldn't wait for me, my treasure?" His chuckle was rough and satisfied.

She answered by pushing him in, joining to meet halfway. Bremen groaned as the last of hard pulses closed around him. They held in place until both needed to move again, faster and more urgent now. He was up to the hilt; she slid against him. He pushed again wild and hard, conjuring the magic electricity. Sometimes she felt so close to him she could slip into his mind to feel what Bremen felt as he thrust within her.

Together they touched and kissed until almost at their peaks. Bremen pushed deeper, harder, her pleasure coming again, with his this time. She cried out his name in perfect fulfillment.

He took her face in his large hands and kissed. Looking deep into her eyes he said, "I love you, Hallie."

She dozed, curled against him for long drowsy moments until the storm came in from the north. The leaves on the trees ripped and droplets of rain flung from the sky as thunder and lightning brightened the blackness over the house.

She leaned against the warm secure chest. Never afraid of storms, she would take walks in the rain or look from the bedroom window to marvel at the primal release unleashed in a tempest. Raging storms such as this made one feel how small one was—a tiny speck of flesh and bone in a mysterious universe so big.

No moonlight or starlight broke though the stormy clouds. She breathed in the black night and felt it dissolve and envelope her. The quiet of the darkness was there under the noises of the storm.

Bremen slid his hand over her arm and clasped tighter. "Are you afraid?"

"No, it's beautiful. Listen. The storm is getting closer."

He nuzzled her hair. "I love you. I would fight each bolt of lightning for you and shield you from each drop of rain. Then kiss you to distract you from the sounds of thunder and cover your body with mine to keep away the cold."

She fell asleep again in his arms as the storm raged.

****

Hallie passed Viola the chamber pot as she held the long russet hair far away. "A cup of chamomile tea will settle your stomach, dear."

Viola retched again. "The hateful morning sickness has become horrible. Just unbearable."

"Then you must stay home. I won't have you feeling more wretched today."

"I know we'd planned to travel to Wrightsville, but between the nausea and frequent bathroom stops, the trip may be too difficult. Mother has agreed to go with you."

"It's all right, my dear. It will just be a quick trip back and forth with only one short night in town. I'll be fine."

Viola gazed up and drew a few deep breaths. "Are you sure Bremen would allow your solo travel?"

"He would understand." She wasn't certain of that, however, she had no way to contact him about the change of plans. It was too late.

"Perhaps your father will go with you?"

"I'm sure, but there is nothing I can't handle. What is dangerous about meeting an elderly man in the lobby of a respectable inn to exchange dolls? Besides, I am a married woman now."

She felt a twinge of regret after leaving Viola's house and heading toward the train station. Not fear, but intuition niggled at the back of her brain and would not be dismissed. Donald pulled up to help her from the buggy, tipping a broad straw hat before leaving her amidst the passengers.

Thrusting worrisome thoughts away, she purchased a ticket to Wrightsville and boarded the morning train. She settled into the cozy ladies' car, the large package of dolls and small overnight case on the floor at her booted feet. Picking up the sewing, Hallie started to make the minute stitches on the christening gown for Viola's babe.

After a few minutes of forced concentration, she peered out the window at the speeding landscape, each mile moving the car further from Mooreland. Just a few months ago, traveling from Wrightsville, she had been a young innocent woman with a silly chaperone as companion. Now, she was a happily married lady with a successful business. Every day she thanked God for the wonderful life she was leading.

When she returned home to Bremen, with certainty she could share the news of expecting a child next summer. Her lips moved up with a smile. Not surprising as most of their waking hours were spent making love.

She removed the letter from Mr. George Smith again, re-read the correspondence, then folded both hands in her lap and rested a few moments. She was looking forward to meeting the gentleman at the Wrightsville Inn for supper as had been planned. She pictured the customer: a thin elderly man who walked with the assistance of a cane, spectacles perched on a short nose, eyes full of emotion as he delighted in the dolls which resembled the four wonderful granddaughters.

She gathered the sewing again, determined to complete the hem work before the train arrived. This time, the minutes sped by and soon she re-gathered the packages and disembarked, walking the few blocks from the train station to the Wrightsville Inn.

"I'd like to check in, please. Mrs. Bremen Tyler." She smiled while following the porter to the room. She would have to travel here with Bremen before the baby was born to relive old memories. After settling into the chamber, there was just enough time for a short afternoon nap.

She was awakened by a knock on the room door. The porter standing there handed over a note:

*Dear Mrs. Tyler:*

*I regret to inform you I am feeling unwell today and will be unable to travel to the Wrightsville Inn tonight. Would you be so kind as to meet with me at my home in Wrightsville, a short distance from the inn? I'll send my carriage at 4:00 p.m.*

*I regret any inconvenience this may cause, but at my advanced age the bad days outnumber the good. You may be assured, your efforts will be well rewarded.*

*Sincerely,*

*Mr. George Smith*

She felt another twinge of discomfort. To meet in a public place was one thing, but to travel, even a short distance, to someone's home was another. Surely an infirm man could do no harm?

She pushed away any feelings of foreboding with the promise of additional business. With a baby on the way, a little extra funds would be welcome, especially from a generous client such as Mr. Smith.

However, it would be prudent to leave a note with the front desk clerk describing the changed plans as a precaution, and in addition, she would even take the little metal nail file as promised to Bremen.

Venturing downstairs, she ate a light meal in the dining room before advancing to the lobby. The clerk was the same one that she had dealt with before, but hopefully there would be no problem such as Bremen encountered last time.

"Sir, I have a message to leave at the desk. I'll return in a few hours to retrieve it but would be grateful if you could keep the paper in your possession until then."

"Of course, Mrs. Tyler."

Proud of the forethought, she slipped back to the room and gathered the wrapped doll boxes for the delivery. When entering the lobby again, a neatly dressed man in workman's clothes approached.

"Mrs. Tyler?"

"Yes."

"Mr. Smith has directed me to provide transport to his home a few miles away. May I assist with those packages?"

Relieved to be rid of the weight, she handed the items to the man and followed to the waiting carriage. It was not as elegant as expected, especially as Mr. Smith had paid such a great deal to purchase the dolls. Perhaps this was only one of many carriages.

She settled into the shabby red velvet seat, the packages placed across on the other side, and they set out. She hoped Bremen's search had already been successful.

\*\*\*\*

It had been a longer trip than expected, but after numerous stops and connections, Bremen arrived in London to meet with the contact. The associate had sent a cryptic message to Mooreland advising Bremen the holder of the Heart Gem was in the Capital, ready to use the object's powers to assist an elderly widower wishing to choose a bride who would ensure the continuation of the esteemed lineage.

Bremen's cab continued through the vast areas of town until the neighborhood started to change, passing from elegant Kensington townhomes to shabby East End tenements. He wasn't alarmed, but surprised at the surroundings. Surely he paid this associate well enough to stay at better accommodations.

Impatient, he tapped a booted heel on the

flooring. In addition to wanting to conclude the business, he missed Hallie already. Tonight would be their first, and hopefully only, night apart since their marriage. He needed to retrieve the missing Gem within the next day or two so there would never be another reason to leave again to search for the damned thing.

Lately, he'd been wondering if Hallie was expecting. She hurried into the bathroom in the morning and seemed not to have any appetite for breakfast. The possibility of a creating a family in the human world with Hallie would make his life complete, but there could be nothing left to bind him to the Ancestrals. The search for the Heart Gem needed to end.

The cab braked hard when the driver stopped abruptly in front of a run-down hotel. "Here, sir. Please hurry."

Bremen had just enough time to grab his case, jump out and pay before the cabbie drove off.

With some reluctance, he examined the shoddy building. Keeping the search secret was of utmost importance, but the contact had selected a seedy establishment to meet. He ventured toward the front door of the East End Arms and rang the bell. A large unkempt woman in a blousy floral gown came out, instantly seeming to notice his well-cut clothing and appearance. If he had known the neighborhood better, he would have dressed down from tailored black suit to simple shirt and pants.

"A room ye be wanting for the night, sir?" she posed in an obsequious voice. "I see there is just one of ye. I can supply a companion if ye be lonely."

He shook his head. "Neither. I'm meeting Mr. Messing. Can you tell me what room he is in? I'm expected."

The woman shrugged plump shoulders. "The man said to expect a visitor. He be in the third-floor room. It be on the right."

She went around to the entrance, unlocked it to let him in, then pointed down the dim corridor. "If ye change yer mind about a room or companion, I'll make sure ye get the best we have here. Just give a shout."

Irritated, he shook his head again, eager to put this adventure behind and depart. Climbing the long narrow staircase, he came to the door of the room and knocked.

"Come in," a man's voice called.

Bremen opened the door and entered the darkened room. Immediately he knew something had gone wrong. He started to turn back, but felt a sharp pain at the back of his head, then all went black.

****

The drive was taking longer than Hallie expected. Her senses were on high alert now as she rapped on the grimy window, "Driver! How much longer?"

After a long moment the man responded, "Almost there, ma'am."

She regretted the decision to travel alone to Mr. Smith's home. Instead, she should have asked the driver to deliver the dolls and taken care of any future business by mail. "Driver, I've changed my mind. Return to the inn, please."

No response. In fact he seemed to pick up speed.

"Driver! I order you to turn around."

A minute of silence ticked by. "Almost there, miss," the man snapped. They were further than expected from Wrightsville, having driven toward a more secluded area. She even contemplated jumping out of the carriage, but knew she could cause herself and the baby injury. She removed a lacey handkerchief from the jacket pocket and wiped the glass. They'd passed from the gravel road to a dirt path, still drivable but overgrown with moss and short grasses. Another bad sign.

After a few minutes of unpleasant rocking in the carriage, the path improved, the cab circling up to a large stone house set into the trees. The building appeared lit from the inside, and she breathed a small sigh of relief. The driver pulled near the entrance, the carriage swaying as the man jumped off the seat.

The buggy door squealed. "Here, ma'am. I'll carry the packages."

Calmer now, she accepted his help to alight and made the way alone the last few yards to the door. She glanced around in the waning daylight, noticing the eerie quiet and emptiness. Also unnerving was the unpleasant house: a dirty-looking two-story brick structure built in the early Victorian style. A heavy wooden door with drab inlaid stained glass centered the residence; mottled ivy grew on the sides and over most of the first-floor windows.

The warm sun felt good on her skin after the clammy coldness of fright during the ride here. Hearing a sound behind, she turned around and saw the driver had taken the buggy and appeared to be driving back in the direction of Wrightsville. She tightened a hand on the purse. Another bad sign.

She chewed the bottom lip and knocked on the door with a heavy iron pull. No one answered. She tried again, but no one responded. Tired of waiting and now feeling irritated for all the inconvenience, she entered the house.

The unlocked door creaked as it opened. The light filtered through the old windows as the draft from the opened egress set the dust motes in flight. The sparse furniture was old-fashioned, and the residence grimy judging by the faint odor hanging in the air.

The atmosphere was unsettling here, with a

coldness that was not attributable to the temperature. "Hello. Mr. Smith?" She would wait one more minute before leaving. In fact, she should probably leave in half a minute to start the walk back to Wrightsville before it got dark.

The sound of shoes beat upon the plank floor before a smiling man came from the end of the hall. She recognized him as the man who had stopped into the shop searching for Bremen a few weeks ago and also just before the wedding. Curious.

"Mrs. Tyler, so pleased to see you. My apologies for the inconvenience."

"I'm waiting for Mr. George Smith."

"Actually, I'm representing Mr. Smith." He offered the same assessing quick glance.

"I was to meet Mr. Smith. If he isn't here at the moment, I'd like to return to the Wrightsville Inn."

"Unfortunately, that won't be possible right now. Come and have tea, Mrs. Tyler, before we discuss my plans."

She was in trouble, but not sure what else to do at this point, so she followed Mr. Smith into the drawing room, where a tea service had been set. She would exude a tranquil demeanor; anything else might work against her favor.

"Please sit, my dear lady. Allow me to offer you some refreshments after the journey." He seemed to notice her hesitation. "My driver is changing carriages and will return in a few moments. I have your cheque here." He patted a jacket pocket. "In a short time you may return to the inn."

Her suspicious body unclenched a little. A cup of tea would settle the upset stomach and screaming nerves. She took a few fragrant sips of Earl Grey but stopped when she noticed the man wasn't drinking from his cup. Her last conscious moment was of panic.

****

Bremen awoke in the East End Arms room, his head pounding in fierce pain. He touched fingers to his aching head and felt the congealed blood around a large goose egg of a bump at the back. Groaning, he sat and focused around the empty space. Against the wall there was a small bed covered in a dirty thin blanket, and the smudged windows allowed in bright daylight, signaling at least twelve hours since being knocked out.

Someone had lured him here but stopped short of killing him. His wallet was in the black coat; the pocket watch still in the side pocket. He gazed to his sore left hand, to the bare third finger. A scraped knuckle indicated someone had yanked off the gold wedding band.

He glanced at the cheap dresser and recognized one of Hallie's dolls propped up alongside a folded paper.

"Hallie." Fear rushed through every cell of his body. Closing his eyes, he prayed, "Please, God, let her be safe."

He rose as quickly as possible and with shaking arms held the letter and read:

*Bremen Tyler - I hold the lovely Hallie at my pleasure. If you want to ensure her safety, return to Mooreland. Wait there quietly for further instructions.*

Blood drained from his body. He grabbed the doll and note before sprinting down the flights of stairs. The landlady, sitting on the couch darning threadbare sheets and clothing, dropped her needle as he grabbed her shoulders.

"Who are you?" he demanded.

"I be the owner, Mrs. Abbers. D-did ye want a different room?"

"Who was in that room? What was his name?"

"I don't know. He paid in coin and didn't give a name. I never ask." Her face was white and strained.

"Tell me the truth or you will not live out the rest of the day."

She put her hand to her chest in pain. "I don't know who he be, I swear. His hat was down over his eyes. I didn't get a fair look. Please. Please leave me be. I don't know wot's happening here. I run an honest business."

"When did the man come?"

"The day before yesterday. Late it was, dark-like. Said he'd have a visitor and just send him up. Then he just went to the room and didn't leave. Is he gone now? I didn't hear anyone go."

Able to determine the woman was in fact telling the truth, he relaxed his hold. He'd have to discover who lured him here and had some connection with Hallie. He needed to return to Mooreland.

## Chapter Twenty-Eight

Pleased with the splendid progression of his plan, George Iberville observed the sleeping woman on his bed.

He'd hired the best: Jackson was expert in these matters, a man skilled in appearing and disappearing without notice. Especially important, Jackson knew how hard to hit a man on the skull. A lightly measured touch could knock a mark unconscious for a few hours; too hard would cause permanent damage or death. He'd paid the bludger handsomely when the wedding band was returned as proof of completion.

Iberville smoothed his hand along Hallie's brown hair. Not light blonde, this one's locks were soft, and with time, he could get used to the chestnut color. He ran a finger over the translucent cheek, marveling at the silky softness. Certainly a woman of charms.

He patted the secret pocket on his chest where the Heart Gem rested for safekeeping, impatient to use the object. No doubt the image would reveal their wonderful life together. To have Hallie Pinefoy Tyler with him as his Heart Match would solve every problem. Bremen Tyler would be under his control and perchance would even secure the other missing three Artifacts. Love, power, money: also a perfect set.

At first he'd thought killing Tyler would be advantageous, but now it was preferable to wait in order to prevent the Ancestral people from seeking revenge. However, Tyler was besotted with this woman. What better way to ensure the man's end to any meddling than through her?

He slunk to the side window to look down on the dupe standing guard in the back. Of course he wouldn't tell Clay Nash the full plans. That was why he chose Jackson to leave the message at the East End Arms. Iberville allowed himself a quiet chuckle. The note directed Tyler back to Mooreland to wait for a reply which would not be sent for a very long time.

He halted as the woman on the bed stirred. She might be reluctant to stay willingly, but fear was an excellent tool. He would enjoy watching her terror when he flaunted Bremen's wedding band, and perhaps would even claim Tyler was dead. He would hold Hallie here until that man comprehended her life was in Iberville's hands. And if the Heart Gem showed she was not for him after all, well, it was not a concern whether she lived. Better she was dead, in fact. Tying up loose ends was always the best route.

Once all was in place, he could even cast suspicions of Hallie's disappearance on her husband, and Tyler would "kill" himself in his grief and guilt. Iberville was happy to help along in that endeavor, and with the Ancestral out of the way, things would settle down and he'd become a most wealthy man. Yes, things were certainly looking splendid.

****

Six nightmarish hours.

Three hundred and sixty terrifying minutes.

Finally Bremen arrived back home to Mooreland. He would not give in to the dark hysteria which could threaten Hallie's life, but instead, with a cool head, thought of how he would kill her abductor once found. There was no way the bastard would survive.

He brought the buggy to a jarring halt and leaped from the seat. "Hallie!" While not expecting to find her at home, he nonetheless searched every corner of the house and property relieved she was not lying hurt or worse.

He'd brought the doll from the hotel room in London in the hopes of tracing some clue to Hallie's whereabouts from the markings. She kept meticulous records. There might be a name or location to start searching from based on the stamping.

Struggling to not be overcome with fear for her safety he charged into Hallie's workroom, and rushed to the desk to pull out the sales records. There was the inked number, hidden by sewed-on petticoats, and tracked to an order for a Wrightsville pickup. It appeared a Mr. George Smith had purchased the doll and collected the package from the postal office.

He felt the blood rush from his face. *George Smith*. That was the name of the man who knew of the Heart Gem's existence and was in France when Count Henri Reynard purportedly committed suicide.

Whoever George Smith really was, the man would die.

****

The man crept out of the room, having once again checked if she was awake. Hallie had pretended to be asleep each time, and now, without making any movement waited a few interminable minutes until hearing the bedroom door lock once more.

By the heaviness of the footsteps, it was certain to be the man, George Smith. Hearing heightened, she perceived the sound of the front door closing and was alone in the house.

Hallie sat up from the bed and looked around the room, disgusted by the faint, dirty smell to the old house. She looked across at the small pillow next to hers and felt the nausea rise. A pile of silver-toned light blond hair, swirled into a grubby mass, lay clumped on the padding.

She jumped from the bed in horror and attempted to slow the frightened breathing. Whatever that was, wherever that came from, she needed to keep sharp wits focused to concentrate on getting out.

Examining the bed chamber for something to use in an escape proved fruitless. Some old clothing in a large armoire and the barest of furniture and linens graced the room. However, there was clean water in a pitcher, and she drank from the urn before washing her face in an effort to remove the remaining grogginess of the drugged tea.

Her fallen purse rested on the shabby rug, and she retrieved it. A few items there could be of assistance. Bremen would be searching, but no time could be wasted by waiting, and she must do whatever possible to speed an escape.

There could only be one reason for her entrapment: the Heart Gem thief wished to exert control on Bremen by using her. A very serious situation, but she would not meekly submit to Smith's intentions. He had underestimated her if the man believed so.

She stepped to the bedroom window and determined the room faced the front of the house. The building was situated on a wooded lot. In the far distance were the buildings and streets at the edge of Wrightsville. As the horse and buggy here had been traveling at a fast pace, she calculated the town was about five miles away. If able to get out of the room and through the front door, she could skirt the woods for cover and reach the town within a few hours.

She took the metal nail file from the bag and worked at the lock on the door. The mechanism made a few popping noises but would not retract. Damn.

There had to be another way out. Panic set in and a film of cold sweat misted her skin, but she was determined to keep calm and not falter. She examined the door and noted the cheap strap hinges. Methodical and careful, she set to work on them finally able to slip out the screws holding the hardware in place. She tossed the nail file onto the bed to free both hands. With a burst of energy, she slid the door off the hinges.

Keeping a clear head, she cautiously advanced into the hallway and forced both wobbly legs to move to the next door. She opened it. The water closet would afford no escape, but she drank some of the cold water and used the amenities.

The next door opened to another bedroom, dirty and filled with garbage. She closed it quickly; the smell was horrific. The last door closed off the stairway landing but as expected was locked, apparently from the outside.

She returned to the bedroom and plopped on the bed trying to think of a plan. The doors would not allow passage, however the windows could provide egress. The bed linens could be stripped and tied to form a rope to climb down from the second floor of the house, and although heights frightened her, the plan was plausible and possible. After working for a few minutes, she held a corded makeshift rope and lifted the porcelain urn to use to break open the window.

She froze. There was a man in the front yard, turned away but with a familiar build. She ducked down to peer over the top of the window trim as he turned around.

It was Clay. Bremen must already be sending out everyone in Mooreland to search. She jumped and waved her arms. "Clay!" Whatever had transpired over the past few months was regrettable, but he would provide assistance. "Here!"

Clay squinted at the window.

The gaze he returned and his determined gait toward the front door was not one of surprise and relief.

Her troubles weren't over. A serious impediment to an escape was racing up the stairs.

****

Bremen wouldn't stay in Mooreland futilely waiting for contact from the criminal who held Hallie. Instead he was determined to ride to Wrightsville tonight, and while it would take hours, even with changing horses in every town, he could reach the city before nightfall.

Before making his way to the main road, there would be one important stop. He pushed the horse to a canter, going through the small side roads until reaching a neat stone cottage.

Viola worked in the courtyard taking down laundry, her extended belly prominent.

He leaped from the horse. "Viola, I thought you were with Hallie?"

She turned with a smile. "I'd planned to go, but was ill." She opened her mouth to speak again but stopped, as the color drained from her face. "She is all right, isn't she?"

"I'm afraid she is in danger."

She sagged into the old chair outside the door, but he had no time for detailed explanations. "Viola, is your grandmother here? I need to speak with her."

She rose quickly, and he followed over to the old woman sitting in front of the fireplace.

"Mrs. Grey, I'm afraid something is horribly wrong. Hallie is missing. I don't know if she is hurt and have no clue what has happened except that she may be near Wrightsville. Can you help me? I know you have some knowledge of the Old Ways."

"Do you believe in the Old Ways, Mr. Tyler?"

"Of course."

"I can sense you do, as much as I."

He stood silently, attempting to wait patiently while she closed her eyes and thought. Finally she spoke, "Search where you said. I'll make sure the one responsible will not escape."

He reached into his pocket ready to pay the old woman for her efforts, but she waved her palm.

"No. Go now to find her. Bring her back home— that will be my reward. Most towns would have set my granddaughter out, but Hallie ensured that did not happen here."

Nelly Grey eased out of her chair and shuffled to the large iron strongbox. She unlocked it with a key hanging from a silver chain around her neck and from the bottom of the box took out another metallic box which was carved and inlaid with intricate designs. Deep in thought, she traced the designs with a finger. She gazed with intelligent, wizened eyes. "I will make a painful end for the black heart who wishes to hurt Hallie Tyler. I will conjure his heart even blacker, black as the burnt ashes in the grate. Of that be assured."

Relief coursed through his body; he nodded his thanks.

He had never ridden so many hours without stopping for rest. Only pausing briefly four times along the way to change horses, he was hungry, cold, and tired but made the ride to Wrightsville with extraordinary speed.

The long time afforded him a chance to think. It would be necessary to kill George Smith—there could be no other resolution. If he let the man go, nothing would prevent the scoundrel from trying again. However, if he killed Smith, the man who held the Heart Gem, Bremen's own life would end along with Smith's.

There was only one magic the Ancestrals had incanted into the Artifacts of Love. If one of their own killed to gain the return of an object, that Ancestral man or woman would die. Although there was no way to circumvent this edict, Bremen had no other recourse and would remain hopeful death could be swift, without pain.

He wouldn't tell Hallie ending her kidnapper's life would end his life too, but wouldn't hesitate to give up life if that would ensure his wife's safety. Nothing else mattered. He would die for her.

The outline of Wrightsville came into view. He pushed the horse harder toward the Wrightsville Inn.

Greatcoat billowing about like batwings, Bremen raced into the lobby, frightening the elderly ladies standing in the lobby chatting about a successful shopping expedition. The front desk clerk appeared alarmed at the sight of his haggard appearance.

"Mrs. Tyler did leave a note here at the front desk with your name on it." The clerk passed the paper over the counter.

Bremen tore open the envelope. "Where does George Smith live?"

"I'm sorry sir, I don't know of a George Smith."

"What? There must be a George Smith in town." Damn. Another obstacle.

"I'm afraid not, sir." The young man motioned to the night maid, "Maria, Mrs. Tyler has gone to the house of a Mr. George Smith. I don't know the name. You know everyone in town, have you heard of him?"

Maria thought for a moment. "Not of a George Smith, but I did see the driver of the buggy Mrs. Tyler went off in. I remember because I thought it was unusual that Robbie was acting as cabbie. Robbie often goes drinking with a new gentleman in town. I don't know the man's name, but heard the man has rented the old Culver house just outside of town."

"Where is that?" Bremen demanded.

"Take this road right here, sir, and follow about five miles. It is a large grey house just past the woods. You can't miss it. It's the only one there."

He flew from the hotel.

\*\*\*\*

Perhaps Clay would help if she could appeal to him on the basis of their past friendship. Raised a gentleman, there must be some glimmer of sensibility left in his addled head.

Heart pounding, Hallie waited as the front door slammed open, then hard steps bounded up the stairs, and finally a key fumbled in the hallway door. It opened with a slam, and Clay stood open-mouthed, staring at the tied-up sheets pooled around her feet.

Dropping the keys out of his hand and extending his palm, the strong smell of alcohol emanating from his presence, Clay surged forward. "Come away now. Smith is gone. We can leave together. Tyler must be dead by now."

A sick fear flowed through at the thought of Bremen dead. Surely he could not be as she would sense if her husband was gone from this earth. "Let me pass. You must know Smith is holding me against my will."

"Go with me now."

"We'll go to the authorities. This madman must be stopped."

"It's too late to be concerned about Smith. Tyler is dead. I'll comfort you. You'll see, you'll forget in time."

She didn't have time to reason. "We'll ride back to town. Bremen might already be there."

"You are driving me mad." He grabbed her by the shoulders. "Why do you still refuse me? I suffered watching you with Tyler when you should have been mine. What did he give you that I can't? You won't get away again."

Revolted by his words and the smell of liquor on his breath, she shoved away causing Clay to lose balance and spill to the floor. He scrambled to his feet and propelled her onto the bed, her hand landing on the mass of blond hair on the pillow. She snatched away, fingertips skimming the metal file lying on the blanket. She took the object and stabbed Clay's neck with the chipped end.

Roaring, he dove again but she halted his approach by scraping the metal across his ear. He screamed and reached out again.

Hallie bounced off the bed and ran out the room then down the stairs toward the front door.

The cold air hit her face with a jolt. It was still light out, so it was urgent to find cover. She would hide in the woods. She sprinted across the lawn to the trees then surveyed the area for a place to hide. Deeper in, there was a thick trunk on its side covered by the fallen leaves. She dove between the trees. Lying in the underbrush, Hallie curled as small as possible by tucking the dress around her body and pushing around the leaves as cover.

The door boomed and Clay's pounding footsteps sounded on the packed dirt. "Hallie!"

She peeked between the leaves. He was running toward the back of the property, blood dripping from his neck and ear. He grabbed the pitchfork set outside the barn door and ran into the wooden building.

"Hallie. Come out." He called her name while driving the tines of the implement into the hard ground, the metallic stab echoing in the quiet evening. She shuddered thinking how easily the fork could pierce her flesh.

She hoped that once he realized she was not in

the barn, he would go down the dirt road, believing she was running to town.

"You bitch," he bellowed as he left the barn, face red in anger. Instead of the road, he headed toward the woods in the direction of the trees. She curled tighter, anxiety rising in her throat as Clay marched closer.

"Hallie, come out. You know I'll find you."

She steeled herself motionless except for sliding a protective hand over her belly. Hallie watched as Clay used the pitchfork to sweep the leaves away from the fallen trees, methodically moving closer to where she lay.

"I know you went this way. I smell your perfume."

Her mind raced through the possibilities of escape. Should she stay hidden or bolt in the direction of town?

Suddenly he ran forward. "I found you! Come with me now." He snatched her shirt, hefted her upright and dragged her along.

"Wait, I'll go with you, Clay. I was wrong, I'll join you, I promise."

He stopped yanking. "I'll not let you make the same mistake again. You are mine and always have been."

He was at the point of senselessness; she needed to calm him immediately. "Of course, we'll leave as you suggest." She tried to pull out of his hold, but his fingers squeezed tighter.

Her top blouse buttons had become undone during the struggle. Clay stared at the top of her breasts, then he pawed at the fabric. "I'll show you what a real man can do."

He pushed her to the ground, her palms hitting the rough twigs and rocks. She was breathless for a moment too long, providing Clay with an opportunity to fall to his knees, his legs pinning her skirt to the forest floor.

"Move off. Now," Hallie demanded, fighting the hysteria cracking through her fear.

"This is the only way to show you I'm the man for you. We can be together once you see that." He put his body over her, while she struggled madly to remove him to no avail. He started pulling the skirt from around her legs as those red-rimmed eyes bored into hers.

"No stop it, Clay! What are you doing? Think about what you are doing!" She cringed as the jagged nails on the fingers of his left hand touched her calf while his vice-like right hand pinned around her neck.

Dizziness was starting to weaken her, but her fingers groped around the ground seeking a weapon. She wrapped her fingers around a small stone, lifted and smashed it into Clay's eye. He roared but tightened the hold of his right hand.

Hallie swept her fingers along the dirt seeking something larger, but only found soft useless leaves. It was becoming more difficult to breathe. His left hand was grasping at her drawers. "No," she rasped in a whisper. Her arm felt as though it was tearing from the socket, but with one last wide swipe along the ground her fingers found a sharp branch. She gripped it in her fist, focused her eyes and speared deep into the back of his shoulder.

He screamed and rolled off her.

She scrambled to her feet and grabbed the pitchfork on the ground a few feet away. Hallie held the tool with both hands, then aimed toward his gut. "I don't want to hurt you, but I will."

He started sobbing, whether from pain or fear she wasn't sure, but he was drunk. Mumbled words were slurring. Sweat poured off him. His mouth bled where a couple of teeth had fallen out.

"Why are you doing this to me?" She made a

small stabbing motion toward him.

His head appeared to clear a little. "I didn't bring you here. It was the other man."

"Who?"

"George Smith. It's his house. He said you would turn to me if I helped him."

"Where is Smith now?"

Clay wiped drool from his chin. "He went into town. Please let me go. It is the drink. The drink makes me do this. If you let me go, I'll never bother you again. I swear it."

She wanted to show mercy but was uncertain. "If I let you live, Clay, do you promise you will leave us alone? Do you promise on your mother's memory?"

Clay nodded. "Yes, I promise. You know what that vow means."

"Leave."

He turned away limping to the barn. In a moment he brought out his horse. She was sure she would never see him again. He didn't look back, but she kept her eyes on him until he was out of sight.

The tension in her body seeped away as she brushed the leaves from the skirt, but her hand paused when the sound of drumming hoofbeats sounded from the other direction.

She needed to find a better place to hide. The woods weren't thick enough to afford cover, and the barn would be the first place Smith would go. No powers on earth could persuade her to seek a hiding place in the house.

The hoofbeats grew stronger. Closer. It was as if someone were riding like mad. She slipped behind the tree again, the pitchfork held in her white-knuckled grip. Hallie whispered a prayer. Smith was planning something nefarious. Clay had been transparent in his intentions, but Smith's agenda was unknown.

A rider came into view, kicking up great clouds of dust in his wake. The horse was a huge black beast, one she'd never seen before. Smith was coming for her, and unlike how she'd handled Clay, she'd have to kill Smith to escape.

Calm and cool now, from the cover of the tree line Hallie watched the horse and rider plow toward the house. She would use the element of surprise and rush him, unseating Smith from the horse and doing whatever was necessary with the steel implement. She swallowed hard, ready to take action.

Now. Forward. Brandishing the pitchfork as a sword, she flew forward aiming at the rider's chest. The steed's hooves raised in alarm, but she skirted their reach. Dust blew into her eyes as she swirled jabbing at the man.

"Stop!" a man's voice yelled while he pulled the horse back a few yards.

Then she noted the whirling coat and the black hair of the man. The figure was familiar, but she grounded her feet until the air cleared to make sure.

Yes, it was Bremen. She dropped the pitchfork and raced to him.

He barely let the horse stop as he jumped off and clamped onto her.

"You are safe, my love. You are unhurt?"

She nodded into his chest and could feel his heart hammering. "Bremen, we must leave immediately. Smith will be returning."

"No. Smith has the Heart Gem. He will continue to search for us as he knows I am pledged to find the object. This must all end tonight. Take my horse and ride through the deepest part of woods into town, bringing help. I'll deal with him."

"I won't leave you alone here. I believe the madness you told me about has now taken hold of my abductor."

246

He took her face in his hands, vowing as he looked into her eyes. "You'll be all right. I promise."

"*We* will be all right," she corrected.

He didn't answer.

"Bremen, I'll not leave you alone. We'll deal with him together. We'll think of a plan."

"Ride into town and wait for me."

"No."

He struggled with the response. "If there ever was a moment for you to finally listen to me, Mrs. Tyler, the time is now."

"No."

"I'm not sure you'll be safe here. I promise I'll do all I can to protect you, but there is still great danger."

"Now that I know you are here, I'm not afraid."

He tilted her head and gazed deep into her eyes. "You know I have to kill him."

"Do what you must."

"I will do so, my love. Remember that. You can only be safe if I kill him. But if you insist on staying, we must set about a plan. First show me how you escaped from the house."

She took his hand and led upstairs to the bedroom. "Picking the door lock did not work, but I was able to loosen the strap hinges. As the outer door was also secured and my file had broken, I prepared to exit through the window." She raised the tied rope.

"I'm impressed by your efforts, and must tell you Hallie, my dove, your resourcefulness is amazing."

"We wanted to get home to you." She took his hand and placed it on her belly.

His smile reached deep into his eyes before he drew her close. "You'll both be home soon."

Chapter Twenty-Nine

Iberville clutched the packages of food and supplies, enough to last for at least a week. He fingered the strong new scissors in their wrapping, this pair sharper than the rusty old ones. He would use these to cut off a lock of Hallie's hair, and maybe even something else if necessary. He chuckled thinking of Bremen Tyler opening a package containing his wife's hair...or more. Slow torture would prove to be a suitable punishment for Tyler's harassment and interference.

He patted the side jacket pocket holding Tyler's wedding ring before touching the center of his vest, the hidden sewed-up pocket over his chest securing the Heart Gem.

The idiot, Clay Nash, wasn't standing near the door as ordered, apparently disregarding directions to be sentinel until relieved from duty. Probably off drinking again.

Remaining on alert for any possible trap, Iberville carefully entered into the bedroom upstairs. Of late it had become difficult to think clearly, calling for a need to remain sharp as the terrible madness churned in his head and pounded dark thoughts and images into his brain.

"So Sleeping Beauty, are you finally awake?"

****

Hallie composed her breathing when Smith entered the bedroom.

She pretended to waken. "Where am I? Why am I here?" She rubbed her eyes and made her words groggy as she sat up.

"You are here because it suits my purposes." The man straightened and raised his head into the air.

"Your plan?"

"You should feel honored to be such an important element in my scheme."

"Is this pertaining to the Heart Gem?"

Smith thought about the question for a moment while tapping a paper-bound package on his palm. "There's no reason to keep this from you, I suppose." He unrolled the paper from the bundle, "Yes, for the Heart Gem...and another more personal reason."

She looked over with what should be meek expression. "Can I see the Gem? I would like to know what it looks like. Do you have it with you?"

"Perhaps yes, perhaps no," he scoffed. "Soon enough we'll see it together. Remember not to disappoint me."

"Together?"

"Don't worry your pretty little head." His smile was malicious. "Speaking of your lovely crown, there is something I will take."

Smith drew a pair of long scissors from the paper and advanced toward her with a determined curl to the thin mouth.

Bremen burst out of the closet, both guns pointed at Smith. "Stop where you are."

Startled, Smith jumped back.

Hallie rolled from the bed to Bremen's side.

"George Smith, or whatever your name is, tell me where the Heart Gem is, and I will consider letting you get out of here alive."

"Mr. Tyler, I know you want to kill me, but if you do, the location of the Heart Gem will remain a secret. I may have passed the object to another or even hidden the Artifact away. You will spend the rest of your life searching. But if I walk out now, I vow to send the Heart Gem to you. You have my word."

Hallie was surprised at the coolness in Smith's voice.

"Your word means nothing to me," Bremen countered, "This will end now."

"I will never divulge the Heart Gem's whereabouts. You know you will have to kill me for it. And I know how you'll pay for that. Are you ready to do that?"

There was some information missing from her understanding, "Bremen, what does he mean?"

"Oh! She does not know?" the abductor responded.

"There is nothing for her to know." Bremen cocked his pistols. "Take off your jacket, everything. Shake your clothing out so I can see if you have the Heart Gem on you."

"No."

Bremen pulled the trigger of the gun in his right hand. A flash came from the barrel. The bullet struck the man's calf, piercing the flesh. Blood pooled on the fabric of his pants.

Hallie flinched but wouldn't look away.

Smith barely cringed. "Mr. Tyler, if you riddle me with bullets, eventually I will die from a loss of blood. Is that what you want? Do you think that is what she wants?"

Bremen shot the left-hand gun at the man's thigh. This time Smith let out a yelp. This time, blood pooled on the floor.

"Tyler, I know I will die either way. But you'll go too."

Bremen raised the gun again, aiming squarely at the man's torso.

Suddenly Smith grabbed his chest as though there was an incredible pain in his heart and fell to his knees in anguish. "Stop the pain!" he screamed.

She was shocked and even forgot herself and started to move toward Smith, but Bremen put out his hand to indicate she should wait.

Now roaring in agony, George Smith ripped open his vest and tore the stitching from the pocket. He pulled out the Heart Gem, but not before it had burned a large black hole into his chest. The acrid smell of burning flesh filled the room. He flung the Gem toward the wall. It struck with a thud while all three watched. Then, like molasses in winter, Smith sagged to the floor.

Bremen moved forward cautiously to inspect the body.

"Is he dead?"

"Most certainly. I can see the floor planks through the hole in his chest."

She gazed to where the Heart Gem had rolled. "It's over?"

"Almost, Hallie." He pointed the gun at the Gem.

She put a hand on his arm. "No, Bremen, return it to its rightful owners. This is part of the Ancestrals' heritage. Our child's heritage."

"You don't know the unhappiness these Artifacts have brought to my family. I want it gone from this world. I will tell my people the Artifact was destroyed as I fought with the thief."

"Do it for me? We can live out our lives without any worries or guilt."

He seemed to be struggling with what to do.

She bent to retrieve the gold wedding band which had been turned out of Iberville's jacket pocket. She took Bremen's hand and kissed his bruised knuckle before placing the ring back on his finger.

Bremen elevated the Heart Gem and extended his palm. "Do you want a view? You can see our future together and be assured we are each other's Heart Match."

"No. I don't need to see anything that tells what

I already know. I love you."

He paused for a moment. "You are sure you don't want a view? This will be your only chance."

"I need no proof. You are my Heart Match, my love. And I am yours."

Bremen clasped her tightly. "We will go together to the Stronghold and return the Artifact."

He put the Heart Gem in his pocket. She took his hand in hers and together they went down the stairs and out of the house.

Epilogue

Bremma Tyler gazed down at the adorable baby napping in the pine crib. How fortunate Bremen and Hallie were to have such a wonderful life and child.

She had shooed the sleep-deprived new parents up to bed with the promise of watching little Kellian as they took some time for rest. However, judging from the glances the couple had been exchanging for the past hour, sleep would not come until much later.

Years ago, when Bremen had first divulged an intention of leaving the Old Ways, she hadn't believed there would be any hope of happiness. After spending the past week in Mooreland, it was obvious the right decision was made after all. Hallie and Bremen were fortunate to have found true love, without even using the Heart Gem.

Bremma looked back down at the babe. She really needed to meet with the Seer. Perhaps there was hope for her too.

## A word about the author...

Isabella Macotte writes the kind of romance she loves to read: a story with delicious dialogue, seductive encounters, a dash of the paranormal, and an irresistible, unforgettable hero.

Passionate about books, Isabella keeps busy reading, writing and working in a library. But if a few moments remain at the end of the day, she spends them with a wonderful family and a sweet bichon pup named Daisy.

Visit her at: www.isabellamacotte.com

Thank you for purchasing
this Wild Rose Press publication.
For other wonderful stories of romance,
please visit our on-line bookstore at
www.thewildrosepress.com.

For questions or more information
contact us at
info@thewildrosepress.com.

The Wild Rose Press
www.TheWildRosePress.com

To visit with authors of The Wild Rose Press
join our yahoo loop at
http://groups.yahoo.com/group/thewildrosepress/